# THE FIRST LADIES CLUB

## J.B. HAWKER

No part of this publication may be reproduced or transmitted in any form or by any means, electronic or mechanical, without written permission of the author.

This book is a work of fiction.
Names, characters, places and incidents are either products of the author's imagination or used fictitiously.
Any resemblance to actual events, locales, or persons, living or dead, is entirely coincidental.

Copyright © 2014 J.B Hawker
All rights reserved.

ISBN-10:1502951150

ISBN-13:978-1502951151

*Dedicated to the spiritual sisterhood
of
pastors' wives everywhere*

# PROLOGUE

An aged gray van winds along the two-lane highway as it meanders through thick stands of evergreen forest on the west side of the Northern California Coastal Range. The road's curves occasionally break through the trees onto breathtaking vistas of the Pacific Ocean below.

These impressive views are unseen by the half-dozen passengers in the windowless back of the van. Hardened criminals - the worst of the worst - on their way to an extended stay at Pelican Bay, California's notorious super-max prison, these men care little for the scenery.

Chains clank when the shackled men shift uncomfortably.

A few of the prisoners manage to carry on desultory conversations with their bench mates, but most prefer to remain silent, only muttering occasional curses in complaint about the hard seats or the guard's driving.

Heavily muscled and tattooed, Carver Schramm is the most silent of the prisoners. No one shares his bare metal seat.

Schramm is headed for a long stretch in solitary confinement as the result of his bad behavior while in the San Francisco County Jail awaiting sentencing for a murder conviction.

His shackles do not connect with those of the other men, but, instead, anchor him on either side to stout iron staples welded into the van's frame. His feet are similarly restrained.

Even his fellow inmates recognize this man as a character best avoided. No one has ventured to speak a word to him since being loaded into the prison shuttle.

Schramm isn't bothered by any lack of conversation. He has done time in solitary before, more than once, and is comfortable with his own thoughts, thoughts that would make those around him decidedly uncomfortable, if they were aware of them.

At this moment, his inner voice rages about only two things: revenge and escape.

Inside Carver's mind images swirled without structure. Unfocused fury prevented his thoughts from coalescing into coherent patterns or plans. His desire to strike out at anyone and everyone grew with each mile as the van rolled along the asphalt highway.

Seeming outwardly calm, on the inside he was like a newly captured predator gnawing on the bars of its cage and taking a swipe at anyone who approached.

Pelican Bay was built for just such human aberrations as Carver Schramm.

No one has ever escaped from the maximum security portion of this prison, although a few have managed to break away from the lower level security of the outer ring of the complex reserved for non-violent offenders.

The van took a hairpin turn too fast, throwing the passengers against one another and initiating a round of obscene catcalls.

Carver's spirits lifted at the thought of the van crashing and giving him an opportunity to get away. He never considered the possibility of being killed in the resulting wreck. Like most sociopaths, Schramm thought of himself as invulnerable.

As it happened, the van and its malignant cargo made it to the prison without mishap.

When the convicts' chains were unclasped from the van, they shuffled out and were escorted into the processing center for body searches, showers and prison uniforms, before being taken to their cell assignments.

Carver Schramm felt his desperation rising as each step brought him closer to the clang of his solitary cell door.

He knew from past prison experiences he could never endure the years ahead in the jungle atmosphere among the prisoners or the constant prying eyes and bullying of the guards.

He was determined to escape, somehow.

One of the prison staff, who was holding a tablet computer containing the prisoners' cell assignments, directed the guards escorting the new arrivals.

Carver began to follow the others, but his guard was stopped and directed to take him down a different corridor.

Schramm supposed this must be a short-cut to the solitary confinement he was promised, so he was surprised to find himself being led out into the minimum security courtyard.

"What's this? A taunting glimpse of how the other guys live before being plunged into Hell?" he muttered under his breath.

He was incredulous when the guard handed him a packet of "house rules" and thrust him into what looked like a cheap motel room, already occupied by a small middle-aged man.

"Here's your new roomie, Halverson. Show him the ropes and keep him out of trouble," the guard instructed before shutting the solid security door with a slam.

Rather than the bars he'd expected, Schramm saw a small wire-mesh reinforced window in the door.

William Halverson, who had been sitting at a desk reading, observed his new roommate with some alarm.

Carver's dark shoulder-length hair, framing a face and neck covered with tattoos, was an unusual sight on this side of the prison.

When Halverson stood to attempt to shake Schramm's hand, the newcomer towered head and shoulders above him.

"William Halverson here, uh…welcome," he said, looking up.

Carver sneered contemptuously at the man's outthrust hand.

"Well," William said, drawing back his hand, "I think you will find things pretty comfortable here. If you have any questions, I'll be happy to help."

He returned to his chair and Carver threw the packet of personal items onto the nearest bed.

"That's my bed, I'm afraid. You can have that other one. They are identical," Halverson said.

"Then you won't mind moving, will you?" Carver said.

His voice was soft, but the look accompanying it pierced Halverson to the marrow.

William was certain this room assignment had to be a mistake. All his previous roommates were pretty decent sorts.

He decided to fill out a new-roommate request right away, during the next recreation period.

"No, of course. Not at all. I'll just take the other bed. Um, er, I didn't get your name."

"Schramm," Carver replied, looking out the mesh-covered window and fighting down an urge to beat the smaller man to death with the metal desk chair.

He knew it must be some sort of computer snafu bringing him to this room, instead of to a concrete block hole in solitary. Sooner or later, the mistake would be discovered and he would be moved. In the meantime, he didn't want to draw attention to himself.

Feigning an uncharacteristic congeniality while attempting a friendly smile, Schramm sat on his chosen bunk and leaned toward William as he spoke.

"So, what's the drill around here?"

The little man gulped, barely swallowing down a scream, as the oddly grimacing visage loomed near.

"The drill? Um, you mean the regular routine?"

Carver wanted to smash his fist into this stupid pipsqueak's idiot face, but instead, forced his mouth into an even more grotesque contortion and nodded.

"That's right. What sort of activities you got? Do you ever get out in the fresh air?"

"We will be released to the yard and recreation center in mid-afternoon, just before dinner."

"You got a cushy set-up here. So nice, they probably don't even need many guards, huh?"

"Oh, we have plenty of guards. The security staff here is very competent. Of course, there are security cameras covering most of the grounds and buildings."

"Most?" Schramm asked. "Where don't they cover?"

"A few years ago there was a fellow who walked away from the garbage dump, when it wasn't covered. I imagine that situation has been rectified by now, though."

"Just walked away, huh? Did they catch the guy?"

"Oh, yes. He was moved to the super-max, after that. I don't know why anyone would ever want to risk it. One hears such horror stories about the place…and, of course, no one's ever escaped from in there."

"Yeah, that's what I hear, too. What sort of activities you got in that rec center?"

"Oh, it's very well equipped. There's the gymnasium with workout equipment…you'll probably like that," Carver glared at him and Halvorson hurried on, "and there's the library and the TV lounge area."

"Library, huh? You got computers? They let you go on-line?"

"Only certain sites. There have to be filters or some of the men, even here in minimum security, might take advantage and indulge their baser instincts."

"Oh, sure. Ya gotta guard against them basic instincts. Well, guess I'll take a rest before rec time."

To Halvorson's immense relief, Schramm swung his feet onto the bed and turned his face to the wall.

An hour later, the doors buzzed and swung open.

A loudspeaker directed the men to leave their rooms and go out to the courtyard.

The inmates were mustered for a head count while the rooms were being inspected, then were free to jog around the outdoor track, toss footballs or shoot hoops.

Those who preferred could use the recreation center facilities.

Carver followed William into the library where he elbowed the smaller man out of his way and grabbed a seat in front of a computer.

Entering a search on "Northern California prisons," he was able to pull up an overhead view of Pelican Bay, including the area in which he was housed.

After getting the information he wanted, Carver stood up and left, turning the computer over to the next impatient inmate.

Newly hired prison security guard, Boyd Lenninger, leaned lethargically against a green metal dumpster. Being low man on the seniority totem pole, he was assigned to patrol the trash collection area during recreation times until a new security camera could be installed.

Bored and resentful of the tedious duty, he was taking advantage of the rare privacy to sneak an unauthorized smoke break.

He did not hear the man creeping up behind him, until it was too late.

# CHAPTER ONE

Naidenne Davidson, her wild red-gold curls bouncing with every step of her long legs, jogged down the potholed side street, hurrying to get to the crosswalk before the only traffic light on this stretch of Oregon's Highway 101 changed to red.

She knew the crosswalk light stayed green only long enough for a person to dash desperately across before it switched back for another interminable through-traffic cycle.

If she missed that light, she was going to be late, again.

Eskaletha hated it when any of the women arrived after the meeting began, and she wasn't shy about letting everyone know it.

Naidenne was in luck! The little walking-man symbol was still glowing when she stepped between the lines of the pedestrian crossing.

She increased her pace when the red hand began to flash its warning, just as a white and black sub-compact, anticipating the green light, surged forward and struck her a glancing blow, spinning her around and sending her skidding along the pavement.

Naidenne scrambled on all fours to the sidewalk and sat on the curb gasping for breath.

When she pulled her toes up to protect them from the vehicles now rushing past, she noticed blood running down her legs, jagged holes in her capris and a painful throbbing in her knees. She eased to her feet, hanging onto the signal pole for support and stood still for moment getting her bearings.

Dazed, Naidenne wobbled along the sidewalk toward her meeting. It was being held in a local restaurant inside the Ships Stores, an upscale shopping mall only a block away.

The mall was on the site of an old dockside processing plant recently converted in hopes of attracting tourists.

Once inside the mall, she made her way to the Boatworks Coffee Shop, where she stood swaying in the entrance trying to regain her composure before joining the others.

Jostled from behind, Naidenne turned to see her friend, Judy Falls, another tardy member of the group.

As usual, Judy's lank and faded blond hair had escaped its elastic scrunchie and drooped messily over her chubby cheeks.

Naidenne was happy to see her kind-hearted friend, even though Judy's wrinkled organic all-cotton blouse and peasant skirt were badly in need of a wash and her leather thong sandals revealed toes coated with dirt.

A throw-back to the hippy era, Judy somehow managed to maintain her voluptuously unrestrained figure on a strict vegan diet. Her politics were extreme, but her genuine love of the Lord earned her a grudging tolerance, if not outright welcome, from her husband's conservative Presbyterian congregation.

"Excuse me! Oh, Naidenne, you look awful. What happened to you?" Judy asked. "Come on, we need to find you a chair."

Naidenne allowed the shorter woman to lead her into the café's banquet room.

She eased down onto a chair near the doorway.

As she'd feared, the meeting had already begun.

"Just a minute, Olivette, I don't think we have everyone's attention," Eskaletha Evans arched her eyebrows as she addressed the tiny gray-haired woman standing beside her at the front of the room.

"You can resume reading the minutes when Judy and Naidenne finally get settled."

All eyes turned toward the late arrivals.

Soon realizing something was the matter, many of the ladies left their seats and surrounded Naidenne and Judy, asking questions and exclaiming in dismay over Naidenne's bloody knees and ruined clothes.

"Ladies! Please, can we have some decorum?" Eskaletha spoke over the commotion and clapped her hands.

Her commands ignored, she strode toward the back of the room, a glower forming on her handsome ebony features.

In high dudgeon, Eskaletha bore a striking resemblance to a bust of Queen Nefertiti, only without the headdress.

"What's going on here? Can't you girls ever take our meetings seriously?"

The group parted, allowing their president to see what was causing this uncharacteristic display of anarchy.

"Goodness, Naidenne! What's happened to you?" she exclaimed.

Turning to the others, she asked, "Is someone getting a first aid kit?"

Eskaletha crouched down and whispered, "Do you need to see a doctor, Deenie? Ooh, your poor knees."

Elizabeth Gilbert efficiently gathered up napkins and a glass of water and dropped to her knees on the other side of Naidenne to dab at the wounds.

While not a large woman, Elizabeth's upright posture, neatly tailored shirtwaist dress, and sensible shoes, with her salt-and-pepper hair twisted into a tidy knot, provided a strong, capable presence appreciated by the members of the United Methodist Church where she and her husband were co-pastors.

"These cuts don't look very deep, but she's lost a couple of layers of skin," Elizabeth explained to the others.

"Well, you're the nurse practitioner in the group, so I guess you should know, but they look pretty bad to me," Judy responded. "Darn it! I forgot my bag when I left the manse. I always carry a jar of my homemade organic herbal salve. Do you think we should get her to the ER?"

"No, Liz is right," Naidenne said. "It's just road rash. Sure does burn, though."

One of the women came back with the first aid kit from the Boatworks kitchen.

Elizabeth soon had Naidenne's wounds cleaned and bandaged.

"We can't do much for your pants, I'm afraid. Were they favorites?" Judy asked.

"No. Just a pair I found in the last tag sale we ran at our church. I liked them because they are supposed to be cropped, so no one can tell if they are too short, but no great loss. Thanks."

"So, tell us what happened," Eskaletha, now back in control, prompted.

"I guess you could say I was the victim of a hit-and-run," Naidenne said, shaking her head.

"What? You're kidding. Someone knocked you down and just drove off?" Judy asked.

"I was crossing the highway when this little car jumped the light and sort of side-swiped me and just kept going."

"Did you get his license number?"

"What kind of a car was it?"

"We should call the State Troopers."

The women were all talking at once, until Naidenne held up her hand, so she could reply.

"I didn't get the license number and don't have much of a description of the car, except it was really small, maybe a Mini Cooper or a Smart car, being driven by a not-too-smart driver. Anyway, it wasn't going fast enough to do any real harm. It just knocked me off balance and I fell."

"Well, if you're sure…I still think we should report it," Olivette offered.

Olivette Vernon was the oldest member of the little group. She and her husband, Kendall, had served the Bannoch Reformed Church for his entire career. Her small stature and mouse-like demeanor belied her tremendous faith, which was matched by her hard-work and dedication to her church.

"If all the excitement is over, perhaps we can resume our seats and get on with our meeting," Eskaletha stated, striding back to the podium.

Olivette scurried closely behind.

"I think it is just awful the way these tourists speed on the highway through town, polluting the air and scattering trash all over creation. Sometimes they don't even stop for that light," Judy commented.

"I know visitors mean more income for the town, but it was nicer before we had so much traffic," Elizabeth agreed.

"Tourists, traffic and all the riffraff coming from California; the Coast isn't the same, anymore," Gwennie Barthlette, wife of the Trinity Nazarene Church minister, spoke up.

"And what about all the underpaid and exploited workers commuting to that new big box store between here and Tillamook?" Judy added.

"Ladies! If we can please return to our seats?" Eskaletha called out.

"You may resume the reading of the minutes of our last meeting, Olivette."

"I'm afraid I don't remember where I left off, Madam President."

"Just start over at the beginning. Some of us missed that part, anyway."

"Oh...good idea," Olivette smiled in relief, squared her narrow shoulders and began reading the minutes of the last meeting in her high, reedy voice.

After the earlier commotion, the ladies sat obediently through the formalities, followed by an orderly discussion of plans for their next community project.

When they were finished, Eskaletha asked a blessing on the refreshments and adjourned this monthly session of the Bannoch First Ladies Club.

Jostling around the snack table to get first dibs on one of Olivette's famous homemade Danish pastries, the women filled their plates before settling in for a serious gabfest, the real purpose of the gathering.

"How are your knees, now, Naidenne?" Judy asked around a mouthful of pastry.

"Much better, thanks."

"I blame all the yahoos coming north from California these days. They all drive like they own the road," Gwennie said.

"Could you tell if the car's plates were out of state, Deenie?" Olivette asked.

"I'm afraid I didn't even look. I was trying not to fall on my face."

"My cousin says she went to LA once and all California drivers are insane. I wish they would just keep their wild rides down there and leave us alone," Gwennie said. "And it's not just their bad drivers, either. What about all the crime we are seeing these days along the southern Oregon coast. I just know we have the stupid California Prison Realignment to thank for most of it."

"I read where some of the hardest hit communities refer to it as a catch-and-release program, like with fishing, when they let the small fish go…even though they are cruelly damaged by the nasty hooks and probably traumatized for life. Blood *sports* should be outlawed…" Judy jumped in.

"As I was saying," Gwennie went on, "in California now, some criminals are arrested, released and re-arrested for new crimes all in the same night. No jail time, let alone counseling and rehabilitation. What can they expect?"

"That doesn't make any sense," Elizabeth Gilbert agreed. "My husband was preaching a series on Responsible Love just last month. It is no kindness to enable a person to continue in their sins."

"That's right. We are not to be a stumbling block," Olivette nodded emphatically.

"Well, their prisons are so over-crowded. What can they do?" Naidenne asked.

"Not send their problems up here, that's what," Gwennie asserted.

Her comment serving as a benediction on this particular topic, the ladies moved on to the more gratifying practice of sharing the frustrations and joys of small town life in the parsonage and manse.

The First Ladies Club was formed shortly after Naidenne and the Reverend Scott Davidson married.

Eskaletha had come to the Bannoch Community Fellowship's parsonage to welcome Naidenne into the ranks of local pastors' wives and the two became instant friends.

Over the following weeks they frequently met for lunch, when Naidenne would seek Eskaletha's advice on her new role. Occasionally, one or another of the other pastors' wives would join them.

Eventually, they decided to schedule regular gatherings and invited the wives of all the pastors in town.

When it came time to name their group, Eskaletha and Peggy Burt, wife of the Missionary Baptist pastor, suggested The First Ladies Club, after the title conferred upon the wife of the senior minister in their churches. Everyone loved the suggestion, so they had been The First Ladies Club, ever since.

The women represented a wide range of Christian religious traditions and styles, so they agreed to concentrate only on their commonalities.

Theological discussions were not encouraged; especially any debate of the prophetic books of Daniel and Revelation. By common consent, conversations about pre-tribulation, post-tribulation, and mid-tribulation, were strictly avoided.

All these women shared a love of God and a desire to serve Him in their community.

Sometimes more than a dozen women were at the monthly meetings, although busy schedules and responsibilities meant at other times only five or six could attend.

The club held regular fund-raisers for various community improvement projects, always being mindful not to compete with fund-raisers or other activities of the local churches.

In deference to her chewed-up knees, Naidenne accepted Eskaletha's offer of a ride home when the meeting broke up.

Relaxing into the soft leather seats of her friend's Lexus, she took a deep breath and allowed herself to think about her accident.

It was a very close call and could easily have resulted in serious injuries, or worse. Remembering the experience made her just a little light-headed.

Eskaletha was looking at her oddly, and her expression brought Naidenne back from her woolgathering.

"Uh, did you say something, 'Letha?"

"I asked are you going to the Women of Faith conference in Tillamook, next weekend," Eskaletha repeated.

"Maybe. I haven't asked Scott what we have planned for that night. Saturdays can be tricky, as you know. I think my sister-in-law, Rosamund, may want to go, though, if she isn't busy."

"Well, since Scott won't be going, I can't see what difference his plans make. It can't interfere with his sermon prep just 'cause you aren't there."

"No, but he may have accepted an invitation for us to call on a member of the flock. He sometimes does on a Saturday. If it's a single woman, you know he can't go alone. I'll just have to check with him."

"It's a crying shame a pastor can't call on a widow woman in her home these days without a chaperone, just so he won't be accused of some impropriety," Eskaletha said.

"I agree, but that's the way it is, shame or not. It frightens me to think of what one false accusation can do to a man's career…but, on the other hand, unfortunately, there actually are predators in the pastorate. I've encountered a wolf in sheep's clothing myself."

"I suppose it just takes one bad apple…still, it's too bad," Eskaletha commented.

"Thanks for the ride," Naidenne said, as they pulled up in front of the drafty church-owned two-story Victorian house she shared with her husband and his sister.

"Call me tomorrow and let me know how you're doing. I'm thinking, by then, you are going to hurt in places you never knew you had," Eskaletha predicted with a grin, before driving off.

Naidenne entered her home and was immediately enveloped in the rich aroma of roast chicken with rosemary.

"That smells wonderful, Rosamund! What can I do to help?"

Her sister-in-law turned from the stove as Naidenne entered the kitchen.

"You can make a nice salad and help me decide what to fix for dessert, if you want…what in the world happened to your pants?"

"Oh, I fell down crossing the highway. A car jumped the light and sort of bumped into me."

"Oh, Naidenne! You're hurt! Are your knees cut up terribly under those bandages?"

"It's not too bad. Could have been much worse, if I'd been any later for the meeting. The car clipped me from behind. I think I was just late enough not to get flattened."

"Don't you worry about helping with dinner. Go have a nice soak in the tub and then rest. Let me know if you need help with fresh bandages."

"Thanks. I'd like to get out of these clothes. A bath sounds nice. But I'll come back to help when I've changed."

## Chapter Two

"Dear, are you sure you don't need to see a doctor about your knees? Is anything else starting to hurt?" Scott asked his wife when she joined him in the old-fashioned formal dining room.

Before replying, she placed a carrot and raisin salad in a pretty cut-glass bowl on the modest pine table.

"Only my pride, as they say. Seriously, I scraped my knees and had a bit of a scare, but I feel blessed it wasn't any worse. Don't worry about me, please. You have enough on your plate these days."

Rosamund came in with the roast potatoes and slipped into her seat, placing a napkin neatly onto her lap.

"What do you have to worry about these days, Scott? Has something happened I don't know about?" she said.

Scott held a chair for Naidenne and took his place at the table.

"Now, how in the world could anything happen around here without you knowing about it, Rosie? Remember how I called you Nosey Rosie when we were kids? Some things just never change."

"Stop being silly and ask the blessing before the food gets cold," his sister scolded.

Following Scott's brief prayer, while the dishes of food were being passed, Rosamund again asked what was causing him concern.

"If you weren't too busy with your new fella to attend the last business meeting, you might have noticed the state of the church budget, Rose. Giving is way down this quarter."

"So what? That always fluctuates. It's never caused you much stress before."

"Well, it's different, now."

Casting a quick glance at Naidenne, Rosamund thought she understood.

"You always trusted in the Lord to provide for us, Scott. Don't you think he will take care of Naidenne, too, since you are married?"

"Of course, I do. But it's different, now," Scott replied with an uncomfortable shrug.

"It isn't just our income Scott's thinking about, Rosamund. All the programs of the church will suffer if the giving doesn't come back up," Naidenne offered.

"There is something else I haven't told you, Sis."

"What's that?"

"I received a Transfer of Membership letter earlier this week from an old adversary who is returning to Bannoch."

The look on Scott's face and his tone of voice gave Rosamund a sinking feeling. The hairs on the back of her neck tingled.

"Who? Not…"

"Maureen Oldham. Yes, I'm afraid so. I'm sorry, Rosie," Scott said.

"I know what a thorn in your side she was before she and Vince moved to Portland. When I saw whose letter it was, I was tempted to mark the envelope, 'Unknown – Return to Sender,' but there really wasn't anything I could do."

"I'd heard about Vince passing away, but it never entered my mind that woman might move back here. I feel sick," Rosamund said, pushing her plate away from her.

"What in the world is this Maureen person like? Why is she so unwelcome?" Naidenne asked.

"Oh, dear…I know this is no way to feel about a fellow believer…I can't seem to help myself. It must be a test."

Rosamund seemed to be talking to herself, and then looked up, "Please pray for me. I can't welcome Maureen Oldham back into my life without God's help."

"Of course," Scott replied.

He took the women's hands in his. Praying for an extra helping of wisdom, courage and strength for them all, he also asked for blessings on the recently widowed Maureen Oldham.

"I could tell you about our history with Maureen, Deenie, but I don't want to prejudice you against her, at least, not any more than we already have done. When she was here before, she was a perfect example of what's sometimes referred to by us pastors as a *well-intentioned dragon*, but widowhood may have mellowed her, you never know. We might be dreading her return unnecessarily," Scott said.

"Please, God, let you be right," Rosamund said.

This conversation left Naidenne itching with curiosity and eager to meet the mysterious woman.

"When will Mrs. Oldham be back in town?" she asked.

"That's the rest of the story. She's already here. She'll be in church this Sunday," Scott said, with a rueful glance at his sister.

Rosamund moaned and got up to clear the table.

After putting the leftover food into the refrigerator, Rosamund excused herself and went up to her room, leaving Scott and Naidenne to finish clearing away the dinner things.

The couple made quick work of the cleanup, moving smoothly around each other, easily reaching the tall cupboards in this high-ceilinged room.

It was fortunate Naidenne shared the Davidson siblings' above-average height. She wondered how a diminutive pastor's wife would survive in such a kitchen.

"Eskaletha asked me about the women's program in Tillamook this weekend. Do you mind if I go with her on Saturday night?"

"Not at all," Scott replied. "That works well. I am on the rotation Saturday night for a ride-along as Sheriff's chaplain."

"Well, then, I'm going to ask Rosamund to come to the program, too. Maybe it will cheer her up."

"Good luck with that. Len Spurgeon books up all of her Saturday nights, lately. Or hadn't you noticed?"

"They have been spending a lot of time together. He seems like a good man. Do you think it is getting serious between them?"

"It is on his part, I'm sure. It's harder to read Rosie."

## The First Ladies Club

"What's your opinion of Len? Do you think he's the man for her?"

"I like him. He's solid on his Bible and appears to be sincerely trying to live his faith. He's a bit pompous, now and then, but, as a banker, that probably goes with the territory."

"If they marry, will you miss your sister? You two have shared this home for a long while, now."

"There was a time when I would have been horribly lonely if she'd moved out. Not so much, now, though," Scott grinned and grabbed Naidenne around the waist.

She nuzzled his neck before hanging up the dish towel to dry.

Switching off the kitchen light, she paused in the doorway, gazing suggestively over her shoulder before exaggeratedly swaying her hips as she climbed the stairs with her husband bounding after her, laughing.

In her bedroom, Rosamund heard the others come upstairs and enter their room at the far end of the hall. Soft voices and throaty laughter were immediately silenced when the door closed behind them.

The many rooms in this over-sized house had become an unexpected blessing when Scott and Naidenne married. There would have been uncomfortable privacy issues for the newlyweds if they were all sharing a modern bungalow. As it was, the distance between the bedrooms prevented Rosamund from becoming an unwitting eavesdropper on intimate moments.

Having Naidenne join the household was all good from Rosamund's perspective. The two were becoming close friends, more like real sisters than sisters-in-law.

Adjusting to sharing the upstairs bathroom was a bit tricky, at first, but mutually accommodating routines were quickly established. Having a downstairs powder room off the spare bedroom eased any traffic issues.

Lately, Len was urging Rosamund to consider moving out of the parsonage to live with him. He'd made it very clear he wanted to marry her.

The two had known each other for almost two years and had been spending much of their time together for many months. Rosamund was certain she loved him, yet she kept dragging her feet about becoming engaged.

She was not usually a superstitious woman. Superstition didn't fit very comfortably with her faith. Still, she couldn't shake the fear that saying yes to Len would doom him, somehow.

The only other man she'd ever loved was killed in action in Vietnam, mere weeks after they became formally engaged. His death devastated Rosamund. She was afraid to suffer another such a loss. Illogically, she couldn't help feeling the engagement had put some sort of hex on the poor man.

Though recognizing her fear was irrational, she couldn't seem to bring herself to become engaged, again. She loved Len too much to risk it.

The past few times they were together, Len subtly indicated he was growing impatient with her.

If she couldn't get over her silly phobia, she risked losing him.

And now, on top of everything, Maureen Oldham was back. Drat and blast the wretched woman to heck, anyway.

Down the hall, Scott and Naidenne were also wondering about Len and Rosamund.

Naidenne sat on the bed drying her hair with a fluffy towel. Her voice was muffled by the thick terrycloth folds.

"I know Rose cares for Len. I've seen the way her eyes light up when she speaks his name."

"Well, he's not the one delaying things. He asked for my blessing more than six months ago," Scott responded from his side of the bed, where he was propped up against pillows reviewing his Bible study notes.

"Do you think it's because she's afraid of the, um, physical side of marriage?" Naidenne asked.

Scott let out a guffaw, and then continued, chuckling.

"Is that side of things so scary, then?"

"Not to me! But, Rosamund has never had any experience and she's been single for a long time."

"Experienced, or not, I don't think my sister is afraid of anything. No, if she's keeping Len at arm's length there must be another reason. Maybe she just likes things the way they are."

"I doubt it. Not that I think she's unhappy living here with us. It's just that almost any woman wants a home of her own."

Naidenne was gingerly pulling a wide-toothed comb through her tangles.

"Come over here and let me detangle that adorable strawberry-blond mop for you."

Naidenne walked around to Scott's side of the bed, knelt on the floor beside him and handed him the comb.

"You know, whatever Rosie is thinking or planning regarding Len is really her business. We just need to let her get on with it and support her whenever she needs it," Scott said, as he tenderly detangled his wife's damp hair.

"I know. It's just that I can tell she's been a bit down, lately. I wish I could help."

"You do help. A lot. I think she was a little lonely before you came into our lives, my love. Having you here has been a blessing for her…and for me too, of course. There, all smooth."

He ran his hands through his wife's shiny hair.

"Thank you, darling," Naidenne said.

Getting to her feet, she hung the damp towel on a drying rack behind the door, slipped out of her robe and into bed.

"Do you have much studying to do tonight, Scott?" she asked, sliding her hand along his thigh beneath the covers.

"Not anymore," he replied, laying the book on the nightstand and turning out the lamp.

"Nothing that can't wait until tomorrow…"

༄

Rosamund stepped onto the front porch as the sun nosed over the mountains behind the parsonage. Turning to look down toward the ocean, she could see the fog was already retreating from the shoreline.

"It's going to be another beautiful day. Thank you, Lord."

Walking carefully in her bedroom slippers onto the still-damp grass, she picked up the morning paper and went back inside the house, scanning the headlines as she went.

Naidenne was fixing the coffee as Scott trotted down the stairs.

"Morning, Rosie," he greeted his sister. "Anything interesting in that thing?"

He continued into the kitchen without waiting for a reply and kissed Naidenne.

"Good morning, Sunshine. How's the light of my life?"

Naidenne smiled and stroked his jaw.

"How would you like your eggs this morning?"

"Just coffee today. I have an early breakfast meeting with the trustees. Something about necessary repairs on the church roof. Those guys love to have breakfast meetings. I think they conjure up issues just for an excuse to eat breakfast out. Some of their wives have gone overboard on the low-fat, high-fiber, no-flavor kick."

"Roof repairs sound serious, though, and expensive."

"We'll see. I'll call you from the office, later, and tell you how it went. What's got your attention in that paper, Rosie?

"Have you heard anything about this during your chaplaincy duties, Scott?"

"About what?"

"It says here, there have been a series of burglaries in the county just south of us. Mostly empty vacation cabins and a few homes ransacked when the people were out," Rosamund replied.

"One of the deputies mentioned a memo going around about being more alert for prowlers, but there haven't been any break-ins here in town. I'm sure you don't need to worry, Sis."

"I certainly hope not. I just don't know what this world is coming to," she replied. "No one is safe, anywhere. One day everything is wonderful and you are making plans for a bright future and then in a twinkling it can all disappear."

Naidenne and Scott exchanged worried glances, while Rosamund poured a cup of coffee and took it out onto the front porch.

"Oh dear…" Naidenne began.

"We can talk about my sister later, hon. I've got to go, or I'll be late. She's probably just moody, anyway. Maybe it's hormones," Scott said, before kissing his wife and leaving.

## Chapter Three

When Scott entered the coffee shop shortly after seven o'clock, the four trustees were already seated at a table with half-empty cups of coffee in front of them.

"About time you got here, Pastor, the day's about gone," red-faced Orville Locke greeted him.

He pulled a bandana from his unbuttoned and overstuffed overalls and mopped his shiny head, already beaded with perspiration.

Scott feared for Locke's health. Orville always looked on the verge of a stroke and the half-eaten doughnut on the table next to his coffee wasn't going to help.

"These youngsters like to lie in bed half the day," Josiah Watkins added in his raspy voice.

Watkins was the oldest active member of the congregation. A small, dried-up twig of a man whose attitudes were firmly planted in the early twentieth century, he still managed to exert a major influence on the business of the church.

"Ah, cut him some slack, you two," Bill Odem said.

"The man's still practically a newlywed," he went on, "I wouldn't want to crawl out from under the covers, either, if my Effie looked like Mrs. Davidson," he added while wiggling his eyebrows and drawing an hourglass shape with his hands.

Bill thought of himself as a funny man, patterning his repartee after 1960's insult comic, Don Rickles, whom he, unfortunately, resembled.

Scott smiled thinly at the others as he sat down.

Bill signaled the waitress and she approached with a coffee pot at the ready to pour refills.

"You gentlemen ready to order? ...and I use the word 'gentlemen' ironically, just so's you know," she added. "Except you, of course, Pastor."

"What'll you have, Padre? Did you work up an appetite this morning?" Bill said with a broad wink, looking around to be certain no one missed his innuendo.

"I'd like a scrambled egg and whole wheat toast, Gladys," Scott answered the waitress, ignoring Bill's comment. He feared Odem was slipping into some sort of raunchy second adolescence.

"So, what's on the agenda for this morning?" Scott asked Orville, the senior trustee, as the others gave Gladys their orders.

"Roof leaks," Josiah interrupted.

"We noticed a big wet patch on the ceiling of the choir's dressing room. Looks like the water's running along the rafters from that flat section near the steeple," Orville explained.

"Probably need a whole new roof," Josiah predicted.

"So, with the budget crisis going on, we wondered what you could offer us to help out, Pastor," Bill said.

"Have you gotten quotes on the necessary repairs? Just what are we looking at?" Scott asked.

"Well, no actual quotes, you might say, but my brother-on-law got a new roof put on his house a few years ago and it was a huge expense, thousands and thousands, and that was a simple house, none of these weird angles like we've got on the church," Orville said.

"We gotta cut expenses somewhere, or we'll never pay for it," Bill insisted.

"We're thinking, since your pretty wife works and you got two incomes, now, we could cut back on your salary to cover the roof expenses, just until it's paid for, of course."

"Hold on a minute. I'm not ready to even consider something like that, until we have firm figures from a few roofing contractors. All we know for certain is we have a leak. Until a professional looks at the roof, we can't tell what sort of repairs are needed, let alone their cost," Scott told the men.

Their breakfasts arrived as Scott spoke.

The trustees exchanged looks and began to concentrate on the food.

Scott couldn't get a single bite past his rising anger. He took a sip of coffee, pushed his plate away and grabbed his check.

"I've got to make a run by the hospital before heading to the church office, so I'll be going now. When you get some quotes on the roof, we can discuss it again."

He made his way stiffly to the cashier, keeping a tight rein on his anger, until he was safely in his car.

"Damn and blast those men!" he cursed, slamming the steering wheel with his fist.

Taking a few deep breaths, he regained his composure and began to share his feelings with the Lord. As soon as he felt calm enough, Scott started the car and drove away.

It was people like his trustees who made too many good ministers decide to leave the pastorate, Scott thought. He had run up against these men, and others like them, throughout his ministry, yet somehow always managed to keep his perspective.

It was different now. He wanted to protect Naidenne from the more challenging aspects of ministry life for as long as possible.

She'd had some unfortunate experiences with churches and church leaders when she was growing up and only came back to God shortly before Scott met her. A tussle with the trustees over his salary could undermine her newly reborn faith in the church as an institution and, possibly, even her faith in God.

After driving by the hospital to avoid having lied to the trustees, he pulled into the church parking lot and parked in his reserved space with the hand-painted "Reserved for Pasor" sign.

This was a fairly recent amenity, an anniversary gift from the church, in lieu of a raise. There was seldom a problem finding parking at the church, but he appreciated the gesture, even with the misspelling.

Once in his office, Scott answered his phone and email messages, looked through his sermon notes and tried to put the breakfast meeting out of his mind.

Shortly before nine, he remembered his promise to call his wife.

This was one of her work days, so he called the property management office.

"Naidenne Grinager Properties, Naidenne speaking," she answered.

"Don't you mean, Naidenne Davidson?" Scott teased.

"Oh, hi darling! How did it go with the trustees?"

"Fine. They just wanted to get my input on some roof repairs. They are going to get some quotes to bring to the full board before we decide how to proceed."

"A few weeks ago, after a particularly heavy rain, I noticed a leak in the choir robing room. I suppose that's what they were talking about."

"Yes. We don't know if it will be a major repair or not, until professionals look at it. But the trustees are a pessimistic bunch, never happy unless they've got a crisis," Scott said.

"It probably makes them feel important, now they are all retired. You know how men are," Naidenne teased.

"Of course. But, I am not retired, so I need to get back to all my very important work and I'll let you get on with yours. I love you."

"You too. See you at lunch?"

"It's the Lunch Bunch today, so I won't be home."

"Oh, I'd forgotten! I didn't make your sack lunch this morning," Naidenne moaned.

"No worries. I'll grab something from the Crab Shack. See you this evening, my love."

After Naidenne put down the phone she finished some escrow papers she'd been working on.

She was coming into the office only part-time since marrying Scott, and had given up the property management side of her business. She limited herself to real estate sales in order to have time to fulfill her duties as a pastor's wife.

Naidenne wanted to help her husband in every possible way.

A single business woman well into her thirties, she'd supposed she would never marry before meeting Scott.

Growing up, from grade school on, Naidenne was always the tallest girl in every class and usually the tallest student, too, until the boys got their growth spurts in the last years of high school.

Being so tall was awkward for the shy girl and she hadn't dated much.

Naidenne was grateful her mother always insisted on good posture, never letting Naidenne get away with slouching to try to seem smaller. It was one of the few blessings she'd received from her mother.

Until fairly recently Naidenne never even bothered to play up her best features, opting instead to be as inconspicuously appropriate as possible, by sticking to a bland uniform of dark suits and white shirts.

She'd spent years struggling to tame her riotous reddish curls, always pulling her hair back into a rather messy knot.

One day a friend suggested to Naidenne that, if she tried a more feminine style, she might have a better chance at an active social life. On a whim, she'd taken this advice to heart and soon caught the eye of the local pastor, who was now her husband.

In the months since, she'd learned how to make the most of her clear skin, willowy long-legged figure and luxurious hair.

Naidenne loved going out with her tall, handsome husband, knowing he was just as proud to be with her. She thanked God every day for bringing Scott into her life.

The little bell over the door tinkled, announcing the arrival of Shirley Griffith, partner in the local crafts boutique the two ran in a section of Naidenne's office.

"Good morning! Isn't it a beautiful day, Naidenne?"

"Hi, what's up?"

"I've got a couple of boxes of crafts out in the car. Can you give me a hand?"

The two women went out to Shirley's car and soon returned, each carrying a large cardboard box.

"What's in this one, a chainsaw sculpture? And the chainsaw?" Naidenne asked. "It's sure heavy."

"Close, but no chainsaws. These are a couple of metal sculptures Maizey Simmon's late husband created. They've been sitting in her garage for years. I was finally able to talk her into trying to sell them on consignment. They are actually pretty good."

"Hey, they really are," Naidenne said when she had the pieces unwrapped. "How did you convince her to let them go?"

Admiring the intricate wire dolphin and a stylized cougar made from cut and welded metal scraps, Shirley responded, "I told her about the new dishwasher I just bought with my own craft sales income. She hadn't realized there was a market for this sort of local artwork."

"The increased tourist traffic has certainly helped our business. I noticed we've been getting more arts and crafts shoppers than people looking for real estate."

"Do you miss the property management income? I know it got you through the housing slump."

"It sure did. But, no, we are managing fine on Scott's salary. My occasional real estate commissions go into the retirement fund, mostly."

"Sometimes I wish our church was affiliated with a major denomination, so we could offer our pastor a decent retirement pension."

"That's a kind thought, Shirley. I'm sure we will be fine, though. God will provide, after all."

"Oh, He gives us what we need, and what he knows is good for us, but that's not always what we'd rather have. I don't like to see a pastor left penniless in retirement, without even a home of his own or the money to buy one."

Feeling a little uncomfortable talking about their finances with a member of her husband's congregation, Naidenne changed the subject.

"Where do you think we should display this new art? What sort of price is Maizey asking?"

"That was really funny. When I asked her, she was torn between paying us to haul it away as junk and putting a sentimental price on it, way above what it might bring. Finally, I suggested a couple of numbers and she picked one she could live with."

"I hope they sell quickly. Does she have more of her husband's art?"

"When I asked her she said the basement and attic are full of it. These two pieces in the garage were just the easiest for her to get to. I don't think she does stairs, anymore."

"The sculptures look quite nice here, don't they? If these sell as well as I think they might, you and I should go over and offer to take a look at the other things for her."

"That sounds like fun. I'll suggest it when I deliver her proceeds from the sale of these."

"Scott's not coming home for lunch today. Would you like to come over and eat with Rosamund and me?"

"Sorry, I'm committed to joining the Lunch Bunch today for our weekly sack lunch and prayer meeting."

"Of course. I forgot you attend, too. We'll have you over another time."

Naidenne felt a twinge of guilt for not participating in the lunchtime prayer group, too.

She supposed it was selfish, but on office days she enjoyed getting home for lunch and was reluctant to add another weekly church obligation onto her schedule.

"That reminds me, I've got some errands to run before lunch. I'll take these old boxes back with me," Shirley said.

"See you later."

Shirley left and Naidenne went back to her paperwork and was undisturbed the rest of the morning.

Setting the sign to let people know she would be open again after lunch, she locked up and went home.

# Chapter Four

When Naidenne returned home for lunch, she was surprised the parsonage was empty.

There was a note on the counter from Rosamund, "Lunch with Len...back before supper."

Naidenne smiled and then set out the fixings for a tuna sandwich.

Sitting at the kitchen table eating her lunch, she thought back to the years when solitary meals like this had been her everyday routine.

She thanked God, yet again, for bringing Scott into her life.

There was a time when she would have shuddered to consider spending time with a member of the clergy, when she consciously avoided so-called men of God, but after meeting Scott she'd discovered there actually were men who lived up to that description.

Naidenne seldom thought about it, now, but when she was only thirteen she was repeatedly raped by a traveling evangelist whom her parents invited to stay in their home during a revival campaign.

When she told her mother what was happening, that saintly woman told her to be grateful to have the attentions of such a godly man and to keep her mouth shut, so she didn't destroy his ministry.

The experience left Naidenne with a rather dim view of organized religion and a permanent lack of respect for her mother.

It had taken Scott to show her a different aspect to the church and those within its circle.

Washing her cup and plate, she glanced again at the note from Rosamund and wondered where Len had taken her for lunch.

~

In Cannon Beach to the north, Rosamund sat at a linen-draped table with a magnificent view of the Pacific Ocean.

She and Len had finished their entrees and were lingering over coffee and dessert.

"How's that chocolate soufflé, Rose?" Len asked. "Looks lighter than air. I hope it has some real flavor."

"It's delicious! The raspberry syrup has just the right blend of sweetness and tang to complement the chocolate. This whole lunch is just wonderful. You are always so good to me."

Len ate the last bite of his apple pie and put down his fork.

"I wanted this lunch to be special, you know."

"Oh, it is, but you always treat me special, Len."

"That's because I care about you, Rosamund."

"I care about you, too."

"Do you? I wonder."

"Why do you say that? Have I done something to upset you?"

"It's more what you haven't done. I think you know what I'm talking about here, so don't be coy."

Rosamund looked down at the remains of her dessert. The moment she'd been dreading had arrived.

"Well?" Len prompted. "Do you love me, or don't you?"

"I do! More than you can ever know."

"Well, then, why do you keep putting me off? At our age we can't afford to play games, Rosie."

"I want to marry you. I really do. It's just…"

"Just what?" Len pressed.

Without warning, Rosamund began to cry. Embarrassment turned her tears into sobs.

"Gosh, don't cry, Rosie! I didn't mean to make you cry. Please stop."

Len scooted his chair closer, patting Rosamund clumsily on the shoulder.

"There, there, it's alright. I won't rush you. I'm so sorry, dear. Please don't cry."

Rosamund's sobs subsided into hiccups and sniffs as she dabbed at her eyes with a napkin.

"I'm sorry, Len. I don't know what's the matter with me. Forgive me, please."

"No, it was my fault. I shouldn't have bullied you like that. We can just forget everything I said. Except don't forget I love you...and whenever you're ready, I want you to be my wife... now don't start crying again, please."

Rosamund excused herself to wash her face and regain her composure in the ladies' room while Len paid for their lunch.

Looking at her splotchy face in the mirror, she thought it was a miracle anyone could want to marry her. She felt tears threatening to fall once more.

"Rosamund Davidson, you are a fool!" she told her reflection.

Len was so kind, but his patience wouldn't last forever. If she hadn't known it before, today's lunch date would have convinced her.

Back in Bannoch, the Lunch Bunch meeting at the church was breaking up.

"Goodbye, Pastor Scott. See you at Bible Study," Hazel Gooding called as she pulled herself up the steps from the basement social hall.

The remaining handful of older women gathered up their things and laboriously climbed the stairs to the parking lot while their pastor lingered in the fellowship hall looking after them with a thoughtful expression.

When this noon-time prayer group first started the idea was to provide a convenient time and place for working people to gather on their lunch breaks to pray for their co-workers and the community.

It was hard for busy people to take a night out during the week for such gatherings and this seemed a good solution.

Women in the church who did not work outside their homes volunteered to provide sack lunches for the others, to make it easy for workers to drop in to eat, pray and leave; getting back to their jobs on time.

At first, the congregation was enthusiastic about the project and made a point of encouraging each other and members of the community to attend. Gradually, many volunteer lunch-makers dropped out. A meagre response from the community discouraged others from participating. Scott felt continuing these half-hearted efforts drained the resources and spirits of a congregation.

He proposed cancelling the project, but, as with many church programs, once begun, no one wanted to acknowledge failure by ending it.

As a pastor, he would rather see ineffectual programs dropped and the energy used, instead, to assess the real needs of the community and to find out where those needs were matched by the resources of the congregation.

Scott firmly believed any church which was genuinely seeking God's will would find it…and if God allowed a congregation to continue, it was because He had work for them to do… in the very place they were planted and with the abilities and talents already present within the congregation.

Like many others, his congregation frequently bemoaned their lack of resources to support the programs they saw in other churches; they wanted to put on grand musical productions, but had few musicians, or to sponsor a foreign missionary when they couldn't even figure out how to fix the roof without cutting their pastor's pay.

Scott's philosophy was to find out what a church could do and then do it. Do it boldly and do it well.

One idea, since the congregation had aged and had few young families, was for the church to start an "Adopt-a-Grandparent" program providing afterschool care and mentoring for children in the community whose parents work and who had no local extended family.

However, the board did not want to pursue his plan when Scott suggested it. They said it would be too much work and probably wouldn't bring in any new members, anyway.

Rather than regretting what they lacked, Scott felt they should take advantage of their abundance.

Every church has an abundance of something. Theirs just happened to be old people.

Identify your abundance and find a matching need to fill with it, was his motto.

The Lunch Bunch program had seemed to fit with this philosophy but, as it turned out, the Bannoch community hadn't seen the need for it.

Scott told his people, over and over, how important it is to get out of the church and into the neighborhoods to find out which needs the community recognizes.

It was discouraging for him to realize, after all his years in Bannoch, he still hadn't been able to persuade the people into his way of seeing things.

Perhaps it was time to move on. He'd run out of new ways to try to reach the people. Maybe they had become so used to his voice they were no longer listening.

Scott turned to his computer and pulled up a listing of churches with open pulpits and active search committees, just to see what his options might be.

☙

When Naidenne returned from her office that afternoon, she spied Rosamund's handbag on the hall table and knew she was home, so she was surprised not to find her in the kitchen.

Going upstairs, Naidenne tapped on the closed door of her sister-in-law's room.

"Rosamund, are you okay?"

"I'm fine, dear, just a bit of a headache from the long drive," Rosamund answered through the door. "We went all the way to Cannon Beach for lunch."

"Can I get you something?" Naidenne asked.

"No, thanks. I'm just lying down with a cool cloth on my head. I'll be up to fix dinner soon."

"Don't bother. I'll throw something together. Would you like a tray in your room?"

Rosamund reluctantly opened the door. Her eyes were puffy and red.

"No, that won't be necessary. I'm feeling much better."

"Are you sure? You're not coming down with something are you?"

"I am feeling a bit sniffly. I suppose it might be a cold, or allergies, maybe. Nothing to worry about."

"Well, you go lie back down. I'll come up when dinner's ready and you can tell me then if you'd rather have yours on a tray."

Naidenne frowned as she went down the hall to her room to change clothes.

Rosamund looked very much like a woman who had been crying, and crying hard, not like she was coming down with an illness.

Naidenne said a quick prayer for her sister-in-law as she pulled on one of her pairs of high water jeans and went downstairs to find something for dinner.

When she heard Scott come in, Naidenne called out, "I decided to fix hamburgers. Will you barbecue them, or shall I pop the patties under the broiler?"

Without answering his wife, Scott came into the kitchen and wrapped his arms around her, taking solace and drawing strength from the physical contact.

"What's the matter, Scott?" she pulled back, looking with concern into his eyes.

"Nothing, really. I just missed you today. Guess I've been dipping my toes into the slough of despond. You are my restful arbor, my love."

"That's very flattering, Pilgrim, but can you leave the arbor long enough to heat up the grill?" Naidenne asked, in an attempt to lighten Scott's mood.

"Sure. Now I've had my batteries recharged, I'm ready to keep on going and going and going. Just let me change into my chef's hat and apron."

He patted Naidenne's bottom and ran up the stairs to change his clothes.

Naidenne was setting out toasted buns and condiments when he reentered the kitchen in T-shirt and khaki shorts.

"Where's Rose? Is she dining out again tonight?" Scott asked.

"She's upstairs lying down. Said she had a headache."

"Sounds like you think there is more to the story."

"When I got home and checked on her, she looked like she'd been crying. I'm afraid she and Len may be having problems."

"That's too bad. I like Len. But, if you're right, there's nothing we can do about it. They are both adults and will have to work it out on their own."

"Oh, I know that. Still, you should be gentle with her when she comes down to eat. Don't let on you know she's been upset."

As it turned out, Rosamund decided to stay in her room and skip dinner. Her excuse was a late and large lunch, but in truth, she was still too agitated to eat.

Finally over her crying jag, Rosamund paced around her bedroom, pausing now and then to stare out her window at the treetops swaying in the gathering darkness.

After one such interlude, she gave her head a shake, squared her shoulders and walked purposefully to her desk, where she opened the bottom drawer and pulled out a box of stationary.

With an air of decisiveness, she sat down and began to write. When finished, she folded the sheet of paper and put it into an envelope.

Pausing for just a moment and taking a deep breath, Rosamund crossed to her closet, pulled an overnight bag from the top shelf and laid it on her bed. She quickly filled it with toiletries and clothing, zipped it up and set it by her door.

She stepped onto the landing and called out a cheerful, "Goodnight!" down the stairs to Scott and Naidenne before returning to her room.

After waiting what seemed hours after hearing Scott and Naidenne come upstairs and settle in for the night, Rosamund felt certain they must finally be asleep.

Tiptoeing along the hall and down the stairs, she placed her envelope on the dining room table and let herself out the back door, locking it softly behind her.

She drove out to the highway where she paused to decide whether to turn north or south before flipping on her left turn signal and pulling out into the late night flow of traffic.

# Chapter Five

"How foolish I am to be running away like this," Rosamund chastised herself as she drove through the night.

The unlighted coastal highway was lonelier after dark than she remembered. Even the usually heavy tourist traffic was sparse, as most travelers had already wisely turned into a brightly lit motel for a good night's sleep.

Driving at a steady five miles per hour under the posted speed limit, she was occasionally overtaken and passed by a more impatient driver who soon disappeared down the highway. Each time, the passage of the bright lights momentarily blinded Rosamund, reminding her of why she seldom drove at night.

Her eyes were readjusting from the bright beams of a passing car when she saw something rush across the highway in front of her.

Thinking it was a deer, she braked hard and swerved to the shoulder to avoid a collision.

Her car's engine stalled from this rough treatment and she sat, shaken, beside the highway as the motor ticked, both she and her car attempting to cool down.

Rosamund's heart rate was just returning to normal when a dark form loomed up in the side window.

A man, his face partially obscured by long, unkempt hair, knocked on the glass.

"Do you need a hand, lady? Open up and I'll help you, and maybe you can give me a ride," he urged.

Rosamund reacted instinctively, quickly turning the key in the ignition and stepping on the gas. The tires spun in the gravel before the little car shot out onto the highway, leaving the surprised stranger shouting after it.

"Oh dear, that wasn't very charitable of me," she said. "He must have been in desperate straits to be alone on foot out here."

Thoughts of the Good Samaritan and those less-good folks who had passed the poor injured man by in the parable almost caused Rosamund to go back and see what the stranger needed.

Before giving in to that generous impulse, her more pragmatic nature asserted itself. A woman alone on a deserted highway in the middle of the night had no business stopping for any strange man who sprang up out of the darkness.

Instead, she made a mental note to call the State Police once she got to her motel in Gold Beach. She would tell them where she encountered the man and let them attend to his needs.

With her mind made up, she continued her journey.

❦

"Naidenne, did you see this?" Scott called to his wife the next morning.

"What 'this' do you mean?" she responded from the kitchen.

"There's an envelope on the dinner table…from the handwriting I'd say it's from my sister."

Naidenne dried her hands on her apron, came out of the kitchen and found Scott in the dining room reading the note.

"Good grief!" he exclaimed.

"What? Tell me, please," Naidenne urged.

"She's gone. My sister got some sort of bee in her bonnet and says she's going to take a few days away to gain perspective. Says she isn't very good company and doesn't want to impose her mood on us. What hogwash!"

"Does she say where she's gone?"

"Not really. Just going to stay some place quiet, so she can think and pray."

"Is there any clue as to what is bothering her?"

"Not that I can see. Here, read it for yourself."

Scott handed the note to Naidenne and the couple walked into the kitchen as she read Rosamund's message.

## The First Ladies Club

"What should we do, Scott?"

"Nothing to do. She's a big girl. If she wants to hare off like this, there's nothing we can do. I'm not about to go after her and drag her home, even if I knew where she went."

Scott sounded angry, but Naidenne knew it was because he was worried about his sister.

"Has Rosamund ever done anything like this before?"

"Only once, a very long time ago. When her fiancé, Roger, was killed, she took off for a week and no one ever knew where she went. When she returned, she refused to talk about it. Rosie's pretty private about her feelings."

"Do you suppose this is about Len? If he hurt her, I'll never forgive him."

"Now, let's not start jumping to conclusions. I think we should give her some space. She'll probably be back in a day or two with everything figured out. Let's have breakfast."

Naidenne scrambled eggs while Scott made toast.

When they sat down to eat, they prayed for God's protection and guidance for Rosamund, along with wisdom and patience for them all to face whatever else was in store that day.

✦

In mid-morning, Len Spurgeon dropped by the church office and rapped softly on Scott's open door.

"Got a minute, Pastor?"

"Len, come in. What brings you here?"

"I've been trying to reach your sister all morning, but she's not answering her phone. I swung by your place on the way here, but she wasn't home. Do you know where she is?"

"She's gone out of town for a couple of days, I think. She didn't tell you she was going?"

"Not a peep about it at lunch yesterday. How long has she been planning this?"

"I think it was a sort of last minute thing. Is it important for you to get in touch with her right away? She shouldn't be gone very long," Scott said.

"Don't you even know when she's coming back?"

"She was sort of vague about it when she left."

Scott was valiantly attempting to avoid telling Len how Rose left, but didn't want to lie to him. He was pretty sure the problem his sister was trying to figure out had Len at its center.

"Well, where did she go, can you tell me that, at least?"

"Sit down, Len, and I will tell you what I know."

The older man sank into the cracked imitation leather visitor's chair and looked at Scott with a worried expression.

Scott came around and leaned against his desk with his hands clasped together, almost beseechingly, as he tried to find the right words. With a shrug, he held up his open palms as though offering a gift and began to speak.

"I don't know where Rosamund has gone, Len. She came home after her lunch with you yesterday, all upset. She'd been crying and didn't join us for dinner. This morning she was gone. We found a note she left for us indicating something was upsetting her and she needed to get away for a few days while she worked it all out. She didn't say what the problem was, but I can't help thinking it has something to do with you. Do you have any idea what could be bothering her?"

Len moaned, leaned forward with his elbows on his knees and dropped his head into his hands.

"Do you know what this is all about, Len?" Scott prodded.

Len sat back in the chair. When he looked up at Scott there were tears in his eyes and his face was pale.

Scott thought the older man looked ill.

"Can I get you a drink of water, or something?"

"No, no. I'm okay. When she wouldn't answer my phone calls, I was afraid I'd gone too far."

"What do you mean, you went too far?" Scott asked, standing to attention, as though ready to defend his sister's honor.

"Calm down, Pastor. Nothing like that. I love Rosamund and I want to marry her. I've told her that over and over, but she keeps putting me off. She says she loves me, too, you know."

"If that's true, then why won't she marry you?"

"I wish I knew. I'm afraid I got impatient trying to figure it out. Yesterday I asked her again. I guess I pushed too hard. You're right about her crying because of me."

"What did you do? You weren't violent, were you?"

"Course not. Don't be daft. I took her to our special place in Cannon Beach, wined and dined her…well dined, anyway…you know she never drinks…then I said I was getting tired of waiting, or something, and she just fell apart. Once the waterworks started, I back-pedaled, but I guess the damage was done. Shoot, I wouldn't hurt her for the world. If she just wants to be friends, I'll take what I can get and make up my mind to be happy with it. I just don't want to lose her."

Scott feared Len was going to start sobbing. He patted him on the shoulder before retreating behind his desk and sitting down, giving the fellow a chance to regain his composure.

So, this was the reason for Rosie's flight. For some reason, she didn't want to marry Len, but didn't want to turn him down, either. Women…go figure.

"Look, Len. This doesn't sound too serious. I mean, Rose will be back before you know it and you can tell her how you feel and everything will be back to normal in no time."

"I hope so. But in the meantime, where is she? What if something happens to her? What if she needs help?"

"God has his eye on my sister, wherever her flights of fancy take her. Would you like me to pray with you before you go?"

The two men prayed for Rosamund's safe return before Len went back to the bank.

Scott tried to concentrate on his sermon notes, but in his mind Len's plaintive words played over and over, "Where is she? What if she needs our help?"

☙

Dinner that night was simple and light because Scott and Naidenne had to go back to the church for Bible Study and choir practice. Simple, due to lack of time, and light because there were always refreshments served for any gathering at the church.

In an attempt to cut down on the number of evenings church members needed to come out, the board had decided to have all the weekly evening meetings on Wednesdays. There were Bible clubs for the children, Bible studies for adults, the Youth Group for teens, plus choir practice and any board or committee meetings.

It worked well in theory, and perhaps with a much larger congregation it wouldn't put such a strain on a church's limited resources.

For Bannoch Community Fellowship it was becoming a combination juggling and tightrope act. The Board members and Trustees were the same people who sang in the choir, led Bible studies and clubs, served on committees and led the youth.

Coming out only once a week had sounded attractive, but the reality might soon result in burnout for the church leadership. The scriptural admonition, "Do not grow weary in doing good," came often to Scott's mind.

Scott had been suggesting they revisit the issue for several months, but no one wanted to go back to the old days of church meetings almost every night of the week. He felt certain there must be a compromise solution, but hadn't been able to come up with one the board would accept.

Returning home later that night, Naidenne checked the answering machine, hoping for a message from Rosamund.

"Pastor, I know you're there!" an imperious nasal voice rasped from the recorder. "You can't avoid me, you know. I want to talk to you about this Sunday. I want to sit in my spot in my usual pew. If anyone else has been sitting there, you better just tell them to find someplace else."

The caller hung up without even identifying herself.

"What in the world…" Naidenne began.

"Dear, I'd like to introduce you to the infamous Maureen Oldham. Doesn't sound as though she's mellowed, after all."

"Scott, you don't suppose Rosamund went away to avoid this woman, do you? She does sound frightful."

"No, I didn't get a chance to tell you earlier, but Len Spurgeon dropped in to see me today. I think you were right about it being romance troubles. Let's go to bed. I'll tell you all about it."

## Chapter Six

The fugitive, Carver Schramm, scrambled through the undergrowth above the northbound lane of Highway 101, making his way to the Canadian Yukon Territory, where he hoped to lose himself.

He hadn't meant to kill that stupid guard at Pelican Bay Super Max Prison. The fool must have had some sort of brittle bone disease for his neck to snap like that.

Schramm wasn't squeamish about a bit of murder, now and then, but he knew killing a guard while breaking out would have every cop in the country on his tail.

Keeping constantly on the move was making him hungry.

The supplies he'd found in the last place he broke into were long gone. He needed to find more food soon.

It had caused him almost physical pain to leave behind all the loot the owners had just lying around in those empty shacks, but he was too smart to take any valuables to sell. He figured the cops would be watching all the pawn shops and he wasn't about to take a chance on being seen in public. His escape plan depended on him staying out of sight and one step ahead of the authorities.

Schramm had expected to be closer to the Canadian border by now, not still tramping through the wilds of Oregon.

He'd already be in Washington if that old bat didn't get scared and drive off into the night. Stupid bitch.

The cabins he was encountering near the highway all seemed to be occupied, but he wouldn't venture far into the woods, not as long as he could avoid it. Carver was a city kid. All these friggin' trees disoriented him and the night sounds gave him the creeps.

A steady hum of traffic on the highway told him he couldn't try to hijack another car here, at least not before nightfall.

Someone traveling alone on a quiet stretch of road was what he needed.

That old biddy had been perfect. She'd looked like the type who would open the door to talk to him long enough to let him get his hands around her scrawny neck, too.

Flexing his fingers now, he could almost feel her windpipe pulsing under his thumbs.

A loud growling from his empty stomach quickly changed his focus from fantasies of violence to his own growing hunger.

Glimpsing a house off to the right in the trees up ahead, about a hundred yards from the highway, he veered in that direction.

As he grew closer it became obvious the cabin was inhabited. Smoke rose from the chimney and washing hung on a wire strung between the pines in the only sunny patch of yard. Battered toys lay scattered among the dusty pine needles.

Schramm hesitated, but only for a moment. Where there were people there was food.

He pulled a wicked-looking hunting knife from his belt, congratulating himself, once again, as he held it up to admire the sharply honed blade. He'd hit the jackpot when he found the weapon in the hunting gear casually stowed in the back of a pickup truck in the dark gravel parking lot of a roadside bar.

Keeping out of the line of sight from the cabin's bare windows, he crouched low and slowly approached the warped and peeling back door.

Carver paused on the sagging doorstep to listen for movement from inside.

Hearing music, he smiled. He liked a sound track while he worked.

The unlocked doorknob turned easily in his hand and he slipped stealthily inside.

In the Lexus's cushy backseat on the ride home from Tillamook Saturday night, Naidenne watched the stars overhead through the open moon roof and listened to the quiet conversations of her friends.

Riding shotgun, Judy was commenting on one of the speakers from the conference they'd attended.

"I just didn't think she was *real*, you know?"

"She certainly wasn't a hologram," Eskaletha snapped, without taking her eyes off the road.

"That's not what I meant and you know it. I didn't feel like what she said was organic, like it came from the heart."

"I know what you mean, Judy," Elizabeth spoke up. "It was like she was saying what she thought we wanted to hear or something. Almost like it was more of a performance than a testimony."

"I imagine giving the same testimony over and over could easily begin to sound like a script, no matter how heartfelt. Remember, these women do this night after night, all over the country," Naidenne felt compelled to add.

"Well, the music was wonderful. I felt like I was in Heaven," Olivette piped up from where she was squeezed in between Naidenne and Elizabeth.

"I wonder…" Eskaletha began, and then paused.

"Wonder what?" Judy asked.

"Well, we always expect beautiful music in Heaven…I wonder if any of what we expect will really be there."

"Of course, it will," Olivette insisted.

"I suppose we will just have to wait and see," Naidenne said.

"Just one of those unanswerable questions, like why God allows so much pain and sadness in the world," agreed Elizabeth.

"Oh, that reminds me! Have you heard about all the break-ins south of us? Mostly empty cabins, but someone's stealing food and trashing everything," Judy said.

"Probably just a bunch of kids with too much time on their hands," Elizabeth offered.

"Kids with no discipline," Eskaletha said. "I blame their parents."

# The First Ladies Club

"You've got to admit there isn't much for teenagers to do in our small coastal towns, though, Letha. That's an issue our First Ladies' Club should address," Elizabeth said.

*❧*

On a well-traveled logging road not far from Bannoch Scott was riding in the less-than-cushy backseat of a sheriff's cruiser. He was listening as the deputies up front conversed quietly over the scratchy, metallic background chatter from their radio.

The dispatcher abruptly squawked out the unit's call sign and began to relay details of a break-in and suspicious death in the hills on the other side of town.

Deputy Williams responded that they were on their way to the scene, ETA ten to fifteen minutes.

*❧*

"And you are sure your uncle was dead before you left the house?" Deputy Williams asked the overweight woman who slouched in the middle of the chaos of her kitchen wearing dirty rubber sandals, cut-off jeans and a man's tee shirt.

The woman's greasy hair, parted in the middle and tucked behind her ears, revealed an array of mismatched earrings suspended above a Harley logo tattooed on the side of her neck.

In the adjoining living room, two preschool age children stared listlessly at the Lawrence Welk Show reruns on the console-style television, seemingly unmoved by the bubbly champagne music.

"Yes, of course. I told you, that's why me and the kids took off down to the neighbors to use the phone. Uncle Virgil's been working on dying for six months or more. Prostrate cancer. Today he finally made good on it. I checked his pulse and everything. Any fool could tell he was gone. Shoot, that old bird outlived most everyone. He was ninety-four on his last birthday."

"Your uncle was suffering from prostate cancer? Who was his doctor?"

"I already told the ambulance crew all that. Can't you just check their records? I've got to get this mess cleaned up and feed my kids…if I've got any food left in the place."

"I've just got a couple more questions, thank you for your patience, ma'am. So, while you and your children were gone, someone came into the house, with your uncle already lying dead in that recliner, there, slit his throat and then made this mess?"

"That's what I said, isn't it?"

"Can you tell me what all has been taken?"

"Well, it looks like they about cleaned out my ice box and pantry. Then they smashed up or just tossed around the stuff they didn't take."

After speaking, the woman looked around at the damage and sank onto a backless metal kitchen chair with a sigh, as though all the air was leaking out of her.

"What are we gonna do, now?" she moaned.

"Do you have family nearby? Or could you go to your neighbor's for a while?"

"Uncle Virgil was my last family and I was his. Why else do you think I had him here? Now, he's gone and took his Social Security payments with him. They say you can't take it with you, but he sure enough did."

Saying this seemed to restore the woman's energy, as she stood up and began sorting through the debris, while cursing under her breath.

She picked up a battered-looking blue box from the floor and shouted, "You kids get in here and find me a pan, so's I can cook up this here mac and cheese!"

Deputy Williams took this opportunity to return to Scott and the others out in the yard.

"Do the people in there need my services?" Scott asked.

"Not unless you want to pay their bills or clean up the mess. The lady of the house doesn't seem the sort to want a chaplain. Apparently, her uncle's death was from natural causes, not connected to the break-in. She'd been expecting it and she doesn't seem to be grieving. It was just a weird coincidence."

"So, someone broke in and just ignored a corpse in the room?"

"Not quite. The EMT said it looked like someone had turned out the old boy's pockets and slit his throat from ear to ear."

"When he was already dead? That's macabre. What sort of person does something like that?"

"Someone desperate and hate-filled, or just plain evil, maybe, but you'd know better than me about that, Padre."

❦

In a large culvert beneath Highway 101, Carver Schramm was tearing into a package of Oreo cookies. Chicken bones from a stolen bucket of fried chicken were scattered around him, along with a couple of empty beer cans.

He reflected on his good luck as he munched a cookie. All that food, plus twenty bucks from the stiff's pockets and all he had to do was waltz in and take it…waltz, yeah. He chuckled to himself as he thought of the old-fashioned music the dead guy liked.

He thought the old geezer was dozing in front of the TV until he'd already cut him.

The puny trickle of blood and the guys' clammy skin told Schramm he'd wasted his efforts with the knife. Still, it was good practice.

Schramm had grabbed a couple of grimy pillowcases off one of the beds and filled them with the contents of the refrigerator and cupboards. He even found a can opener and some forks and spoons when he dumped a drawer on the floor.

It was like one of those shopping spree shows he'd watched when he was a kid. He took everything he could stuff into the two cases and left.

When he heard the sirens he was already a quarter mile away from the cabin, chewing on a chicken leg as he hurried away.

It occurred to Carver to hope the cops wouldn't try to pin the dead guy on him, but then he reminded himself he would already be in the Canadian wilderness when they connected him with the burglary, if they ever did. And one more body wouldn't make much difference, with his record.

Finally, completely full, he made himself comfortable and settled in to sleep until after dark.

This lucky break could be a sign he would snag himself some wheels that night.

❧

The remainder of the night's ride-along was without incident, giving Scott ample time to think about the burglarized cabin.

He didn't like to think someone was capable of such an act as the wanton slashing of an elderly man just to steal some food.

Scott preferred to think the burglar had not known he was attacking a dead man. Murder in the commission of a robbery was at least understandable, but desecrating a corpse seemed so depraved.

Whether the burglar knew he was defiling a corpse or thought he was committing murder, Scott didn't like knowing he was wandering around so close to his own hometown and loved ones.

The people of Bannoch were seldom exposed to such evil and might not be able to defend themselves.

Returning home following his shift, Scott checked to be certain Naidenne was safely tucked into bed, then locked the house up tight and left the outside porch lights on, just in case.

Scott thought about his old dog, Reacher, and lamented anew his faithful companion's death from old age the previous summer. He began to think it was time to stop mourning the loss of his friend and protector and to start looking for a replacement.

## Chapter Seven

The next morning Scott leaned down and pressed a kiss on his sleeping wife's bare shoulder.

Naidenne opened her eyes and smiled up at him.

Spying the coffee mugs he carried, she sat up. Scooting back against her pillows, she took one of the steaming cups.

"Thank you, darling. How are you this morning?"

Scott settled on the edge of the bed beside Naidenne and sipped his coffee before replying.

"Not still upset about last night, I hope?" she asked.

"No. It was only a routine burglary and the death of a very old man from natural causes. I've seen much worse on these ride-alongs. I was a bit unsettled last night, though, thinking about what sort of person would slit the throat of a dead man before stripping him of anything valuable. I know evil exists in the world. It's just hard to take when it pops up so close at hand."

"I guess it has always been this way. One of the conference speakers from last night was talking about the origins of the Hebrew word, *hamas*. She said it means random destruction for its own sake. That's practically the definition of evil. If the ancient Hebrews needed a word for it, even in Old Testament times, it shows how long wickedness has been around."

"…and on this beautiful Sunday morning, oh, Best Beloved, we need to remember Christ has already defeated Satan and his minions, including last night's housebreaker, they just don't know it, yet," Scott added.

"You look very handsome in your go-to-meeting clothes this morning, Pastor. Too bad you are already dressed for church. Otherwise, I might try to convince you to have a little cuddle before you go," Naidenne patted the mattress beside her as she spoke and rolled her eyes.

Scott laughed, kissed his wife on the nose and went downstairs to grab his sermon notes and Bible before heading to the church, where it was his practice to spend at least thirty minutes in prayer and quiet preparation before worship.

Naidenne finished her coffee, then climbed reluctantly out of her warm bed to dress and have breakfast.

She paused before the open window, breathing deeply of the fresh sea air.

She relished these precious peaceful moments before the day's activities began, since Sunday mornings for a pastor's family were usually hectic.

She would follow her husband to church later, arriving in time to teach the primary age Sunday School class.

Once arriving at the church, both Scott and Naidenne would be fully occupied until after the worship service.

The couple seldom had a moment alone on Sundays, especially if they were invited out to dinner or shared their own mid-day meal with a church member, as was often the case.

Naidenne always dashed from her classroom as soon as the last small child was collected and frequently barely made it to the choir room in time to run through the morning's music.

It wasn't until she was donning her robe on this particular Sunday morning that she overheard a chance remark and remembered this was the day she would finally meet the infamous Maureen Oldham.

Jack Griffith, Shirley's husband, was getting his own robe from the rack.

"Where's Rosamund this morning, Naidenne? She caught the flu bug that's been going around?"

"No. She's fine, just taking a little vacation out of town."

"Really? Well, I guess she deserves one. I can't remember her ever taking a trip before."

Naidenne was uncomfortable skirting around the whole truth of Rosamund's absence and quickly changed the subject.

## The First Ladies Club

"Say, I hear a former parishioner has returned to town. Do you remember Maureen Oldham?"

"Oh...Maureen...er yes, I remember her."

Now it was Jack's turn to feel uncomfortable.

"We'd better get to our places. The director's ready to run us through our paces," he urged.

About fifteen minutes later, following the choral call to worship, Naidenne sat in the choir box at the front of the sanctuary looking out over the congregation, observing a few latecomers finding their seats.

A short, stocky woman, whose frizzy orange-dyed hair haloed an over-sized head and a generous beak of a nose, entered the sanctuary. She looked from left to right over the congregation, bestowing a tight smile here, a nod of the head there, in regal acknowledgement of those who recognized her.

Reaching a pew on the left, about half-way down the aisle, she stopped abruptly, hands on hips, and directed a glare of consternation toward the pastor.

Scott's dismayed expression alerted Naidenne; this was the notorious Maureen and Scott had not followed the voice mail instructions about preserving her special seat.

Maureen leaned into the face of the unsuspecting claim jumper and snapped, loudly enough for all to hear, "You're in my spot."

Shock drained the face of the woman seated in the pew, who then flushed bright pink. Quickly gathering up her purse and Bible and sidling awkwardly along the pew, she accidentally plopped down painfully onto the bench's low wooden sidearm and dropped everything into the far aisle.

An usher helped the flustered women retrieve her things and gave her shoulder an encouraging squeeze before he returned to his post in the narthex, throwing Maureen a disapproving scowl as he passed.

His look was wasted on Maureen who was complacently settling into her chosen roost, oblivious to the general atmosphere of reproof.

Scott stepped into the pulpit and began the worship service with an unusually emphatic and heartfelt invocation of the presence of God and His Holy Spirit.

Fighting off a twinge of guilt for missing church that morning, Rosamund was sitting on the oceanfront balcony of her third floor room at the Gold Beach Inn.

Finding it difficult to concentrate on reading, she set her devotional book on the ornate patio table, took a sip of Constant Comment tea and gazed out on the magnificent view of the ocean.

Earlier that morning she thought she'd caught a glimpse of a migrating whale and been stirred by the majesty of God's creation.

She'd always been openly disparaging of people who claimed not to need a church building to worship the Lord. Such sentiments seemed to her like rationalizations for following one's own inclinations on Sunday mornings. Looking out on the waves, now, she thought perhaps a sincere person could praise God as well outside of a sanctuary, after all. Occasionally.

After riffling through her mental file drawers, she finally recalled the last time she had skipped church. It had been the terrible winter when she caught pneumonia. She'd missed two Sundays in a row then, more than half a dozen years ago.

Perhaps the Lord would give her credit for time served and give her a pass for this morning's dereliction of duty.

She decided this resort, near where the Rogue River empties into the Pacific Ocean, might well serve as an open air cathedral. There were many easy paths to the beach and even little secluded garden areas scattered about. One couldn't help but think of God amid such natural beauty.

Rosamund had been fortunate there was a vacancy when she arrived so late at night without a reservation.

She was surprised by the quality and variety of the free breakfast bar selections that first morning. She put off eating lunch until late afternoon each day and was making her money stretch by buying only one meal per day at a nearby restaurant.

This could be a perfect vacation spot, but as she turned from the views and grounds to look into her lovely room with its king-sized bed and matching recliners, she couldn't help picturing Len here with her.

Getting away from home had calmed her frazzled nerves and helped her reclaim a bit of perspective. She was finally over her crying jags, too.

With each passing day, she became more certain she wanted to marry Len. Nevertheless, she couldn't get past her unreasonable fear of an official engagement. She loved Len too much to risk tempting the bad luck which had taken her long ago fiancé.

Once again she poured out her heart to God in prayer, begging his forgiveness for her ridiculous superstition and asking him to show her the way.

Sitting with head bowed, she'd almost dozed off in the balmy breeze from the ocean, when the barking of sea lions on the nearby rocks caught her attention.

Smiling, she watched the creatures' antics for a few moments before suddenly sitting up straighter and saying aloud, "Of course!"

She jumped up, hurried inside to the telephone and began to dial.

&

"What a day!" Scott said, after draping his suit jacket over the back of a nearby chair and folding his long frame onto the living room sofa.

He tugged off his tie and leaned his head back, the picture of a thoroughly exhausted man.

Naidenne came from the kitchen holding a glass of red wine.

"Here, this will help, at least a little."

"I'd drink a gallon, if only it would wash away the memory of today's episode with Maureen."

"Why on earth did you agree to have dinner with her after church, when you dislike her so?" Naidenne asked.

"It's because I don't like her. I'm the pastor. It's my job to love the unlikable."

"I suppose. Still, she does seem to go out of her way to provoke you. She certainly made some nasty cracks about Rosamund. I admired the way you kept your cool."

"That's the power of prayer for you," Scott said with a laugh.

"What's so funny?"

"I was actually praying for the ground to open and swallow her up. It was that mental image that kept me smiling through all of her venom. I expect I'd better ask forgiveness…but I can't genuinely repent just now. That woman is really something."

"She is a good cook, though. I enjoyed her pot roast and I wasn't just trying to make points when I asked for her recipe for the apricot dessert. I want to fix it for us some time."

"Everything tasted like dust to me with Maureen spewing nastiness across the table. If you say the food was good, I'll take your word for it."

"Honey, try to forget her. We're home, now, and you can relax."

"Did you hear what she said about the church roof? How can she be meddling already, when she's scarcely unpacked?"

"What did she say? I didn't hear her."

"Oh, never mind. She was just repeating a wacky idea the Trustees had about taking the price of a new roof out of my salary. It's nonsense. I shouldn't have mentioned it. I was just so annoyed at seeing her already back to her interfering ways."

"But, why would they want you to pay for the roof? That's silly! You didn't make it leak."

Scott stood up, put his arms around Naidenne and pulled her to him.

"It was a stupid joke one of the trustees made, not seriously, I'm sure. It takes an old harridan like Maureen to try to act on it."

"Are you sure?"

"Of course. One lasting blessing of Maureen's all-too-brief absence from Bannoch is she is no longer a church officer. She's not on any of the boards, so she is in no position to make any real trouble."

Naidenne began to protest, when Scott kissed her.

"Come on, we've given Maureen Oldham too much of our time already for one day. That glass of wine and your beautiful gray eyes have gone to my head and given me much better ideas of ways to spend the rest of the evening."

Naidenne laughed and turned out the lights while Scott locked up, then followed him upstairs.

Carver Schramm awoke after dark with stabbing pains in his stomach, a raging thirst and a splitting headache. It took a moment for him to clear his head enough to see he was still in the culvert beneath the highway where he'd dozed off after feasting on his haul from the cabin.

Finding a half-full can of beer near his hand, he greedily gulped down the contents and immediately began to vomit.

When the spasms passed, he wiped his face on his shirttail and tried to assess his situation.

After heaving up his guts, he felt even worse than ever. Something was definitely wrong.

It must've been the leftover chicken, or something else he'd eaten. He should have known better. That place was such a dump; there could have been all sorts of microbes crawling around in the food.

He couldn't stay here. He might die lying out in the cold when he was so sick. He had to find shelter where he could hole-up and recover.

Schramm rolled over and rose shakily to his feet. He made his way, retching, stumbling and crawling, out of the gulley and up into the woods above the highway. Sweating and fighting a wave of nausea, he was forced to ease down against a tree to catch his breath before moving on.

## Chapter Eight

"Thanks for coming with me this morning, Deenie," Shirley said, as she drove over the rutted track to Maizey Simmons's place.

"I'm happy to come. I want to see the look on Maizey's face when you hand her that one hundred dollar check for her husband's sculptures."

"Yes, I'm pretty sure the poor dear can use the money. There she is, now."

Shirley parked in the gravel drive and waved to an older woman standing in the open doorway of a modest two-story farmhouse.

"Come on in, you two. Coffee's on and I just took a batch of biscuits out of the oven," Maizey called out.

"Homemade biscuits! Now, I'm really glad I came," Naidenne remarked as she got out of the car.

Stepping through the wood framed screen door into the old-fashioned kitchen was like walking into another century.

Well-scrubbed butcher block counter tops and a square porcelain farmhouse sink would cost a small fortune in a trendy home supply store, but the signs of years of wear declared these were not some designer's retro fashion statement.

A round oak claw-footed dining table, draped with blue and white checked oil-cloth, filled the center of the room, while open shelving lined the walls.

Maizey set a heaping basket of hot biscuits onto the table beside a mason jar filled with wildflowers and a dish holding a dripping honeycomb.

"Do you keep bees, too, Maizey? I haven't seen a honeycomb in ages," Naidenne said.

"My old man was the beekeeper, but I've managed to keep one of the hives alive. That's bramble blossom honey, just as tasty as you'll find anywhere."

"This is wonderful," Shirley said, as she added honey to a biscuit already dripping with melted butter.

"Eat up, you two. It'll only go to waste, otherwise, 'cause my waist sure doesn't need any."

The women chatted through several biscuits and refills of coffee.

Shirley wiped her hands on one of Maizey's handmade cloth napkins and pulled an envelope from her purse.

"Here's the proceeds from the sale of those two sculptures, Maizey. Do you think we can take a look at what else you have?"

"Why, this is too much! Did folks really pay fifty dollars apiece for those piles of scrap metal?"

"Yes, indeed," Naidenne replied. "We can sell more, I'm sure. Your husband was a very good artist."

"Well, I never! Imagine that."

Maizey sat quietly, just shaking her head, before looking up with a grin.

"The attic and basement are full of the dang things. Help yourself, girls. You can haul it all off and I'll just start making plans for spending the loot."

She chuckled, adding, "Seems I owe Mr. Simmons an apology. I was always after him for wasting time and making a mess, when it turns out he was a real artist."

Shirley and Naidenne tackled the basement first and found many obviously unfinished pieces. They pawed through a maze of decomposing cardboard boxes filled with old clothes, moldy toys and empty canning jars, before uncovering three sculptures worth toting upstairs.

Setting these finds beside the door, the two women spied their hostess outside taking clothes from the line.

Shirley went out to tell Maizey what they'd found and to get directions to the attic.

When she returned to the house, Shirley led Naidenne through the back hallway to the narrow attic stairs.

Halfway up, Naidenne was overcome by a wave of nausea and sank down onto a step while it passed.

"Are you okay, Deenie?"

"Just a touch of vertigo, I guess. These stairs are a bit steeper than I'm used to. I'm fine, now."

The women emerged into the dark disorder of the attic.

Shirley crossed to the window and pulled back the ragged and crumbling curtains, letting in just enough light to see a chain hanging from the single bulb affixed to a beam in the roof. She pulled the chain with a click and the small dusty bulb cast a watery light over even more boxes and clutter than they'd encountered in the basement.

"This is going to take a while," Naidenne sighed.

Carver Schramm, weak from vomiting and dysentery, watched from the trees as an old woman unpinned sheets and towels from a clothesline in the farmyard below.

He had been forced to move away from the highway due to his ill health and the lack of cover on the road approaching Bannoch.

Ill and weak, he needed a place to hide out until he was well enough to continue north.

Even in his weakened state, he felt certain he could overcome an old woman. This isolated farmstead was just the sort of place he'd been looking for.

Before he could make his way down the hill into the yard, Shirley stepped out the back door and walked over to join Maizey at the clothesline

"We've found several really nice pieces upstairs, Maizey. I called Jack to come help us get them down from the attic and haul them to the shop in his pickup. Let me help you with those sheets while we wait."

When Naidenne came out to join the others, Schramm couldn't take his eyes off her.

In all his dreams while incarcerated, this was the woman who filled his twisted fantasies.

In his feverish state, Carver made up his mind. Before going any further north, he would have this tall, golden-haired female.

He had to lie down for just a moment to catch his breath before he dared to tackle all three women.

Schramm needed to rest and regain his strength. A few minutes should give him all the energy he and his knife would need to eliminate the old broads and convince the tall one to make his dreams come true.

Awakened by sounds of a pickup truck bouncing over the rutted drive, Schramm sat up suddenly and nearly swooned.

When he saw the truck pull up to the farmhouse and a man hop out, Carver was filled with rage. He knew he'd missed his opportunity.

Keeping out of sight, he crept closer until he could hear the conversation going on near the open door.

"Say, you've got quite a haul here! Did you leave anything at all in Maizey's attic?" Jack asked.

"Don't worry, Jack, they didn't get anything I wanted to keep. If they'd even tried I'd a' just grabbed my old man's trusty shotgun I keep by the door here and dusted their backsides with buckshot," Maizey responded.

"Don't be silly, you two. Let's get these pieces loaded into the truck. Naidenne needs to get back home to fix the pastor his supper," Shirley said.

"Rosamund still out of town? I thought she did most of the cooking in the parsonage," Jack said.

"Yes, she's still away, so I'm afraid Scott will starve if I don't get home soon, you know what rotten cooks preachers are...always expecting divine intervention in the recipes."

Naidenne joked to cover her unease about Rosamund's continued absence.

In only a few moments the sculptures were loaded and the departing vehicles were throwing up a cloud of dust on their way back to the paved road.

Schramm had heard enough to learn Naidenne was the wife of one of the local preachers, a man named Scott.

Hearing about the old woman's shotgun changed his mind about taking over this particular farmhouse and he began shuffling, weakly, in the general direction of Bannoch.

※

Maureen Oldham was fussing around a shelf filled to overflowing with birds.

There were stuffed birds, ceramic birds and crystal birds of every size and shape. A glance around the crowded sitting room revealed even more avian examples.

One could easily identify Maureen's chosen decorating theme.

"I just can't seem to get these right," she spoke to herself as she rearranged the ornaments.

"If Vince was here, he would give me his opinion...it would be wrong, of course, but it would help me see what I was after. Just hearing him say some stupid thing was always helpful, somehow."

She sighed and gave up on the birds for the moment, deciding she needed a cup of tea.

Once in the kitchen, she heard a robin's chirp coming from her Birds of the West wall clock and knew it was late enough to find something for dinner.

A woman had to eat, even though it wasn't much fun cooking for one.

She'd enjoyed putting on a big spread for the pastor and his new wife on Sunday, but she didn't feel like thawing out the leftovers for herself; too much fuss with all the various dishes.

Maureen rummaged in the freezer and finally selected a bag of individually wrapped fish fillets.

If Vince were here, she'd whip up a beer batter coating and deep fry them to serve with corn fritters and coleslaw. That seemed like too much work, just now, so she popped a single fillet into the microwave, cut up a tomato and buttered a slice of bread.

The tomato didn't look like the ones she used to grow in her garden, but there hadn't been time to plant a garden after moving back to Bannoch. Next year she'd get one in, for sure.

## The First Ladies Club

This little house on the far southern edge of town had plenty of room for a nice garden and very few nosy neighbors to bother her.

She'd never thought twice about people observing her working in the garden until Vince brought home a couple of those wooden signs to put in their yard, the ones showing a gardening man and woman from the back, all bent over pulling weeds. All you saw was their great broad derrieres. From that moment, Maureen couldn't bend over in the garden without wondering what sort of picture she might be presenting to passersby.

Vince thought those signs were hilarious, of course. Maureen happily sold them in the yard sale before they'd had to move to Portland to that special housing unit for folks, like Vince, with Alzheimer's.

The assisted living apartment was a nice enough place, but it wasn't her home.

She'd missed Bannoch and all her church activities too much to remain in Portland once Vince was gone.

A note on her bird-themed kitchen wall calendar reminded her of a women's mission society meeting coming up soon.

Maureen was eager to get back to the work of the church. No telling how the other ladies might have let things slip while she was gone. They never seemed to know what to do unless she was there to tell them.

That new wife the pastor got for himself didn't look like she would have been much help. Too tall, for one thing.

Height was all right for a man...why, her Vince was nearly six feet tall when they got married, but women should be modest about everything. Any woman as tall as Naidenne was just showing off.

The microwave dinged and Maureen slid the fish onto her plate next to the bread and tomato, sprinkled everything liberally with salt and pepper and took it to the sitting room.

She set her plate on the coffee table and turned on the TV. It was time for her shows, Jeopardy and Wheel of Fortune.

Carver Schramm gulped cool water from the hose attached to the back of the garage beside Maureen Oldham's house. He was severely dehydrated and needed to rest. Seeing his fantasy woman in the flesh had given him a temporary a surge of strength, but it soon left him while tramping through the coastal wilderness.

He leaned against the garage and slid down to the grass. He needed to rest a bit before checking out this house and deciding his next move.

Rest now; track the woman down later, when he had the strength to really enjoy it.

Schramm drifted off with his mind full of all the things he would do once he got his hands on his tall, golden fantasy girl.

## Chapter Nine

In the chill morning fog, the growling of the garage door opener roused Schramm as he slept slumped on the damp grass behind the garage.

Still groggy with sleep, he heard a car engine and the door rolling back down, followed by the sounds of tires crunching on gravel as Maureen drove away.

He couldn't believe it. He'd slept clear through the night, but at last he seemed to be feeling a little better.

If the people who lived here had driven away, now would be a good time to check the place out, see if he could keep any food in his system and get cleaned up.

Not bothering to try to be quiet, he picked up a pink painted rock from the flower border and smashed it through a window pane on the backdoor before reaching in to unlock it.

As mean as he still felt, if anyone remained in the house Schramm would enjoy using his knife, again…on a live victim, this time.

He was almost disappointed when he failed to encounter anyone while checking out the small bungalow's rooms.

Once he was certain the place was empty, Carver backtracked to the kitchen where he ate a carton of yogurt.

While waiting to see how his stomach reacted, he returned to the bedroom and looked through the closet for some clean clothes. Schramm wasn't the most fastidious of men, but even he was disgusted by his filth and the reminders of his illness.

Rejecting the old-fashioned suits hanging in the back of the closet, he grabbed a dusty white dress shirt and a pair of green polyester slacks, and then rifled the wardrobe drawers, finally grabbing a pair of white cotton boxer-style granny panties, in disgust.

After showering, he donned the shirt and slacks over Maureen's clean underwear.

Passing a mirror as he left the room, Carver fancied the lady's undies made him mince ever so slightly and he kicked out, shattering the mocking reflection.

He rummaged through the cabinets, drawers and purses in the house, uncovering around fifty dollars in small bills and change, which he thrust into his pockets.

His insides seemed to have been soothed by the yogurt and he began to feel real hunger, so he returned to the kitchen for a more substantial meal.

As he ate, Schramm began to feel stronger and decided to stay put in this cozy spot until he was well enough to pursue his long-legged goddess.

He would deal in the usual way with the people who lived in this house, whenever they returned, and would not leave until it suited him.

❧

Oblivious to the danger awaiting her at home, Maureen was busily reestablishing her dominance over the women of the mission circle. The six elderly ladies who had turned up for the monthly meeting were taken completely unaware when she showed up and were woefully unprepared for her onslaught.

"So, that's what we will do for now. I'll call you all individually later in the week with more detailed instructions. Any questions?" Maureen asked before immediately going on to her next topic.

"Now, the issue of the church roof has come to my attention. Apparently we need a whole new roof and the only way to pay for it is to cut the pastor's salary."

One of the ladies gasped.

"Oh, don't be like that," Maureen snapped. "His fashion model wife makes plenty of money. She could probably make up the difference by cutting back on shopping and beauty parlor treatments for a few weeks."

"But, Maureen, what do we have to do with the roof? That's the trustees' concern," another woman spoke up, tentatively.

"I will stay in touch with the deacons and trustees and get back to you. We may get some grumbling from the pastor about this, so we need to present a united front. Since there is no more business for today, this meeting is adjourned."

"But, Maureen...."

"I've got to get back home. There's so much to do since moving back here. Just not enough hours in the day. Bye!"

The other women metaphorically peeled themselves off the floor where Maureen's steamroller tactics had left them, and shakily began to discuss the morning's events to try to decide what they were going to do now the infuriating woman had returned.

Maureen was backing out of her parking slot, intent on getting back to her household chores, when she spied Josiah Watkins coming out of the utility shed with a pair of hedge clippers.

She stopped her car, blocking the entrance to the parking lot, and walked over to her informant and comrade in arms to see what progress had been made on the roof repair plans.

"Howdy, Maureen," Josiah greeted her as he began haphazardly snipping at stray branches on the Japanese holly hedge bordering the parking lot.

"How's tricks?" he asked her.

"I'm overworked and underappreciated, as usual. Nothing changes around here, does it? I've been trying to straighten out the women's missionary circle this morning. They haven't accomplished very much since Vince and I had to move away, but I'll get them back into shape. You'd think the pastor would have picked a woman with some leadership ability for a wife, but she doesn't seem to have taken charge of any of the women's work."

"Well, she is one of them modern women who work outside the home, you know. Doesn't leave much time for the church."

"That's what I wanted to talk about. Orville mentioned the trustees' plan to reduce the pastor's salary to offset the cost of a new roof, now that he has his wife's income. I just want you all to know the women's mission circle supports that idea one hundred per cent."

"Good to know. The pastor didn't take to it much, so we may have a bit of a tussle on our hands."

"You can count on me to rally the women of the church, Josiah. If my Vince were still head of the deacons, he could have pushed it through. As it is, I'll be doing all I can…and you know that's a lot. Gotta run home, now. Too much to do and too little time."

Josiah nodded and went on with his desultory clipping while Maureen bustled back to her car and drove off, without even a nod to her longsuffering pastor waiting patiently in his idling car to drive into the parking lot.

Scott pulled into his space, waved a greeting to his dour sexton, and walked into the church.

Velma Parker, one of the members of the mission circle, was coming up the stairs from the fellowship hall as he entered.

"Can I give you a hand, Velma?"

"Thank you, Pastor Scott. Can you take these dishes, just until I get up the steps?"

"I wish we were in a financial position to provide a ramp or a lift from downstairs for you ladies. Unfortunately, the balance in the building fund never seems to get big enough for such improvements," Scott said, as he went down and took her tote bag containing the empty serving dishes.

When she reached the landing, Velma paused with an indecisive expression before turning to Scott to retrieve her dishes.

"I um, I understand we have a new expense coming up requiring almost all those building funds," she said.

"There seems to be a leak in the roof over the choir room, but we haven't gotten any quotes from roofers, yet. We won't know how big a hit the fund will take until we do."

"Oh, that is good news! Here, I can take that, now."

"Let me carry it to your car for you. Don't worry about the roof until we know the extent of the repairs. 'Sufficient unto the day are the troubles thereof,' you know."

"Of course. Thank you, Pastor Scott. Please give my love to Naidenne."

Velma drove away, leaving Scott to return to the church.

"So the rumor mill has already begun grinding," he mused.

୶

Once more headed back home, Maureen remembered she needed to pick up some bird seed and detoured to the grocery store, where she dashed inside, still intent on getting home as soon as possible.

Rushing to the pet supplies section, she ran headlong into Orville Locke.

"Whoa, there, Maureen. Where you headed in such an all-fired hurry?"

"I've got things to do, Orville. What are you doing blocking the whole aisle, anyway? Other people like to shop, too, you know," Maureen snapped.

"Just settle down, now. No call to run around like a chicken with your head cut off. What's so important you can't stop to gab with an old friend, anyway?"

"I've still got boxes to unpack at home, from the move and all. And I've been trying to get the women's work at church straightened out, too. There's never enough time to do everything on my plate."

"Why not take a little break? What did the ladies at the mission circle think of our idea for paying for the new roof? Was there any grumbling?"

"Of course not! Why would there be? Every one of those ladies agrees with me. We need a new roof and there is no reason the pastor shouldn't pay his share. Why, we've been supporting him for years, when all he does is teach a few Bible studies and preach for half an hour once a week. We don't get paid to teach Sunday school or listen to his sermons, do we? He's had it too easy for too long. He should be happy to pay for the roof now that he has his wife's money, too."

"I wonder if she's tithing that extra income... I'll have to take a look at the treasurer's records. I know where my Gladys keeps them."

"You know, that's a good idea, Orville. If she hasn't been giving her share, and push comes to shove, we can say the roof would make up for what she's been holding out on God."

"Course, we couldn't say how we know. Gladys is pretty particular about people's privacy, even the pastor and his missus."

"I don't know why they should object to the whole church knowing their giving habits. They are supposed to set us an example in every area of Christian life. They should be volunteering the information."

"Yeah, like the Good Book says, they shouldn't be hiding their light under a bushel. Why would they want to keep it secret, unless they're ashamed?"

"You just remember that at the next meeting of the Boards. I've got to get my bird seed and head on home, now. Give my regards to Gladys. Tell her we missed her at the mission circle, but I'll be calling her to let her know what jobs we've assigned to her."

With that, the little woman trotted down the aisle, grabbed the bag of seed and impatiently made her way to the line at the check stand.

"Do you mind if I go next?" she asked the woman already in line, as she insinuated herself into the space in front.

"I've only got one item and I'm in a dreadful hurry. So many responsibilities to take care of all by myself."

The woman frowned, but took a step back, allowing Maureen to take possession of her place in line.

Maureen fidgeted and tapped her foot while the clerk rang up the purchases of her current customer.

Dropping her bag of seed onto the counter before the clerk had even handed the previous customer's receipt over, Maureen elbowed her way into position and swiped her debit card.

"It's not taking my card," she complained.

"Please wait until I complete this transaction, ma'am," the clerk said.

"I'm in a terrible hurry. I have important things to do," Maureen said and swiped the card several more times, before the machine was ready to begin the new sale.

"These things are supposed to save us time, but they are more trouble than they are worth, if you ask me."

The clerk quickly scanned the birdseed and put it into a bag.

"Please press the green button, ma'am."

Maureen pressed the red button in her haste, voiding the sale.

The clerk sighed, saying, "Please swipe your card, again. You just cancelled the transaction."

"I did not! Your machine is defective. Oh, never mind. I'll pay cash. I don't have time for all this incompetence."

Maureen fumbled in her purse, scattering pennies, tissues, old receipts and chewing gum wrappers on the counter in the process of pulling her wallet out.

The clerk re-scanned the birdseed and announced the charge, "That will be $5.98, please."

"Oh, for goodness sakes! I never paid that much for bird seed in all my life. It is only $4.75 in Portland."

"I'm sorry, but that is our price. Do you want the seed, or not?"

Maureen swept all the detritus back into her large handbag and snorted, "I do not! For that price you can keep it. I can always drive to Tillamook where I won't get robbed."

She stomped out of the store, still fuming under her breath, leaving the clerk and the next customer exchanging looks and shaking their heads.

# Chapter Ten

"You know, Tyrone, I think Elizabeth is right," Eskaletha Evans commented to her husband as they were eating lunch in their spacious, modern kitchen.

"What about? I can't always read your mind, you know."

"I wouldn't be surprised if you could, to tell the truth. I never seem to be able to surprise you. Elizabeth is right about what she said the other night. We do need to do something about giving our young people in this community more healthy outlets for their energy."

"Who's 'we' in your statement?"

"We are the First Ladies Club, for one, but now I think about it, 'we' should be all the churches in town. I'm putting the topic on my agenda for tomorrow's meeting. You should bring it up at the next Ministerial Association meeting, too. If we each attack the problem from our own angle, we might make a real difference."

Tyrone carried his empty plate to the sink, rinsed it and placed it on a rack in the dishwasher before replying.

"That is a good idea, my dear. I'm going back to my study at the church, now, and the first thing I'll do when I get there is try to come up with some suggestions for the Ministerial to consider. I've found that having something to tear apart helps the group to come up with ideas of their own."

Eskaletha was rapidly clicking the keys on her laptop as her husband kissed her on top of the head and left.

"I'll put Liz in charge of the sub-committee on this…perfect," she murmured to herself as she wrote.

Elizabeth Gilbert rode up to the garden in back of the Presbyterian Church parsonage and hopped off her bike. She pushed open the recycled crib headboard now serving as a gate and walked in, looking between the rows of lush greenery to find her friend, Judy.

She was startled by a well-padded bottom emerging from a patch of pole beans nearby.

Judy backed onto the path, pulling a basket filled with fresh-picked produce behind her, and stood up, wiping her hands on an already soiled multi-layered gypsy skirt.

"Hi Liz! Where did you come from? I didn't hear your car."

"I rode over on my bike. I came to get some of those veggies you offered me. I thought I would make a pasta primavera for dinner. Some cherry tomatoes, asparagus, beans and peas would be more than welcome."

"Oh, sure. The asparagus is almost finished, but I think I saw a few late tender stalks this morning. I've got tons of all the rest. Happy to share the wealth."

"I appreciate it. I just don't have the time or energy for a vegetable garden. That doesn't stop me from wanting to eat homegrown produce, though."

The two women wandered in the garden, with Judy picking a generous selection of vegetables for Elizabeth as they walked, collecting them in a layer of her skirt pulled up into a sling.

When they gathered all Elizabeth could use, the two friends walked over to a garden table made from a large wooden cable spool Judy had rescued from the dump.

Elizabeth sat on one of the converted-barrel chairs and watched Judy transfer the vegetables into a hand-crocheted string bag.

"Do you ever have anything new, Judy? Everything I can see around here is made from something else. I admire your ingenuity and industriousness."

## The First Ladies Club

"I enjoy making other people's discards into something useful. When you think about it, everything in creation is recycled, in a way. God created all the raw materials and we just keep converting them into different shapes and sizes for our own use. Mankind can only manipulate the things God has created."

"That's very profound. I think I might work that into my next sermon. Gil is preaching this month, so I've got time to work on it. Thanks for the raw material for me to recycle into a Sunday message."

"I've got to hand it to you, Liz. Being both a pastor and a pastor's wife has to be hard sometimes."

"Oh, sure. Sometimes I don't quite fit into someone's concept of either one, and that can cause difficulties. Most of the time I revel in the freedom it gives me. "

"What do you mean?"

"Well, if someone wants me to do one of those jobs always thrust onto a pastor's wife and I don't feel qualified, or interested," she grinned, then went on, "well, I can always say I'm too busy with pastoral duties."

"Sneaky!"

"And, on the other hand, when I'm frustrated, or even inspired, I can talk about it in my sermon, rather than try to convince my husband to address the issue."

"Ooh, I'd love to be able to do that! Ken never uses any of my suggestions in his messages."

"Well, I'd better get going. I've got to cook the pastor's dinner, as a good pastor's wife should. Then, I must work on my co-pastor's article for the church newsletter. Thanks again for the garden goodies."

Elizabeth placed her bag of vegetables into the bicycle basket and rode off sedately as Judy called, "See you at the Ladies Club tomorrow!"

☙

Carver Schramm was making himself at home in Maureen's house. After eating a hearty meal, and leaving his dirty dishes and scraps scattered around the kitchen, he grabbed a can of diet soda from the refrigerator and sprawled on the sofa. Stretching to his full length, he heaved his muddy shoes onto the well-polished coffee table. Grabbing the remote, he settled down to watch TV and await the return of the home's legitimate occupants.

❧

Maureen left the supermarket in a worse temper than usual. As she drove, she composed a letter in her head, complaining to the store manager about her mistreatment.

There was no reason for that snippy young clerk to be so rude! And they should fix their faulty card scanner. And the prices! Something should be done about those. Maybe she could organize a boycott? When would she ever find the time?

Everything was so much more complicated since Vince passed on. He'd always been so annoying, Maureen never expected to miss him, but, somehow, life just wasn't as much fun with him gone.

Thinking of her late husband reminded Maureen of her promise to check in on his cousin in the local nursing home.

She checked her watch and, seeing it was already afternoon, decided to grab a hamburger at the fast food drive thru, eat in the car, and then make her duty visit before returning home.

Once that was done, she could just relax for the rest of the day, and tackle the unpacking again tomorrow.

Everything seemed to take so much more time than it used to and she wore out so much more quickly, too. Sometimes she wished she'd been the one to pass over, instead of her husband.

❧

At the combination real estate office and craft boutique, Naidenne had just returned from showing a property when Shirley Griffith popped in.

"Hi, Shirley. How did this morning go while I was out?"

"It was terrific. That's why I wasn't here when you got back. I sold three of Maizey's largest sculptures. I wanted to get the money into the bank right away. This office is empty so much of the time; I don't feel safe leaving cash here."

"Wonderful. Maizey will be so pleased."

"While I was at the bank I was chatting with my friend, Kathy, who works there. She told me her boss, Len Spurgeon, took a vacation all of the sudden and she and the other staff are all wondering why. Did Rosamund say anything about it?"

"Why, no. I haven't spoken with Rosamund about Len recently," Naidenne replied with an inward grimace.

"Oh well, I sure hope there's nothing wrong. Len is a nice man. He's got a good bass voice, too. We'll miss him in the choir if he's gone very long."

Shirley busied herself with rearranging the home crafts to fill the gaps left by the sculptures, and then went home.

Naidenne sat at her desk, thinking.

Could Len have been so upset about Rosamund he had to leave the area? Or had he gone off to look for her?

Why hadn't they heard anything from Rosamund?

She picked up the phone to call Scott, and then decided to wait to talk about it with him that evening.

Gwennie Barthlette was arranging flowers in the foyer of the Trinity Nazarene Church when one of her parishioners stopped by to drop off a bundle for the community clothes closet run by the congregation.

"Say, Gwennie, you will not believe what I saw today."

"What was it, Julia?"

"You remember that horrible little woman from Bannoch Community Fellowship? You know...the one who always tried to run things whenever we had joint women's activities. The awful Oldham woman."

"Oh, yes. She moved away a while back, didn't she? I thought I heard she'd gone to Portland, or Seattle."

"I don't know where she went when she moved away, but she's back!"

"What, for a visit, you mean?"

"Oh, I can't be sure, but she didn't sound like she was here on a vacation."

"What did she say?"

"It's not so much what she said, as what she did. I was in the grocery store, waiting in line like a civilized person, when she squeezed right in front of me. Acted like she was entitled."

"That sounds like her, alright."

"But that's not all. After being rude to me and the clerk and everyone, she couldn't figure out how to slide her payment card and ended up throwing things at the cashier and storming off without her purchases. It was like she was crazy."

"Oh, dear. Perhaps she's had a stroke or is getting dementia. We need to pray for her, Julia, not gossip about her. Remember, 'there but for the grace of God,' it could be one of us one day."

"I expect you're right, Gwennie. But it was sure a sight."

"If Maureen Oldham's back in town, she's probably back at her church. I'll ask their pastor's wife if she knows what's up, when I see her tomorrow."

"And I'll pray for her, Gwennie. Say, should I call the prayer chain?"

"Everyone needs prayer, but please be careful about how you ask. It's a prayer chain, not a gossip grapevine."

"Of course!"

When Scott got home later that afternoon he found Naidenne on the utility porch putting a load of laundry into the dryer.

"Hi Honey, how was your day?" he asked before giving her a kiss.

"It was good. We sold three more metal sculptures for Maizey and I showed a few houses to a couple who seem like serious buyers. How about you?"

"Pretty routine, I suppose. I'm happy to be home, though. What's for dinner?"

"Oh, gosh! I haven't even thought about dinner. I have been so spoiled by Rosamund, I've gotten out of the habit."

"Not a problem, we can go out or order a pizza. What do you feel like?"

"A pizza sounds perfect and I can at least call in the order, so I'm not a total failure," Naidenne laughed.

"Speaking of Rosie, she didn't happen to call, did she?" Scott asked.

"I'm afraid not. And I heard something disturbing today. Did you know Len has gone away suddenly, too?"

"Where'd you hear that?"

"One of the tellers at the bank, a friend of Shirley's, told her he went off on a sudden vacation, with no warning and no explanation."

"That's not like our local bank manager, at all."

"You don't suppose he's gone to look for Rosamund, do you?"

"How could he? He wouldn't know where to look any more than we would."

"I hope he wasn't so upset by your sister's disappearance that he felt compelled to get away, too."

"Len doesn't strike me as the emotional type, Deenie. I would wager he had some sort of family emergency and just didn't have time to tell his employees all the details…or maybe didn't want to. He is sort of private…like Rose that way."

"You're probably right. I'll go call in the pizza order while you get changed out of your preacher clothes. Thin crust Canadian bacon, with extra mushrooms and bell peppers, right?"

## Chapter Eleven

Maureen sat behind the wheel of her car in the nursing home parking lot following a depressing visit with Vince's elderly cousin, Gladys. That poor woman was in her mid-nineties, suffering from dementia and very frail.

Maureen wasn't certain Gladys enjoyed the visit, either. It had been obvious she was only dimly aware of her surroundings, but it was equally obvious she didn't want to be where she was.

Gladys spent most of the time moaning softly, but had a brief moment of lucidity as Maureen prepared to depart.

She grabbed Maureen's wrist in a surprisingly strong grip and said, quite clearly, "Why won't they let me die?" then her hand dropped and she resumed making unintelligible sounds.

The episode shook Maureen and she was trembling as she walked from the room.

Sitting in the car, she imagined she could still feel the pressure of that claw-like hand.

Maureen never thought of herself as old, but when she calculated Gladys was only a half dozen years her senior it forced her to reconsider and contemplate a similar future.

"Most merciful God, creator of life and death, please take Cousin Gladys very soon," she vehemently and uncharacteristically prayed, concluding with, "and please, please, please, spare me from ending up like that. Amen."

With all her errands now completed, Maureen drove directly home and soon pulled into her garage, anticipating a light supper in front of the television and an early night.

Inside, Schramm heard the car return and jumped up from the sofa where he'd been dozing.

Which way would the people enter?

When he noticed the security chain was still fastened on the front door, he dashed into the kitchen, arriving just as Maureen came in through the back entrance, looking down at the broken glass crunching underfoot.

When she looked up, she was shocked to see a strange man in her house, but she stubbornly held her ground.

"Who are you? You don't belong here! Get out!" she screeched.

Carver rushed toward her, pulling his knife out, ready to plunge it deeply into her neck.

Before he reached her, Maureen felt a brief searing pain in her upper chest and back, and then nothing more, as she crumpled onto the linoleum floor at Schramm's feet.

"What the... I never even touched her," he complained.

Maureen's open eyes, staring right at him so fixedly, made Schramm uneasy and he looked away as he knelt beside her body feeling for a pulse.

What about that? The old bat just dropped dead.

Schramm began laughing, but stopped when he felt the knife in his hand, unneeded, yet again.

He gave Maureen's body a frustrated kick and decided to drag her out to the garage before she could stink up the place.

This house would suit him fine, now, at least until he got his strength back. He wasn't ready to move on, not yet. He wanted to be at full strength when he hooked up with his dream girl. And when he was through acting out his favorite fantasies with her, his knife would finally get a workout, too.

"...so now, the latest big controversy in our congregation is about changing the name of our mid-week Bible Study. One of the members read some crazy thing somewhere saying if we call it *Bible* Study it turns people off! Can you believe it?" Judy Falls complained to the other ladies.

They were sitting around enjoying snacks following another meeting of the First Ladies Club.

Olivette Vernon was hosting the group in the damp and musty Reformed Church parsonage, her home for more than three decades.

"What do they want to call it, then?" Peggy Burt asked, reaching for another of Judy's chewy granola cookies.

"Small Group Study, can you imagine? Not very descriptive, considering every group at our church is a small one. Ken says it's all part of the effort to make churches less intimidating for visitors, or something. I think it's just silliness, especially when there are real issues to get worked up about, like global warming and vivisection and genetically modified food."

"Changing the name may seem silly to us, but I've found over the years that most folks are simply trying to do whatever they can to help their church grow," Olivette said, and sat down next to Peggy.

"I agree. It's tempting to grab onto whatever is the latest fad when your church is struggling," Peggy said. "I know I've sometimes tried to convince my husband to try some exciting new church-growth programs. Once he looks them over, he usually tells me they've already been tried under some other name. It's disappointing."

"We all want to help our husband's ministries, especially when we were fresh out of seminary," Olivette said. "I remember in my early days as a pastor's wife, I often had inspirations for sermon illustrations, sometimes in the middle of the night, and I would write them down for Kendall to include in his message. He occasionally tried using one, but it inevitably fell flat. I thought it must be his delivery," she laughed. "It finally dawned upon me, if God wanted to inspire Kendall, he didn't need to go through me to do it and, if those illustrations really were divinely inspired, they were meant for my benefit."

The others chuckled or nodded in agreement.

"There are many opportunities for spiritual growth living in a parsonage, all right," Elizabeth commented.

"Well, I grew up in a series of run-down old parsonages, and we kids were lucky to have grown up, at all," Judy said.

"What do you mean, dear?" Olivette asked.

"My brothers and I were always in trouble, in the way, or in for a beating. Between having a sanctuary full of self-appointed foster parents bent on either keeping us on the straight and narrow, as befit the children of their pastor, or tattling to our parents about how awful we were...I remember one time we went skinny dipping with the Baptist pastor's kids in the Baptist church's great big baptistery the night before a baptism. You would have thought we'd committed a crime, the way folks carried on. We always envied those Baptist kids for that big indoor pool."

"I never knew you were a PK, Judy," Elizabeth said.

"Oh, yeah. And it was a sort of lonely life, even with my brothers for company. I sure never planned to spend my whole life in the stained-glass fishbowl, but God had other plans, as he often does."

"My good friend, Bunny, was a pastor's wife. I remember her saying she sometimes felt isolated, but I haven't felt that way since marrying Scott," Naidenne commented.

"You probably will, from time to time. It's the nature of the beast, I'm afraid," Olivette said.

"As long as churches are filled with people, there will be those who are difficult to love and who will make things uncomfortable for the pastor and his family."

"Speaking of that," Gwennie spoke up, "I hear a particularly difficult person has returned to your church, Naidenne."

"Oh? Who do you mean?" Naidenne hedged.

"She means Maureen Oldham, of course!" Judy stopped picking the chia seeds and cookie crumbs off her blouse and chimed in.

"Maureen has come back to the church, yes. But I don't know her very well, yet. I only saw her briefly this past Sunday."

"When you do get to know her, you will wish you hadn't," Judy said.

"Let's not gossip, ladies," Eskaletha said in her club meeting voice.

With that, the women began gathering up their things and thanking Olivette for her hospitality.

Naidenne stayed to help Olivette clean up after the others were gone. She admired the older woman and enjoyed spending time with her.

"Olivette, did you know Maureen Oldham very well when she was here before?"

"She wasn't part of our congregation, of course, but we were on several community committees together over the years."

"Was she as awful as the others say?"

Olivette sighed, put down the cups she'd been gathering up, and sat on the old-fashioned maroon horsehair-covered settee which had come with the house.

"I remember her as a very forceful woman, pretty determined to have her own way. She didn't seem to be overly concerned with the feelings of others. But she was a very hard worker and I'm sure she meant well. Who can know what burdens she carried, then or now?"

"I was intrigued when Rosamund and Scott talked about her coming back to Bannoch, but now I'm mostly intimidated, I think. How do you handle these hard-to-love members of the congregation?"

"Not as well as I should, I'm sure. However, I do pray for them and I always try to act as if I really like them. May seem hypocritical, but sometimes I actually forget I'm acting."

She sat quietly for a moment, and then went back to clearing the clutter from the meeting. On her way out of the room she paused and asked, "Is your sister-in-law back in town, yet? I miss Rose in the quilting circle."

"We expect her back soon," Naidenne replied.

"Good. Miss Dot from up Cannon Beach way is going to be our guest speaker at our next meeting. Rosamund wouldn't like to miss that."

Rosamund paced in front of the large window in the boarding lounge of the Medford airport. She stopped every few moments to look toward the security screening area, lines of anxiety marring her brow.

# The First Ladies Club

While gazing unseeingly out the window, where planes were landing and taking off, she noticed a change in the reflection on the glass and turned quickly.

"Len! You made it," she cried out.

"I wouldn't have missed this for the world. I can't believe we are actually going to..."

Rosamund stopped him with her hand over his lips.

"Not one more word. Remember your promise."

Len kissed her finger tips, then pulled her into a quick hug before stepping back to look at her.

"You know, I think your little impromptu vacation has done you good. You look rested and even more beautiful than ever."

"Oh, go on!" Rosamund said.

She was blushing happily, almost simpering, when the boarding announcement sounded.

Len took her hand and the two stepped into line.

Schramm spent the next couple of days watching TV and eating all the food in Maureen's house. When he began to get restless, he found a phone book and began calling the area churches.

He'd remembered the conversation he overheard at the farmhouse and that his tall goddess was married to a preacher named Scott.

He began calling the churches in the listings, asking for "Pastor Scott."

Since small town churches can seldom afford full-time secretaries, the phones frequently went unanswered or were picked up by machines. Those he marked to call back at another time. He could afford to be patient. He knew he would hit the right one, eventually.

There weren't that many churches in the town and two of those were Catholic, with no pastor's wife in the rectory.

On the sixth try the phone was answered by a man with the words, "Bannoch Community Fellowship, Pastor Scott Davidson speaking," and Schramm knew he'd hit the jackpot.

Hanging up without speaking, he noted the address of the church and began to make plans to follow the preacher home later in the week.

Carver Schramm was no stranger to stalking a victim and looked forward to the next few days with relish.

"They always say getting there is half the fun, don't they?" he spoke aloud to himself.

"Looks like this long, slow walk up the coast is going to be its own reward. Gettin' sick on that spoiled chicken must have been fate."

## Chapter Twelve

"Ken! Please don't put your nasty bacon down on my prep counter. Now, I have to purify it again before I can fix my food," Judy complained to her husband at breakfast.

"Oh, for crying out loud. I must be the only Presbyterian minister in the country who must put up with a 'kosher' kitchen in the manse."

"I don't keep kosher, you silly thing. But, you know I'm a very strict vegan. I can't have the juices of a poor murdered animal mixing with my food."

"Vegan schmeegan! It's a lot of hogwash, if you ask me. God put the creatures on this Earth for man's use, not the other way around."

"The Bible clearly tells us to be good stewards of creation. It takes so many more acres to feed cattle than to grow soy beans and other wholesome organic produce, it just makes good sense to eat veggies."

"And would you starve off all the food animals? They do still need to eat, right? So, we feed them and care for them and get nothing back, is that your plan? And what about dairy products? How does not eating them work into your stewardship plan?"

"It's exploitive to take a mother animal's food away from her babies! And, and, um, to keep her either pregnant or lactating all the time, and not even let her raise her own babies."

Judy paused for breath while her husband smirked.

The couple had been over this same territory uncountable times, without resolution, but it never failed to get Judy wound up.

The buzz of the doorbell interrupted the discussion and Judy wiped her hands and went to see who it was.

She was surprised to find a strange man on the steps, with the identical copper-colored hair and round, pink faces of her fourteen year-old twin daughters peeping out guiltily behind him.

"Paisley, what's up? Who is this man? Why aren't you and Astilbe in class?"

Her daughters merely looked sullenly at the ground.

"I'm Officer Harness, are you Mrs. Falls?"

"Yes, what's this about?"

"May we come in?"

"Oh, yes, of course. But why are you here and what are you doing with my daughters?"

"I'm the school attendance review officer and I'm afraid we need to talk."

"Please sit down," she said, obviously flustered. "Excuse me, I need to get my husband."

When Judy padded into the kitchen, her husband was seated in the breakfast nook eating his bacon and eggs and reading the paper.

"Ken, the school attendance review officer is here, and he brought the girls with him."

"What, you mean the truant officer? For Heaven's sake, what have your daughters done now?"

Ken slammed his paper onto the table and strode into the living room.

"Reverend Ken Falls, Officer. What can I do for you today?" he introduced himself before sitting in one of a pair of tapestry-covered wingback chairs and leaning forward intently, gesturing for the officer to take the other chair.

"Well, Reverend, I'm afraid we have a problem with your daughters' school attendance."

"Please explain," Ken said.

"We've sent letters before now, but their attendance hasn't improved. I'm afraid with their absences this week, we have escalated beyond warning letters."

Ken turned to his wife, standing nervously beside him.

## The First Ladies Club

"Judith, you didn't tell me the girls were missing classes. I wasn't aware they have been ill."

"They haven't. I've sent the girls off to school on time every day, without fail. They are almost never sick...we are vegans you see, Mr. Harness, and only eat certified organic foods, no genetically modified freak-food or junkie snacks in this house...I can't remember the last time they stayed home from school."

"You may have been sending them off, as you say, but I assure you the girls' actual attendance this year has been spotty, at best. They haven't attended many classes this week."

"You mentioned warning letters," Ken said, then turned to his wife, "Judith, why haven't you shown these letters to me?"

"But, I never got any letters, honestly...Oh, Paisley! Is this why you've been volunteering to go pick up the mail every day? I was so pleased when you wanted to help. Mommy's very disappointed!"

"I guess we know what became of those letters, Officer. What happens, now?" Ken asked.

"You and the girls will appear before the school attendance review board. They will review and rule on the situation. I came today to deliver this summons in person," Harness said as he leaned forward, handed the envelope to Ken and stood to go.

"I'll leave now and give your family privacy to talk this over. The time and date of the board hearing is noted on the summons. I'll see myself out."

The silence after he left lasted for several seconds before Judy began shaking her head and emitting a soft clucking sound, like a distressed chicken.

"How could you girls do this to Daddy and me? Why, you have been lying to us for months!" Judy said, her voice rising as she spoke.

"You girls go to your room. No TV, no computer, no electronics of any kind," Ken instructed, then stopped the girls as they turned toward the stairs. "And leave your cell phones."

The girls began to protest, until their father demanded, "Hand them over. Now."

Paisley pulled her phone from her backpack and reluctantly placed it in Ken's hand.

Astilbe ran to her mother, threw her arms around her and begged, "Please, Mommy! Don't let him take our phones. How will we talk to our friends?"

"The phone, Astilbe," Ken said, with his hand outstretched.

"Do as your Daddy says, now, sweetheart. I'm sure it will be for only a short time. Daddy's doing what he thinks is best, because he loves you. We both love you and Paisley, very, very much. But you've been very, very naughty," Judy said.

After the twins' bedroom door closed with a bang, Ken returned to his breakfast, Judy following behind.

"This coffee is cold," Ken pronounced and then retreated behind his newspaper.

"Here, let me get you some fresh," Judy said, taking his cup.

When Judy returned to the table, Ken put the paper down and looked at her for a few moments without speaking.

Judy was about to get her own breakfast when he spoke.

"Sit down, Judy. I need to talk to you."

"Of course. What is it?"

"When I married you twenty-two years ago, I overlooked the difference in our ages. In fact, I appreciated your youthful enthusiasm. Knowing I can occasionally be a bit too serious, I felt you were a good balance and I was convinced you would mature with age. Recently, I've begun to feel like I am the only adult parent of three teen-age daughters. This morning was a telling example."

"But, Ken, I thought the girls were going to class!" Judy protested.

"It appears you were mistaken. If you were being a proper mother to the girls, rather than trying to be what's currently referred to as their BFF, you would have known something was going on. Your daughters have made a fool of you and you had no hint. I have enough on my hands taking care of the congregation. I leave it to you to run our household. You have failed. This state of affairs cannot be allowed to continue. I am very disappointed."

"I'm sorry, Ken. I will try to do better, really. Please don't be angry."

"Very well, but I trust there will be no more episodes like this morning. I must get to the church, now. I have a counseling appointment. Make certain those girls stay in their room the rest of the day. Tomorrow you will accompany them to school and see that they stay there."

"Please don't be too hard on them, Ken. It's not very interesting for teens in a small town like ours."

"Oh, please! The other pastors were going on about the poor, bored teen-agers at the last ministerial meeting. There seem to be plenty of interesting things keeping your daughters out of school. These youngsters have every entertainment device available to mankind and they complain of boredom. We should put them to work for a change. That's what I told the other ministers, too."

"Good-bye! See you at dinner," Judy called to Ken's retreating back and began to put away the breakfast things. While she worked she planned a little picnic to carry up to the girls for lunch.

Olivette Vernon and her husband, Kendall, were just finishing breakfast in their dark and ancient parsonage.

Kendall carried the dishes from the rectangular chrome kitchen table to the chipped and stained enamel sink and began to squirt dishwashing liquid into the running water.

Olivette sat on one of the matching red vinyl and chrome chairs, sipping her tea.

"You never told me what you got up to at the ministerial meeting this week, dear. Was there anything interesting?" she asked.

Kendall rinsed a plate, set it on the draining board and turned to his wife, drying his hands and slinging the towel over his shoulder.

"Well, it was mostly just the usual, but there was one new topic. Dr. Evans, from the AME Church, suggested we create a sort of rotating youth club among the community churches."

"What's a rotating youth club?"

"The way Tyrone explained it, each church would take one afternoon or evening each week to open their social hall for the teen-agers to hang out and do their homework. He figured we'd provide a place to play Ping Pong or Foosball and board games and we'd have snacks for the kids. He said it would give them a safe place to gather and keep out of trouble."

"Sounds like a good idea. We were talking at the First Ladies Club about needing something like that."

"It may sound good to you and me and Dr. Evans, but the whole idea was picked apart pretty quickly by some of the others."

"That's too bad. What was their objection?"

"Oh, they had a list. Seems like having young people in the church building, when it's not during a regular service, is asking for all sorts of trouble. Then there were the complaints about not having enough volunteers willing to come out, utilities costs of keeping the building open, security, liability insurance, and on and on. One fellow actually said he wouldn't like 'unchurched' kids mixing with the children of his congregation. Can you imagine? It was very discouraging to hear."

"Did the naysayers manage to quash the idea completely?"

"I'm happy to say they did not. We are each to broach the subject with our boards and return next month to report."

"Oh, good. I will tell the ladies at the Club meeting, so we can try to drum up support with the women in each of our congregations. This may be too big a project for one church to handle, but with all of us together, I'm just certain something good can be accomplished. Don't you agree?"

## The First Ladies Club

"I do, God willing," Kendall replied.

☙

Elizabeth and Gil Gilbert were sitting at their desks in the pastor's study of their church talking about the rotating youth club idea discussed at the recent ministerial association meeting.

"So that was your idea, was it?" Gil asked with a smile.

"Well, not really. All I said is our First Ladies Club should do something about the dearth of wholesome activities for our young people here in Bannoch. From what you tell me about Tyrone's suggestion, I'd say Eskaletha took my comment and ran with it. She's not one to sit on her hands when there's work to be done."

"I chatted with Tyrone after the meeting. He said the rotating youth club idea was just something he thought up to get the ball rolling, never expecting it to be the final outcome, but I told him I thought it was workable."

"Were the other pastors as agreeable, dear?" Elizabeth asked.

"Not so you'd notice," Gil remarked with a crooked smile. "You really should come to the meetings, too, you know. Then you wouldn't need to ask me what happens."

"No thanks. I went a few times when we were first called as co-pastors to this church, if you'll remember. It might have been different if I'd been a female pastor, on my own, but being there with you, I was relegated to the role of pastor's wife, not co-pastor. I fought that fight in seminary and don't feel like I need to conquer Bannoch's misogynistic ministerial association."

"Don't you think that's a little harsh, Liz. Misogynistic? Really?"

"Perhaps not, but I felt their resistance to accepting me on an equal plain. I just don't need to put myself in that situation, unnecessarily. So, I'm happy to get all the news second-hand from my ever-helpful husband," she smiled. "Were there any comments about the return of that Oldham woman to our community? I heard Naidenne say she's coming back to Scott's church."

"I don't think so. I remember her from working on the joint Good Friday service one year, though. She's really something. I feel for Scott."

## Chapter Thirteen

When Maureen failed to make good on her promise to call the ladies with further helpful instructions during the week, no one complained, but when she did not appear in church on Sunday, Scott reluctantly decided to make a pastoral visit on the following day to check on this most annoying member of his flock.

When he phoned Maureen the night before to schedule a visit, he received no answer, nor did he on Monday morning when he called again, so he decided to drive over on his way to the office.

Noticing magazines and newspapers sticking out of an overflowing mailbox as he pulled into Maureen's driveway gave Scott an uneasy feeling.

He tried phoning her again from her front porch and could hear ringing in the house, but there was no response.

It was likely Maureen had simply gone out and this was a wasted trip. He would have preferred to leave, but, since there was always a chance the irascible woman was ill and unable to come to the phone, as in the "I've fallen and can't get up" scenario, he knew he couldn't just walk away.

In the past, Scott had been forced to break into a house to help an elderly member of the congregation, so he knew what had to be done.

Walking around to see if the back door might be unlocked, he was shocked to find the glass shattered and the door hanging open.

This changed everything and Scott began dialing his phone while hurrying back to his car.

This was a job for the sheriff.

Carver Schramm cowered under a large rhododendron shrub at the far edge of Maureen's backyard and watched the visitor go back to the street.

He had seen Scott drive up and, realizing his hide-out was no longer safe, he quickly dashed out of the back door, leaving it wide open.

As soon as Scott was out of sight around the house, Schramm stood up and crept quickly and quietly into the woods, making his way out of the area long before the deputy pulled up next to Scott's car.

"What's up, Padre?" the officer asked.

"I came to check on a member of my church, but she's not answering her phone and the back door looks like someone broke in. I thought I'd better let you check it out before walking into trouble on my own."

"You did the right thing. Show me this door."

The two men walked around to the back and the deputy went inside with his gun drawn.

Naidenne was at her desk checking emails when Shirley entered the combination realtor's office and crafts boutique.

"Oh, this is awful!" Naidenne exclaimed.

"What?" Shirley asked, plopping onto the visitor's chair.

"It's this email I'm reading from our old friend Bunny. She has some terrible news."

"Bunny? I haven't heard from her in weeks, maybe longer. Tell me what's happened," she urged.

"You remember that airplane shot down over Eastern Europe a few months ago? Well, her husband, Max, was on it. He was killed," Naidenne said.

"That's horrible. Poor Bunny! Whatever was Max doing flying over a war-zone in Eastern Europe?"

"He was on one of his frequent business trips, according to Bunny."

"But why didn't we hear about this before?" Shirley asked.

"Becoming a widow again seems to have knocked Bunny for a loop. She apologizes for not letting us know sooner and says she has been trying to come to terms with it and deal with all the details of funeral, insurance, etc."

"Oh my goodness. What will she do, now?"

"That's a bit of good news, sort of, at least for us. She's going to come to the Northwest to visit her sisters soon and will be swinging by Bannoch to see us."

"We'll all be glad to see her, again, but I'm so sorry to hear about Max, even though I never really took to him, much…I guess I shouldn't have said that. Is she planning to stay in Texas?"

"She doesn't say. Boy, you never know what is going to happen, do you?" Naidenne said, just as her phone rang.

Still shaken by her friend's unexpected news, she responded with a simple, "Hello?"

"Naidenne? It's Scott."

"Oh, Scott. We just got some sad news."

"You've already heard? Who told you?"

"Bunny. I got her email this morning…who told you?"

"No one. I was here when the body was found."

"What are you talking about? Max's plane blew up over a field on the other side of the world."

"Max? Max Banks is dead?" Scott asked.

"Isn't that why you called? What body are you talking about?"

"It's Maureen. I came to check on her this morning and found her."

"How awful for you. I didn't realize she was ill. Was it a heart attack or a stroke or what?"

"We have to wait for an autopsy, before we will know."

"Well, she was a believer and had a good long life," Naidenne said.

"Yes, but it may not have been natural causes. Her home was broken into and we found her body in the garage, wrapped in a piece of carpet."

"Oh, my…"

Shirley leaned over the desk and whispered, "What's happened, now? Who else has died? These things come in threes, you know…"

※

Carver was stomping through the woods above Bannoch, muttering angrily and looking for another likely place to hide out.

He was angry at himself for not making plans in case someone came to the old lady's place. He didn't even have time to take any provisions away with him; nothing but the clothes on his back, such as they were, and his trusty knife.

He should have been looking for his golden dream girl already. They could have had plenty of fun in that house. He'd gotten lazy and careless.

Now he'd need to locate the woman and another place to put her, too.

He headed toward town intent on locating the Bannoch Community Fellowship and this Pastor Scott who would lead him, unwittingly, to his prize.

※

The Davidsons' dinner that night was a somber one, with Naidenne and Scott thinking of the two deaths.

Naidenne had called and talked with her friend in Texas before dinner.

They'd had a long chat and caught up on the highlights and low points of their lives since they last spoke.

Bunny seemed to be taking Max's death better than Naidenne expected. She said as much, now, to Scott.

"I was surprised at how calm Bunny was when we spoke."

"Well, she has had a couple of months to adjust," he said.

"Yes, but Max was the grand love of Bunny's life, remember? When they remarried it was like something out of a fairytale. I sort of expected her to be completely devastated at losing him so soon."

"And she isn't?" Scott asked.

"She's grieving, of course. But she is already making plans and moving on with her life. I can't wait for her to come for a visit, so I can get the whole story in person."

"When is she planning to be here?"

"Pretty soon. She's going to California for a few days, first, to see Jean, and then stopping in Boise at Linda's place. After she's seen her sisters, she's coming here."

"It will be good to see her, won't it? Did you invite her to stay with us during her visit? We've got plenty of room," Scott said.

"I did, actually. She turned me down, saying something about her last stay in this house. I'd forgotten she stayed with you and Rose before."

Scott chuckled.

"Yeah, I don't think we were very good hosts. Rosie stuck her in that pokey old spare room off the back porch. Bunny was gracious about it, though."

"Why did Rosamund do that?"

"She thought Bunny had her heart set on becoming the lady of this house. Rosie thought she wanted to marry me," he blushed.

"That's silly! If Bunny hadn't set you and me up, we wouldn't be married today. She practically threw me into your arms."

"I was very happy to catch you, my love. I guess we owe her a lot. Maybe you can convince her to stay with us, if we promise Rose will let her have her pick of the guest rooms."

Naidenne began to clear their plates.

"How can we let your sister know about Maureen? If she knew, she might come back."

"Rosamund won't be happy to hear her old nemesis is dead, you know. In fact, if I know my sister, as well as I think I do, she will be mortified over her unkind thoughts about Maureen."

"From what I've heard about that woman, all of Rosamund's hard feelings were completely justified," Naidenne said.

"Still, it's hard to believe someone would kill her."

"Are the police sure she was murdered?"

"How else would she have ended up bundled into an old piece of carpet in her garage?"

"So, either murder, or someone was hiding her body for some reason?" Naidenne asked.

"That's how I see it. We'll just have to wait for the official report."

※

Meeting this week in the Methodist parsonage, the First Ladies were agog at the news of Maureen's death.

Eskaletha attempted to get them settled down with her basilisk-like gaze. When that failed to work, she tried speaking over the hubbub and finally resorted to banging her gavel on the fireplace mantle.

"Thank you, ladies. If we can all get seated quietly, we can begin our meeting."

"But, Madam President!" Judy Falls called out, waving her hand for attention.

"We can't just go on, business as usual, when there's a murderer in our midst."

Her comment threatened to wind the ladies back up again, as several echoed the sentiment.

"Can we please come to order," Eskaletha said. "While I recognize your feelings, we can't let recent events take over our meeting. There will be plenty of time to discuss the Oldham woman's death during our fellowship time."

"Olivette, will you please read the minutes of the last meeting."

Later, Peggy Burt, carefully balancing a coffee cup and a plateful of tasty snacks, took a seat between Judy and Elizabeth.

"I feel like I should keep Paisley and Astilbe home, just so they'll be safe" Judy was saying. "You know, I homeschooled them for years, but now they are in high school they begged to join their friends at the public school."

"I'm sure your twins will be fine, Judy. There's been no hint of any danger to our schools," Elizabeth offered.

"I heard the police aren't even sure Maureen Oldham's death wasn't natural causes," Peggy added.

"Oh, right! The old thing pitched a fit and wrapped herself up in a carpet and rolled into the garage as she died," Judy scoffed.

"Is that how she was found? I hadn't heard that," Peggy said.

"Well, I wasn't supposed to say anything, but one of Ken's trustees has a brother in the Sheriff's office and he told him all about it. The place was ransacked, too. It looked like the killer had been staying in the house for a few days."

"How odd," Elizabeth replied. "Well, we still shouldn't speculate, until we have all the facts. I'm sure there's no reason to think anyone else is in danger. This is an isolated incident, after all."

"Oh, yeah? What about all the house-breaking and thefts, lately? That could be the same guy," Judy insisted.

"I'm going to be sure to keep my doors locked, just in case," Peggy said.

She finished her last cookie, emptied her coffee in one gulp and stood up.

"In fact, I'm going home right now and make sure all the windows in our old parsonage have working locks."

"That's probably prudent, in any case. See you next week," Elizabeth said.

"Aren't you worried, at all, Liz?" Judy asked when Peggy was gone.

"Not especially. There are always evil people around. I don't feel in any greater danger today than before learning about Maureen. I am saddened to think Mrs. Oldham may have been killed, of course," she replied.

"Well, I felt pretty safe in little old Bannoch before this, but now, I'm worried. I wish I could feel as calmly about it as you, but I just can't. Naidenne, what do you think about it?" Judy asked when Naidenne joined them, taking Peggy's vacated chair.

"About what?"

"The murder, of course."

"Oh, Maureen...Scott says we won't know if she was murdered until the autopsy report is released. It does seem odd, though."

"That's what I say. It is obvious she was killed," Judy said.

"It's too bad, though. All the speculation about how Maureen died is taking center stage. No one seems to be mourning her death," Naidenne said.

"That may not have happened, in any case, Deenie. Maureen Oldham was not very well-liked, you know."

"Oh, I know. I didn't get very well acquainted with her, because she'd moved away before Scott and I married and she hadn't been back in town very long, but I heard the tales about her. Still, I think she meant well."

"If the road to Hell is truly paved with good intentions, she must have had a relatively smooth exit from this world," Elizabeth remarked.

"Why, Elizabeth! What a thing to say," Naidenne said.

"Mrs. Oldham must have gotten under your skin to provoke you to say something so harsh," Judy said, with eyebrows raised. "Tell!"

"Oh, I shouldn't have said anything. Forgive me. No matter what she did, like you said, Naidenne, she meant well."

"I would love to stay, but I have an appointment with the doctor, so I'd better be going," Naidenne said.

"Is anything wrong?" Judy asked.

"No, no, just a check-up. See you later," she waved to the others and left.

"I do hope Naidenne is not having health problems. She is such a dear girl," Elizabeth said.

"She's been a real asset, all right. If she hadn't inspired us to start this club, none of us would be real friends, now, would we?"

"Probably not. We were each wrapped up in our own little church-worlds before. We sometimes worked on community committees when our circles overlapped, but nothing like the fellowship we have now."

Saying this, Elizabeth got up and began to collect the empty cups and plates.

"Ooh, it's late! I've got to go, too," Judy said and dashed out in a flurry of gauzy garments, briefly snagging one flowing sleeve on the door handle on her way out and nearly flinging herself back into the arms of another member who was leaving.

## Chapter Fourteen

While Naidenne was driving the Coast Highway to Tillamook for her doctor appointment, Carver Schramm was loitering in an alley across the street from Bannoch Community Fellowship, waiting for the pastor to emerge.

Earlier that afternoon Schramm saw the man who'd come to the old lady's house enter the church building and heard a woman greeting her pastor by name, conveniently identifying Scott.

Schramm was waiting for the pastor to come out and lead the way back to his delectable wife.

Schramm was prepared to wait as long as it took, but in only a few moments Scott came out, got into his car and drove down the hill toward the highway.

Carver cursed under his breath.

Being ill must have made him stupid. Of course, he couldn't follow the man on foot.

He picked up a pinecone and hurled it after Scott's car in a rage, just as a rumpled elderly man carrying a sack of mulch came out of the shed next to the church parking lot.

Schramm trotted across the street and hailed the old guy.

"Excuse me!"

"Yeah?" Josiah Watkins responded.

"I'm looking for Pastor Scott. I, uh, have an appointment with him."

"You just missed him, fella. You sure you had an appointment?"

"Yeah, but I think maybe I was supposed to meet him at his house, not here. Say, I forgot to write down the address. Can you give me directions? I sure don't want to be late. The preacher said he might have a job for me."

"Sure," Josiah said. "Just go on up this road here, turn left at the corner where the old Billings barn used to be, travel about one hundred and fifty yards 'til you hit the little rise where the Miller's car broke down during the snowy winter of '87, turn right by the blighted oak tree, keep going 'til you see the house, you can't miss it, it's a big old two-story with green trim."

"Hold on, I'll never remember all that. I don't suppose you can just write down the address for me?"

Josiah pulled a small lined tablet from his jacket pocket, along with a stub of a carpenter's pencil, scribbled a few lines and ripped out the sheet of paper.

"Here you go, sonny. Can you read plain writing any better than you can remember simple directions?"

Schramm fought the urge to flatten Watkins for his snarky comment. He swallowed his rage, took the paper and thanked the old man, instead.

Josiah merely waved his hand, dismissively, and began spreading mulch in the flowerbed, mumbling under his breath about tattoo ink killing brain cells.

Carver followed the scrawled directions and soon found himself outside the Davidsons' home, where he settled down in the shrubbery across the street to wait for the leading lady in his erotic daydreams to make an appearance.

When wandering over the hills and through the woods on his way to the church earlier, Schramm passed an obviously empty house, one with a crooked and faded For Sale sign in the yard.

It was set back from the roadway on the edge of town. There were no near neighbors and no traffic on the rutted gravel lane leading to the house. There were stacks of building supplies and a cement mixer in the yard with weeds growing through its wheels, as though remodeling work had been started, then abandoned some time ago.

Schramm checked the place out, breaking the flimsy lock on the back door.

A quick look around had convinced him this was the perfect location to act out all his lurid fantasies.

Naidenne sat in her car in the medical clinic parking lot. After sliding the prescription slips into her handbag, she tried to come to grips with the results of her exam.

"Congratulations, Mrs. Davidson," the physician's assistant had said, reading from her notes.

Naidenne was still trying to take in the news. She was so sure her recent symptoms were either early onset menopause, or something really dire, she was having trouble accepting what she was being told.

"You mean I'm pregnant? Are you sure?"

"Oh yes, it's definite. I'd say you are about four months along. I'm going to write prescriptions for you, both prenatal vitamins and something for the nausea and we'll want to see you again in a month."

It was simply incredible.

Scott was going to be over the moon.

He didn't talk about it much, but Naidenne knew he still grieved for his first wife and little daughter who'd died together in an automobile accident a few years before he'd accepted the call to the church in Bannoch.

This new life now growing inside her could never replace the child he'd lost, but it would do much to ease his pain.

Naidenne, who had resigned herself to childlessness, was in a mild state of shock.

She suddenly laughed, remembering how the PA referred to her as an "elderly primipara." At thirty-nine, she didn't consider herself elderly, but she had to admit it was a bit late in the day to be having her first child.

In only five months, she and Scott would be parents. Their lives would be forever changed. It was a daunting thought, but they would travel this new path together and try to wring every ounce of joy from the adventure as it unfolded.

Resolving to see only the joy and none of the fear of the experiences to come, she started the car and began the drive home, her mind filled with baby names, nursery decorations and the myriad delights to come.

❧

Scott was frustrated. He had driven all the way to Cannon Beach to see Miss Dot, only to find her cabin empty. He kicked himself for assuming the elderly lady would be home, rather than calling ahead. He had driven to her neighbor's too, but no one was home next door, either. Finally checking his appointment calendar, he saw his notation of Miss Dot's request for prayers while she was in Seattle this week at a quilter's expo.

He must be getting absent-minded, not to have even looked at the calendar before starting out. Now, he would be late getting back to Bannoch and he'd accomplished nothing.

❧

Naidenne stopped at the big discount store to stock up on non-perishables on the way home. She was eager to get back and share her exciting news with Scott, but she still couldn't resist dawdling in the baby section, dreaming.

With her shopping done, she pulled back onto the highway, her mind filled with the anticipation of Scott's reaction to learning they were going to have a baby.

Once home, she pulled into the driveway and walked up to the house carrying two bags of groceries, fumbling with her door key as she walked.

"Excuse me, ma'am!"

Naidenne did not see Schramm standing in the shadows. His greeting startled her and she dropped her keys.

"Here, let me get those," he picked up the keys and handed them to her, saying, "I didn't mean to scare you. My car's broke down and I wondered if I could come in and use your phone to call my auto club."

Carver thought mentioning an auto club would lend his request more respectability and was proud he'd thought to add that bit.

"My cell phone is still in the car. Just let me put these bags down and I'll come back out and get it for you," Naidenne replied.

She didn't like the rough look of this man. She doubted his story about the auto club, but was willing to let him make a call and offer him a cold drink.

"Wait here," she said, as she unlocked the door and stepped inside.

Setting her bags down on the kitchen table, she turned to go get her phone and almost crashed into Schramm, standing right behind her.

He grabbed her in a bear hug, making it hard to breath.

"What are you doing?" she gasped.

"Just taking you for a little ride. You and me are going to have some fun."

Naidenne shouted for help and kicked at his legs, struggling to get free.

Schramm punched her on the side of the head, knocking Naidenne down and startling her into silence.

"That's enough of that. You've been coming into my dreams and teasing me since I was a kid. You've driven me mad with all your temptations and you aren't going to cheat me out of everything, now that I've finally found you."

Naidenne was confused and even more frightened by Carver's senseless rambling.

What was she going to do?

Schramm pulled her roughly to her feet.

He snatched Rosamund's aprons from a hook behind the door and bound Naidenne around the ankles and knees and tied her hands behind her. He stuffed a potholder into her mouth, gagging her, before pushing her onto a chair.

Looking wildly around for a way to escape, her eyes fell on the Scripture calendar on the wall. This month's verse was Psalm One Hundred Twenty-one, "I lift up my eyes to the mountains—where does my help come from? My help comes from the Lord."

Reading those words, she was washed over by a wave of peace.

The loving God would never let Scott lose another wife and child. She would get out of this, somehow. She would trust in her Lord's divine deliverance.

Rummaging through Naidenne's bags of groceries on the table, Schramm pulled out the Sam Adams winter sampler carton of beer she'd impulsively picked up as a treat for Scott, and the bottle of rum for baking fruit cakes.

He stuck the flask-shaped rum bottle into the waistband of his grubby jeans, tucked the beer under one arm and grabbed the car keys off the table. Cramming them into his pocket and clutching a knot of her hair with his free hand, he pulled Naidenne up and shoved her outside where he forced her to shuffle to the car. When she stumbled or tried to pull away, he jerked her up by the hair.

Throwing her to the floor of the back seat, he jumped behind the wheel and quickly drove off, his head filled with the sadistic sexual exploits he had planned for his dream woman.

Lying on her side, wedged on the floor between the seats, Naidenne tried to spit out the gag, but it was jammed into her mouth too tightly. No matter how she pushed with her tongue, it wouldn't budge. Her mouth was sore and dry and her scalp was on fire where he'd pulled her hair.

With her ankles and knees bound and her arms pulled behind her back, she was almost immobile, but she continued to test her bonds, twisting and squirming until she was crouching on her knees. A strong push with her legs lifted her onto the backseat, where she pitched over, in an almost fetal position.

She needed to sit up. It was still daylight and they would be driving through town to get away from the parsonage. If she could look out the window, someone might see her and call for help.

In the driver's seat, Schramm's head was filled with tantalizing visions; he was having difficulty concentrating on maneuvering the car inconspicuously through the streets.

Looking in the rearview mirror, he noticed Naidenne on the backseat. She was using her shoulders and the leverage from pushing her feet into the back of the front seats to slide her head up the passenger door toward the window.

He reached back to grab her, briefly swerving into the oncoming lane, then quickly swung back onto his side of the road, accompanied by the blare of horns.

Naidenne took advantage of his momentary distraction to press her face against the window, wildly wiggling her eyebrows and shaking her head to indicate her distress to anyone who might be watching.

Schramm again reached over the seat with one brawny arm and grabbed the front of Naidenne's sweater, flinging her back to the floor.

Assuming a benign expression for the sake of any onlookers, he told her in great detail just what would happen to her, if she tried anything like that again.

Scott returned home, tired and frustrated and looking forward to a good meal before going out again to the monthly church Board meeting.

When he didn't find Naidenne's car in the driveway, he assumed she was late returning from her appointment in Tillamook.

He stepped inside just long enough to leave a note on their family message board in the entry hall to let her know he was going to grab a bite at the Crab Shack before the meeting.

Scott was disappointed their paths hadn't crossed before he needed to go out again, but he wasn't worried.

He liked to have a time of prayer before the deacons and trustees arrived, anyway.

Leaving the porch light on for his wife, in case she got back after dark, he drove off to get some dinner before enduring the dreaded meeting.

## Chapter Fifteen

In Reno, at the El Dorado Resort, a door opened into the Spa Tower Suite.

A California king bed with a pop-up forty-two inch flat screen television built into its footboard dominated the luxury suite, which also featured a small living area and a spacious bathroom with a jetted spa tub and walk-in steam shower.

A uniformed bellhop carried in two small suitcases, set them down and held out his hand toward the couple entering behind him.

"Of course you can't carry me! Do you think I went to all this trouble protecting you from harm, just to see you break your back on our wedding night?"

"Oh, Rosie, you wouldn't hurt me. Why, you're such a slip of a girl, I could probably carry you with one arm behind my back," Len responded, with a huge grin.

Rosamund shook the waiting bellboy's extended hand, ignoring his astonished expression, and firmly ushered him out. She closed the door behind him, getting rid of the unwanted witness to her bridegroom's silliness.

Turning to Len, her air of no-nonsense slipped away and she melted into his arms, eagerly expressing all the emotions suitable to a new bride on her wedding night.

"...and that's why I move the pastor's compensation package be reduced by the amount of one thousand dollars per month until the new roof is paid for."

"I second that!"

"Wait just a minute, now. We haven't even seen an estimate on the repairs that are needed. What makes you so sure we need a new roof?" Scott asked.

"That roof is too old. No point in putting patches on patches. Just rip 'er off and get a new one," Josiah said.

"Yep, that's just good stewardship, Pastor," Bill Odem agreed.

"But, you can't honestly expect me to foot the bill for the entire church roof. That's unreasonable."

"Oh, I don't know so much about that, Pastor. I've been looking at the budget reports…we all get a copy, nothing private there…and I can't say as I see much of an increase in income since you got married," Orville offered.

"What does that have to do with it?" Scott asked.

"Just seems to me, with your wife working and all, there should've been a nice little bump in your tithing, and we should've seen it in the income reports."

"Hold on, you're going too far, now…"

"Not at all, Pastor. You're our example of how to live, remember, and it says right in the Bible you got to run your household well. I reckon that means seein' your wife gives the Lord his share," Bill replied.

"How could you know whether my wife is tithing, just from the monthly report, even if it was any of your business? It is possible the giving didn't go up because others were giving less, isn't it?"

"There's a motion before the floor. I call for the question," Josiah interrupted, bringing the discussion to an end.

Lucy Metzger, the church moderator and Bill Odem's sister, called for the vote.

"All in favor of the motion to deduct one thousand dollars per month from the pastor's compensation to pay for a new roof, say aye…opposed, nay…put your hand down Pastor, you know you can't vote. It's unanimous, the ayes have it."

"You forgot to say when we start taking the money in your motion, Josiah," Bill said.

"I move we start takin' the money with the next paycheck, then."

"I second," Bill stated.

# The First Ladies Club

"This is ridiculous!" Scott said as he scooted his chair back.

He stood beside the table staring at his church board, with his mouth opening and closing, too furious to speak.

When Scott looked around the table, the members of the board became absorbed in the papers on the table in front of them, unable to meet his eye.

Scott shook his head. He couldn't believe what had just happened. Taking a deep breath, he squared his shoulders and left the room, feeling nauseated and shaken.

He knew he had to pray. He knew all the encouraging Bible verses he should be reciting to keep his faith strong, but filled as he was with dismay and anger, he was in no fit state to receive comfort.

Surely this too would work for good, but, right at that moment, he couldn't see it and he was unable to bring himself to speak to God when he had no charity in his heart for the men and women he'd just left in the meeting room.

What was he going to tell Naidenne? What would she think of her church family, now?

Scott stopped at his office on his way out and printed the listing of open pulpits he'd downloaded earlier in the week. After the breakfast meeting when the Trustees hatched this harebrained scheme, just downloading the list made him feel better and he hadn't felt the need to follow up on any of the openings.

Tonight's meeting made it abundantly clear it was now time for him to seek another pastorate.

Driving home, he thought about how upset his sister would be to have to move and leave Len. Would she be willing to relocate? She might decide to stay in Bannoch, but how could she continue to worship with people who'd treated her brother like this?

Scott wanted to talk to Rosamund. Where the heck was she, and when was she coming home?

He needed the comfort of his family tonight. He yearned for Naidenne to hold him in her arms and make this whole evening go away, for at least a little while.

He was surprised her car wasn't in the driveway when he arrived home. The only light in the house was the one he'd left on earlier.

Scott parked his car and pulled out his phone to call Naidenne, but his call went straight to voicemail.

Beginning to become concerned, Scott called Shirley to see if Naidenne had gone to visit her friend.

Shirley's husband answered.

"Hi, Jack. My wandering wife isn't at your place, by any chance, is she?"

"Sorry, Scott. I haven't even got my own wife here, tonight. Silly woman took it into her head to take a yoga class at the high school. Did you ever hear anything like it? Maybe she talked Naidenne into going with her."

"Maybe. I'll check it out. Thanks."

Before driving over to the high school and embarrassing Naidenne by barging in on her yoga class, he called a couple of her other friends, but no one had seen her since the First Ladies Club meeting.

At the high school, women were coming out of their class when Scott drove up.

"Hey, Shirley!" he called, as she walked by.

"Hi Scott. What's up?"

"Was Naidenne in your class tonight?"

"No. I invited her, but she was going to be in Tillamook all afternoon and didn't want to be out tonight, too. Isn't she home, yet?"

"Well, she might be, by now, but she wasn't when I left to come and look for her. Guess I'd better get back before she goes out looking for me, too. We could chase each other all night, at this rate. Thanks, Shirley. See you Sunday."

"Night, Pastor," Shirley replied, looking after him with a puzzled expression as he drove away.

The house was still dark when Scott returned.

Maybe Naidenne was inside, lying down in the dark with a headache. He hadn't even gone inside before beginning to call around and look for her.

Scott felt a little foolish as he went into the house, turning lights on as he went from room to room.

His anxiety returned when he reached the kitchen and saw an overturned chair and groceries scattered on the table and countertop. The grocery bags had the logo of the discount store between Bannoch and Tillamook. Naidenne had apparently stopped there on her way home and gotten back earlier.

Scott ran up the stairs, hoping to find his wife in their room, resting. He told himself she must've had a sudden headache, interrupting her in the middle of putting away the shopping.

When he didn't find her upstairs, he began to be seriously worried.

It was getting late. Naidenne would never stay out like this without letting him know. It just wasn't like her.

Not knowing what else to do, Scott called the Sheriff's office to see if they had a report of an accident.

"...Well, thanks, Deputy Williams, but I'm really getting worried. She's never stayed out like this without letting me know...I see...At least twenty-four hours, if there's no sign of foul play. Got it. I don't suppose a tipped-over chair and some spilled groceries count, do they? Yeah, like you said, she'll probably walk in at any moment with a perfectly good explanation. Well, thanks again."

Scott hung up and proceeded to make equally unproductive calls to the regional hospitals.

He couldn't just go to bed without knowing where Naidenne was, so he went out to his car and headed for the highway.

Even though the evidence pointed to Naidenne having returned safely from Tillamook, Scott had to do something, anything. All he could think to do was drive the same route she'd driven, looking for her disabled car. She must be out there somewhere, and he had to find her.

Schramm got confused trying to find the house he'd checked out earlier. Scenery and landmarks looked different while driving than when he'd been on foot.

After a few wrong turns, he got back on the right road and eventually parked in the gravel driveway outside his chosen love nest.

He left Naidenne trussed up in the back seat while he took the alcohol into the house.

He came back, drinking from a bottle of beer, and paused in anticipation before opening the passenger door. With an evil grin, he jerked it open and pulled Naidenne out by her bound feet. She fell heavily onto the gravel, moaning softly.

"Oh, I knew you'd be a moaner. I'll have you moaning like you've never moaned for your preacher-man."

Schramm kneeled beside his captive and began to run his hands over her, from the top of her head, down over her face and shoulders to her breasts where he paused, breathing heavily, and pushed Naidenne's sweater up under her chin, uncovering her bra.

He pulled out his knife and slid it under her wispy bra and between her breasts. With a quick upward thrust, he cut the fabric apart and brushed the two halves aside, leaving Naidenne's naked upper body exposed to his stares and the chill night air.

Taking the point of the knife, he lightly pricked first one nipple then the other, grinning widely when she flinched.

"I knew they'd be pink…I just knew it," he muttered.

With the flat of the knife, he caressed each breast in turn, as Naidenne tried desperately to block out her awareness of his touch. She strived to fill her mind with happy memories, prayers, math problems, anything to lift her consciousness away from this present horror.

Sliding the knife blade down her stomach, Schramm inserted it under the waistband of her slacks where, with another sudden slice, he cut off the button and the top part of the zipper.

Schramm's arousal had reached fever pitch; he was unable to control himself and flung his body across Naidenne's still tightly bound legs, his body weight grinding her knees together painfully.

She felt first his hands, then his lips and tongue, sliding over her breasts. Having this beast licking and sucking where she'd hoped to feed her baby made her feel sick.

Schramm fumbled with his jeans then began to thrust himself against her thighs. When he began to slide his fingers beneath the front of her pants, Naidenne was suddenly thirteen years old and back in her childhood bed being assaulted for the first time.

She vomited into her mouth behind the gag and began to retch and choke.

His climax quickly spent, Schramm noticed her distress and pulled the filthy gag from Naidenne's mouth.

She coughed and spit and began to breathe again, lying limply on the gravel.

"Don't you worry, little lady. There's plenty more where that came from," he said, taking a long drink of beer. "I can take my time, from here on in."

Just then, a pickup went by on the road and Carver realized he needed to get rid of the car.

"But first, we need to get you settled in a nice quiet place to wait for our next go-round."

Schramm pulled Naidenne to her feet and half dragged her into the house, where he led her to a windowless room with acoustical walls and ceiling. The beer and rum were on the floor.

He threw her down on the plush carpet, kneeling down to run his hands over her, once more. He leaned forward to kiss her, but stopped.

"Phew! Puke breath! Here, take a swig of this," he said and poured beer into her mouth.

Naidenne choked and spit it out.

Grabbing her chin in his rough hand, Schramm forced her lips open and splashed more beer into her mouth, then pressed her jaws together until she swallowed with a cough.

He finished the beer in one swig, and then uncapped the rum.

"That's better. Now you just stay here while I put that car of yours out of sight. We don't want to be interrupted before we've had our fun, do we, now?"

Taking a long pull from the rum bottle, Schramm pushed his hand between Naidenne's still-bound thighs, leaned down and nipped at her breast and began to breathe heavily, once again.

Sitting back on his haunches, he pulled out his knife and cut a thin, wavy line from her breast to her navel, and then hesitated as he held the knife over the apron tied around her knees, shaking his head.

"Nah, gotta get rid of the car first. But I'll be back, never fear, I'll be back, real soon."

He finished the rum, grabbed another beer and left.

## Chapter Sixteen

She was alone.

Naidenne felt the sting of the shallow cut on her abdomen and a trickle of blood running down her side. She knew the man planned to rape and kill her when he returned.

Now was her one chance to escape.

Naidenne knew this house. She sold it to the owners and followed the progress of their renovations before their money ran out and the house went into foreclosure.

This room had been remodeled into a media room, but it was originally the home's formal dining room. The built-in media cabinet on the far wall hid a Victorian-era dumbwaiter.

Below there was a full basement.

The lower level kitchen suffered from wall seepage issues and the buyers had boarded it off with a false wall, rather than deal with expensive foundation repairs.

Naidenne had watched the couple slap cost-cutting cosmetic cover-ups on several of their remodeling projects. If only they had done the same with the dumbwaiter, it could be Naidenne's way out.

She was afraid to try to leave the way she'd come in. Schramm could come back that way at any moment. Hobbled as she was, she'd never get far enough away to elude him.

Her only hope was to hide.

She rolled onto her stomach and tried to wriggle over to the media cabinet, the carpet pulling at her wound, leaving streaks of blood behind her. Rolling onto her back, she was able, by means of a scooting hop on her bottom, to make awkward progress.

Coming up against the cabinet, she managed to get to her knees. Turning her back to the wall, she used her hands on the shallow bottom shelves to push herself to her feet, ignoring the intense pain in her shoulders.

She shuffled sideways until she was in front of the deeper middle shelf meant to hold the TV. Getting a grip under this shelf, she pulled up and felt it move. Little by little, she pushed her hands further under the shelf, until she was able to get an elbow underneath and create a larger opening.

She swiveled around, ducked her head into the space and beheld a gaping well of darkness beneath.

She was in luck!

Thinking she heard her attacker returning, she pushed her upper body through the gap and kicked off with her feet, plummeting down the chute into the blackness; the loose board dropping back into place behind her.

His focus clouded by drink and his plans for Naidenne, Schramm was having trouble keeping the car on the winding mountain road. He took a hairpin curve too fast and veered off into a gulley where the car banged into a pine tree.

The collision popped open the driver's door and Carver fell out, his head bleeding from the impact. He got to his feet and staggered a few steps before sinking unconscious to the forest floor.

Scott saw the light of dawn illuminate the window as he sat at the kitchen table, a half-full mug of long-cold coffee between his outstretched hands.

After driving back and forth on the highway for hours, he'd returned to the parsonage to wait for word of his missing wife.

When he returned home, there was a message light on the answering machine and he eagerly grabbed up the phone, but it was only a prayer chain call about a church member's upcoming hernia operation.

Scott tried to remain calm and believe everything would be okay, but as the night passed, his hopes had grown weaker.

Although the twenty-four hour time limit to report a missing person had not passed, Scott called the Sheriff's Office again, reporting the continued absence of his wife.

The officer he spoke with promised to ask all the units to keep an eye out for Naidenne and instructed Scott to call back, if she failed to turn up that day.

He didn't know what to do, but he couldn't go on as if everything was normal.

Scott showered and put on fresh clothes, then began calling Naidenne's friends, again.

"That was Scott Davidson on the phone, Tyrone. He said Naidenne is missing. No one's seen her since our meeting yesterday," Eskaletha Evans told her husband as he sat at the table finishing a bowl of oatmeal.

"Where does he think she might be?"

"He has no idea. Deenie has never gone off like this. He sounded seriously worried. We've got to help him find her."

"If her own husband has no idea where to look, what makes you think we could find her?"

"I don't know, but we've got to try," Eskaletha insisted.

"I've got a funeral this morning, so I'm afraid I can't be much help on your wild goose chase, my dear. Why don't you ask your First Ladies to form a posse? You are always looking for unsolvable problems to tackle."

"You can make light of this if you want, but Deenie is my friend. I think I just might take your suggestion."

After her husband left, Eskaletha made some calls and an hour later she was calling to order an extraordinary, emergency meeting of the First Ladies Club in her living room.

"We need to retrace her steps. She told us she was going to a doctor in Tillamook. Anybody know which one?" Judy asked.

"Didn't Scott say she came back from there before she disappeared, though?" Olivette said.

"He said he thought she had, but that was only because of a couple of grocery sacks. I don't think we should assume anything," Peggy offered.

"Ladies! We need a plan of attack, and Judy is right. First things first. We must start at the point where she was last seen by all of us, and track her movements from there," Eskaletha stated.

"So, who knows which doctor she was seeing?"

The women looked at each other, but no one spoke up.

"Well, then, Scott will know. Who would like to call him?"

Elizabeth raised her hand, and then took her cell phone into the dining room to make the call.

"What do we do when we find out which doctor?" Gwennie asked.

"We will call to determine if she actually made it to the appointment, and try to find out if she said where she was going when she left."

Elizabeth came back into the room.

"I just spoke with Scott. He already called Naidenne's doctor and verified that she left after her appointment. He said he'd gone to the discount store where the bags came from and a checker remembered Naidenne stopping in yesterday. But, it's an odd thing. The clerk remembered her because she was buying rum and made a special point to let the man know it was for fruit cakes, not drinking. He thought it was funny."

"So why is that so odd?" Judy asked.

"The odd thing is that there was no rum at the house with the other groceries. Scott found the register slip, and there was a carton of beer missing, too."

"Surely, he doesn't think Naidenne went on a drinking binge or something." Peggy said.

"I don't think so, but it is odd," Elizabeth replied.

"What are the police doing about this, anyway?" one of the women piped up.

"They don't want to be bothered until she's been gone so long no one can find her!" Judy said.

"You know, they might get involved sooner, if we put a little pressure on them," Eskaletha remarked.

# The First Ladies Club

"Let's go over to the Sheriff's Office, right now, and launch a protest!" Judy suggested.

"A sit-in!" Gwennie agreed.

"I don't think we need to make a scene, but going over there together to talk to the Sheriff and let him know we think this is a serious matter, couldn't hurt," Elizabeth added.

After the First Ladies Club descended upon the sheriff, firmly impressing upon that good man the seriousness of the situation, he assured them he would instruct his officers to look into the disappearance of their friend, beginning immediately.

Convinced that Naidenne's unexplained absence was finally being taken seriously, the women dispersed to their respective homes.

After they left, the sheriff made two phone calls. One was to the husband of the missing woman, requesting him to come to the office and answer a few questions and the second call was to Portland, requesting help in a missing persons case.

"Sit right here, Mr. Davidson," Detective Rasmussen, the man sent down from Portland to handle the investigation, directed Scott to a chair in the small interrogation room.

"Thanks."

"Now, if you can just tell me in your own words what happened to your wife."

"I don't know what's happened. That's why I reported her missing. That's what I've been telling the other officers all morning. I want someone to find her," Scott replied.

"Are you saying you refuse to cooperate, Mr. Davidson?"

"Of course not! I'll tell you anything I can to help, but I don't know where Naidenne is."

"Okay, if you want to be that way…let's go back to the beginning. When did you last see or speak to your wife?"

"We were together at breakfast yesterday. I went to the church around eight. I called my wife before noon to let her know I had a lunch meeting and was going out of town after that. She had a club meeting in the early afternoon and an appointment with her doctor in Tillamook later. We said we would see each other at home for dinner, but when I arrived, she wasn't there."

"Why was she seeing a doctor? Had you hurt her?"

"What? Of course not. She's been having some women's complaints she needed to get checked."

"Who was this lunch meeting with?"

"I met with a member of the congregation, Harvey Wilson."

"What was this meeting about?"

"The Wilsons are going through a rough patch. Harvey needed to talk."

"So, you were commiserating with another guy with marital problems, huh?"

"Don't be ridiculous. I am his pastor. And my wife and I do not have any problems."

"Then why did she run off?"

"She didn't run off!"

"And you know that because you know where she is, don't you? Where is she, preacher? What have you done with her?"

"Nothing!"

"Okay, so you went out of town after lunch. Where did you go?"

"To call on a former church member in Cannon Beach."

"I suppose this former member will confirm your whereabouts…"

"Well, no. She wasn't there. I'd forgotten she was going to be in Seattle this week."

"Convenient. So you don't have an alibi for the time you say your wife went missing, is that right?"

"I don't know why I would need an alibi. I don't know why you think I would hurt my wife, but you are wrong. I love Naidenne, she's missing and I am worried about her. I didn't do anything to her."

"I understand your sister has recently disappeared under suspicious circumstances, as well. Did you kill her, too, just to whet your appetite, maybe? How many others have there been, preacher?"

"What's the matter with you? My sister isn't dead. She just went out of town to clear her head about her romantic relationship."

"Oh, yeah, the banker. Now, that's a funny thing…he's gone missing, too. What are you, an equal opportunity killer, or did he catch on to what you were doing and need to be eliminated?"

"You must be out of your mind. Do you think we're in a television show, Detective? All your unreasonable and unfounded accusations would be funny, if my wife wasn't missing. I hope there are saner men out looking for her, right now."

"Oh, there are; men and dogs, and we'll find her, too. Why not save us all the time and money and just tell us where you stashed her body."

Scott paled at this casual reference to Naidenne's dead body.

She was still alive, somewhere. She had to be.

"That's enough. I want a lawyer."

"Why do you need a lawyer, if you're so innocent? Come on, man, tell the truth and get it over with."

"Lawyer," Scott replied through clenched teeth, then put his head down on the table and began to pray.

The detective threw Scott a look of disgust and went out, slamming the door.

## Chapter Seventeen

Shirley Griffith returned home from the Sheriff's Office, where she had gone to support Scott. She had called him that morning and was shocked to learn of Naidenne's disappearance.

"Jack, you won't believe this!"

"What is it, Hon? How's Scott holding up?"

"I wasn't allowed to see him. The officers acted like he's a suspect in Naidenne's disappearance, or something."

"That's ridiculous! Scott doesn't actually worship his wife, but she's up there right under the Lord in his heart, I know."

"Exactly. I don't know what they can be thinking."

"Oh, I suppose they have to consider the husband whenever a wife goes missing, but one look should have convinced them that was a non-starter in this case."

"I'm just so worried about Naidenne and now this. What can we do?"

"We can be character witnesses for Scott, if it comes to that, I guess. In the meantime, we can pray," Jack suggested.

"Of course!" Shirley exclaimed and ran to the phone to start the prayer chain for Naidenne and Scott.

At the Boatworks coffee shop, Bill Odem slid into the booth next to Josiah, who was sitting across from Orville.

"Is it true what's on the prayer chain? Did the pastor finally snap and do away with his pretty wife?" Bill asked.

"He was surely angry when he left the meeting. Looked mad enough to kill, all right," Josiah said.

"Now, we don't know anything, for sure. Innocent until proven, and all that. Still, it's got me thinkin'..." Orville paused.

"Thinkin' what?" Josiah asked.

"Pastor Scott was the one who found Maureen's body all wrapped up like a burrito, right?"

"Yeah?" Bill prompted.

"Well, what if he's the one knocked her in the head and rolled her up in the carpet? He never did get along with her, we all know that."

"Was she knocked in the head? I thought nobody knew how she died," Bill said.

"Well, no one's said, yet, but it could have happened that way."

"Just think, the man's been our pastor for years and no one ever guessed in all that time he was a wolf in shepherd's clothing," Bill said.

"They're sayin' over to the Sheriff's Office they think he did away with that sister of his, too," Josiah said.

"I wondered why we hadn't seen her in church, lately. She's such a busybody, always flitting here and there, telling the ladies what cookies to bring, and all."

"It's going to put a kink in our plans for the roof, though," Josiah said.

"What d'ya mean?" Orville asked.

"With the preacher in jail, he sure won't be on the payroll, anymore, so we can't deduct the money to pay for the roof from his paycheck."

"Heck, we will be saving his whole salary, until we call a new pastor. If we drag our feet long enough, the roof will be paid for," Orville assured the others.

"I hadn't thought of that. We will want to take our time picking a new guy, anyway. Don't want another Jack-the-Ripper in the pulpit," Josiah said.

"You just never know about people, do you?" Bill said.

"Nope. It's a real shame, too. I'm going to have some of that marionberry pie, how about you guys?" Orville said and signaled to the waitress.

❧

"Thanks for letting me know, Elizabeth. You're right. We will have to do something ourselves, after all."

The news Elizabeth had shared was even more shocking than Naidenne's disappearance. Eskaletha found it hard to believe the authorities could be accusing Scott of doing something to his dear wife.

Eskaletha sat on the chintz-covered loveseat in her sunroom and prayed for God's leading.

She sometimes seemed like a person who liked to be in complete charge, but she never began anything new without bathing it in prayer and asking for divine guidance.

It was many minutes before she lifted her head and reached again for her phone and began to make calls.

❧

The women of the First Ladies Club were gathered in Naidenne's real estate office.

Eskaletha's first call was to Shirley Griffith, who met the group and let them in. She was seated at Naidenne's computer, pulling up information as Eskaletha directed.

"Ladies, we are lucky that Naidenne hasn't had too many houses on her books in the past few months. That will make our jobs a little easier. After Shirley prints out the addresses, we will divide them up among ourselves and check out each one. It is possible Naidenne was called out to show a house to a prospective buyer and became ill or had an accident."

"Or it could have been one of those scammers who lured her out for nefarious purposes, like those Craigslist robbers," Judy piped up.

"Yes, unfortunately, that is also a possibility. So, we will go in groups of three, each with a well-charged Smartphone. This is serious business; we don't know what we might find and it could be dangerous."

"If either group sees anything suspicious, we need to contact the other groups and the sheriff, right away," Elizabeth added.

"I heard they have some officers with dogs out searching, too. What if we run into them at a house?" Gwennie asked.

"If the officers are already at a location, there's no reason for us to search it," Eskaletha replied.

"Okay, ladies. I've got your lists and keys to the lock boxes on the houses. Now who goes where? I want to come, too. I'm not in your club, but Deenie was, er...I mean *is*, my best friend," Shirley said, with tears in her eyes.

Carver Schramm came to, damp and cold and with a terrible headache.

He got to his feet and climbed with effort back to the roadway.

When he reached the asphalt and looked back toward the car, he discovered the wreck was well below his line of sight. He had accidentally found the perfect spot to ditch it.

It took him a few moments to reorient himself and remember which way he'd come. Eventually, he started walking back in the direction of the house, picking up the pace as he thought of all the delights awaiting him in that windowless, sound-proofed room.

He'd driven a few miles before driving off the road the night before and he hiked more than an hour before spying the house where he'd left Naidenne.

Making a quick tour of the property to be sure no one had been there in his absence, he went inside, where he flung open the door to the empty media room.

Where was she? The bottles were there, but the woman was gone.

He noticed smears of blood leading to one side of the room, where they stopped abruptly in front of the built-in cabinets.

He jerked open all the cabinet doors, revealing only more empty shelves.

She seemed to have disappeared.

The blood trail must have been a trick, but with her knees and ankles bound and her hands tied behind her, she couldn't have gotten far.

Schramm began searching the house. Not finding her on the main floor, or in the empty upstairs rooms, he opened the basement door and stepped carefully down the narrow stairs to the dark and dank-smelling underground rooms.

There were narrow basement windows looking out on weed-filled window wells on one exterior wall, allowing very little light to penetrate the gloom.

Feeling his way along the walls, Schramm attempted a thorough search, finding nothing but dust, grime and mold. The basement seemed to be empty.

Carver stood at the bottom of the steps, thinking.

He was wasting his time in this creepy cellar; no way the woman could have climbed down the stairs trussed up like she was.

Climbing up the stairs in defeat, he paused when he thought he heard a noise from behind one wall. He stood completely still and strained to hear, but as there was no repeat of the sound, he shrugged, assuming it was the rustling of some woodland creature, and left the basement to search the grounds, again.

Behind the false wall concealing the ancient kitchen area, Naidenne moved again and moaned as she regained consciousness.

She lay crumpled at the bottom of the abandoned dumbwaiter where she'd fallen. There was pain in her head and shoulder from her impact on the pile of rags and cardboard boxes in the bottom of the chute.

Struggling to wriggle out of the cramped space introduced more aches and pains, but she ignored them. She had to try to straighten up to assess the damage she'd caused in her swan dive to freedom.

Uppermost in Naidenne's mind was the safety of her baby. So far, she hadn't felt any abdominal pain or cramping, so her hopes were high the child remained unharmed.

Dim light filtered through the narrow and filthy basement windows into the closed-off room, allowing Naidenne to get a good look at her surroundings.

## The First Ladies Club

The kitchen fittings had been left in place when this room was boarded up.

She spied the drawers beneath the metal draining board. If only the owners had overlooked a knife or can opener when clearing out this area, she might have a chance to cut through the fabric ties restricting her movements and find a way out. If not, she had only exchanged a torture chamber for solitary confinement, or possibly, a tomb.

She pushed hard with her legs and flopped out onto the floor on her stomach.

Inching across the room on her knees and shoulders was painful on the cold, rough cement, but she was determined to reach the drawers.

Once across the room, she got her knees under her and lifted her head and shoulders, bringing her mouth level with the drawer handles.

Gripping the cold metal handle made her teeth ache.

Pulling back the first time failed to budge the drawer. The handle slipped from between her teeth and her jaws clicked jarringly together, bringing tears to her eyes.

She tried again and again before the drawer, finally, began to move.

Images flitted through Naidenne's mind of how snaggle-toothed she was going to be after this adventure, but she kept at it.

When the drawer was half-open, she tried to use her chin to pull herself up, but fell back to the floor on her side, feeling as helpless as a supine turtle.

How was she ever going to get to her feet without the use of her hands?

Carver decided to check the nearby grounds more thoroughly.

Walking a dry creek bed leading from the house, he heard a vehicle pass on the road above and saw a Sheriff's unit driving by.

127

If they were looking for the woman out this way, it was only a matter of time before the empty house caught someone's attention.

When he'd returned to find the room empty, Schramm briefly considered the whole episode might have been a fantasy brought on by booze and the crash.

Seeing the empty bottles and the blood in the media room reassured him it was all real.

Real or not, it was time to abandon his dream girl and get back on the trek to the Yukon and safety.

He hadn't been able to act out many of his fantasies, but what he had seen and done would provide fuel for richer, more graphic dreams in the future; fantasies he knew now he could live out whenever he chose, any time he found a tall, shapely woman with wild red-gold hair.

Carver had tasted of the reality and hungered for more.

With renewed determination, he plunged deeply into the woods, striking out for the freedom of the far north.

## Chapter Eighteen

"Thanks, Will. I'm sorry to get you mixed up in this, but when they started accusing me of hurting Naidenne, I knew I needed a good, honest lawyer," Scott addressed the casually dressed man sitting across the interview room table.

"I'm glad you called me, Scott. I only just got in from a camping trip with the boys in my church youth group when I got your message. I came straight here. Now, tell me everything…"

After Scott told his friend what had been happening, he stood up, hands clenched at his sides.

"None of this is finding my wife! What's happening to her while these stupid people play out their TV detective fantasies with my life?"

૭

"I'd hate to be checking out these empty houses at night. They are creepy, even in broad daylight," Judy commented to her search party companions, Peggy and Shirley.

"Too bad we didn't get a list of houses in town, instead of all these clear out here in the boonies," Peggy agreed.

"If Deenie ran into trouble in one of the houses in a downtown neighborhood, don't you think she would have been able to call for help, before now?" Shirley said. "I think our list has some of the best prospects on it."

"Have you known Naidenne a long time, Shirley?" Peggy asked.

"Only a few years, actually. We were introduced by a mutual friend. But we've grown really close. In spite of the difference in our ages, we have so much in common, I feel as if I've known her forever."

"That's the way I feel about all my friends in the First Ladies Club. We come from different backgrounds, cultures, decades and denominations, but we love the same God," Peggy said. "And we wouldn't have ever gotten to know each other, if not for Naidenne."

"We've just got to find her!" Judy said.

"What if something really bad's happened to her? I don't know if I want to be the one to find her that way," Peggy admitted.

"We can't think like that. She's going to be okay and we are going to help find her," Shirley insisted.

"Here we are, this is the next place on our list," Judy said, turning the car between two rock columns standing sentry at the entrance to a gravel driveway.

Inside the rustic log cabin chalet at the end of the winding drive, Bunny Banks was busily airing out the place, opening doors and windows and putting fresh linens on the bed in the loft.

"I wonder where everyone could be?" she murmured, talking to herself as she worked.

"Naidenne never answered my calls or emails, and she must not have gotten my voice mail message asking her to open up the cabin, either. I guess I should have waited in Idaho at my sister's place until I got in touch with the folks here. I probably would have, if Linda hadn't gotten on my nerves trying to help me 'work through' my bereavement."

Bunny had been looking forward to a return to her vacation home in Bannoch for months...ever since she'd gotten over the shock of Max's death.

"I was sort of anticipating a much warmer welcome than this, though."

Stepping out onto the porch to shake out a comforter, she saw a car coming up the drive.

"That must be my welcoming party now! I guess I can stop feeling sorry for myself, after all."

She leaned over the railing to wave at her approaching guests.

"Bunny! That's Bunny!" Shirley squawked.

"Who?" Peggy asked.

"What? I'm going to hit a bunny? I don't see any rabbits," Judy said.

"No, that woman up there. That's my friend, Bunny. She's Naidenne's friend, too."

"Maybe she will know where Naidenne went," Peggy offered.

"You don't suppose they are having some sort of gal pals retreat, do you?" Judy said.

"…and causing all this trouble? How thoughtless," Peggy added.

The car stopped and Shirley jumped out. She ran up the porch stairs and greeted her friend with an enthusiastic hug, almost tumbling them both over the railing.

"Bunny! When did you get here? Why didn't you let someone know you were coming?"

"Hi, Shirley," Bunny replied with a grin. "I just got in a few hours ago. Didn't anyone get my messages at Naidenne's office?"

"No, we haven't been working today…" Shirley began.

"Then how did you know to come here?" Bunny interrupted. "Who have you got with you in the car? Welcome, ladies! Come on up."

"Bunny, these women are friends of Naidenne's; members of the First Ladies Club she belongs to, Judy Falls and Peggy Burt."

"I'm happy to meet you. I was beginning to think I wasn't going to have much of a welcome in Bannoch. Come inside and I'll fix us some tea."

"We aren't on a social call, I'm afraid," Shirley said.

"What do you mean?"

"I didn't know you owned this chalet. It was still on Naidenne's property listing."

"That's probably because, after we bought it, she agreed to look after the place when we aren't here. But, I still don't understand…"

"Naidenne is missing," Judy stated. "No one's seen her since yesterday afternoon."

"We're part of the search party," Peggy added.

"Your place was on our list of empty properties to search," Shirley said.

Bunny grabbed the porch railing. Her knees had gone weak.

"How can she be missing? Where is Scott?"

"I'm afraid the police are holding him. They suspect he might be responsible," Shirley told her.

"Please come inside and tell me everything. I've got to sit down."

Bunny led the ladies into the great room, where they sat on built-in banquettes in the conversation pit in front of an empty river rock fireplace.

"Please tell me everything you know," she asked again.

After the women explained, Bunny was quiet for a moment, taking in the awful news.

"What does Rosamund say? She always kept pretty good tabs on the comings and goings in the parsonage. Didn't Naidenne give her any hints of where she might be going?" she asked.

"That's part of the mystery. Rosamund went missing before Deenie did," Shirley said.

"What? Is there a search party out for her, too?"

"Well, no. Scott and Naidenne said Rosamund went on a little trip, but then he told the Sheriff they don't really know where she went. Apparently, she left a note saying she needed to get away to think, but didn't say where she was going. They haven't heard from her in weeks."

"Now, they think Scott did away with his sister, too!" Judy added.

"Oh, for Heaven's sake! Anyone with half a brain knows Scott Davidson would never hurt a fly, let alone the two women he loves. Does he at least have a good lawyer? Should I call someone?"

# The First Ladies Club

"I think he called Will Stockman. He's a lawyer and a good friend of Scott's."

"Well, if he isn't able to get Scott released, I know some fairly high-powered attorneys, friends of my late husband, who can. I think I should call one of them, just in case. Excuse me."

Bunny got up and went into the kitchen to get her cell phone and make some calls.

"So, this is the famous Bunny we've heard so much about. Kind of a take-charge gal, isn't she?" Peggy said.

"I don't remember her being quite so assertive, to tell the truth, but a take-charge type may be just what's needed here," Shirley responded.

"Scott! Naidenne! We're back!" Rosamund called out from the living room in the echoing parsonage.

"Where is everyone?" Len asked. "Shouldn't they be home from work by now?"

"They certainly should. Maybe something's happening at the church. Let me check the calendar," Rosamund said, as she walked into the kitchen.

Scott had fixed himself a bowl of cereal the morning after Naidenne disappeared.

Rosamund was dismayed to see a bowl of soggy cornflakes and a carton of spoiled milk, slowly turning to cottage cheese, on the counter next to the sink.

With a little mental shake, she reminded herself this was no longer her kitchen, and walked over to the calendar where the events of the church were recorded.

That day's square was blank.

"Something's wrong, Len," she called to her new husband.

"What do you mean? How can you tell?"

"I just feel it. Don't you? This house is too empty. Like I imagine it would look and feel the day after the rapture."

"Well, we'll never know for sure, will we...we'll be gone to Glory," Len quipped.

"Be that as it may, something here is not right. I'm going to call Maureen Oldham."

"That old biddy? Why her? You don't even like her. Of course, nobody does."

"Maureen always keeps tabs on the pastor and his family. She will know where they are, if anyone does."

When she tried to call Maureen, the phone was "no longer in service," according to the recorded message.

Rosamund called Shirley next and Jack answered.

"Hi Jack, it's Rosamund. We just got back and…"

"Rosamund! You're here? In Bannoch? Get yourself over to the Sheriff's office, right away, woman. They think Scott did you in," Jack told her.

"Whatever are you saying," Rosamund stammered, but Jack cut her off, telling her to waste no time getting to the Sheriff, and hung up.

"I told you something was wrong, Len. We've got to get to the Sheriff's Office, right now."

They hurried to the car and drove off, Len restraining his curiosity until they were well on the way.

At the Sheriff's Office, Rosamund and Len approached the reception counter.

"Excuse me. We are here to see Reverend Scott Davidson, please," Len told the duty sergeant.

"What's your relationship to Mr. Davidson?" he asked.

"We are his sister and brother-in-law," Len replied with a proud grin, in spite of the circumstances.

"Names?"

"Rosamund Davidson Spurgeon and Len Spurgeon."

Hearing Rosamund's name, the sergeant looked up, alertly.

"Have a seat over there, someone will be with you shortly," he directed, before stepping away from the counter and making a phone call.

Soon the couple was ushered into an interview room, where they waited several minutes before being joined by the detective on the case.

"You are claiming to be Scott Davidson's missing sister, is that right?" he asked, without preamble.

"No indeed," Rosamund snapped.

"I was told…"

"I am not 'claiming' anything. I am Rosamund Davidson Spurgeon and I have been Scott's sister since the day he was born…longer actually, since the day he was conceived."

"Do you have some identification?" the detective asked.

"As a matter of fact, I have my driver's license and my birth certificate, as well as my marriage license."

"How is it you just happen to have all that?" the detective sneered.

"We were recently married and haven't had a chance to unpack and put our documents into a safety deposit box at my husband's bank. He is the manager of the local branch. Do you need proof of that, too?" Rosamund retorted, handing over the papers.

The detective examined the identification documents, as though suspecting they might be counterfeit, then handed them back.

"Everything seems to be in order. Do you mind telling me where you've been for the past few weeks?"

"I don't see that it is any of your business, officer," Rosamund replied.

"Now, Rosie…I don't mind telling you, detective. We've been getting married and on our honeymoon," Len said.

"Why the big secret?"

"When you get to be our age, you don't necessarily want a big to-do of a wedding."

Rosamund smiled at Len, grateful he hadn't told the detective about her foolish superstition.

"May we see my brother, now?" she asked.

"Wait here."

In a few moments the interview room door opened, again, and Scott entered.

"Oh, Scott! I'm so sorry! I never guessed my little trip would get you into trouble," Rosamund wailed, throwing her arms around her brother.

Scott patted her on the back then gently pushed her back.

"You didn't get me into this, Rose. Naidenne is missing and I don't know where she is. The police just naturally assumed foul play and I guess the husband is the prime suspect."

"Missing? What do you mean?" Rosamund cried.

After Scott recited the story, Rosamund was stunned.

"What can we do to help you find your wife, Scott?" Len asked.

"I don't know…I just don't know," Scott said, sitting down at the table and putting his head in his hands.

"I've been praying since we heard you were in trouble, even before this awful news about Naidenne, and I know you have been, too, but there must be something else we can do," Rosamund said. "At least I can fix you a decent meal. Let's go."

"I'm afraid I'm still in the frame, as they say, for Naidenne's disappearance. I don't think they will let me go," Scott told his sister.

"Well, we can ask," Len stated. "Where's your lawyer? Can't he get them to let you go home?"

"Will left me about an hour ago to talk to someone. I'm afraid I didn't pay much attention. He should be back soon, though."

Will tapped on the door and came in just as Scott spoke.

"Rose! Welcome back. I don't know where you've been, but you made a timely return. I'm not sure I could have convinced these folks to let your brother go home, if you'd still been missing, too."

"But, I wasn't missing! I told Scott and Naidenne I was going."

"Only not where you were going, how to reach you or when you'd be back," Scott pointed out.

"Oh dear," Rosamund sighed.

"Now, don't fuss, Rosie. We're back now. And didn't you hear the man say Scott can leave? Let's get the boy home," Len said.

"Oh, yes. You'll feel better after I fix you a good dinner."

"I don't think I'm going to have much appetite as long as my wife is missing. But thanks, anyway. I'll be happy to get out of here, though. Thank you, Will."

"We may not be out of the woods, yet. The detective did tell me they had a report from someone who thought they saw your wife in the backseat of her own car, making faces at folks. This person said the car was being driven by a long-haired man, but the police don't seem to think this is a serious lead. If Naidenne, well, if she isn't found, we will probably have more dealings with the police," Will said.

"Don't even think that!" Rosamund cried.

"Come on, Scott. Let's get you home where we can talk this over and make plans to find your wife," Len urged.

## Chapter Nineteen

"My attorney friend in Houston is going to contact the local authorities and find out more details. If it looks like Scott needs him to intervene, he'll fly out in the morning," Bunny told the others when she returned from her phone call.

"That's really wonderful," Peggy commented.

"But, it's not going to help us find Naidenne," Judy said.

"Right. Let's go to the next house on our list. She's obviously not here at Bunny's cabin," Shirley agreed.

"Wait. I've only been here a couple of hours and haven't been all over the house or the grounds. Deenie could have come to open the place up and fallen down the cellar stairs, or something. Don't you think we should at least look?" Bunny said.

"You know your house the best. Tell us where we should check," Judy replied.

Bunny sent the women to check the cellar, utility room, closets and guest room, while she did a tour of the yard, even peering under the deck. There was no sign of Naidenne.

"Okay, it was worth making sure she isn't here, but now we really need to move on," Judy said.

"Can I come, too?" Bunny asked.

All four women piled into Judy's car and drove back out onto the road for the next empty property on their list.

"Is that it, up there?" Peggy asked, pointing to the house with all the construction materials in the overgrown yard.

Shirley checked the list and nodded.

"This is the place. See the realtor's sign?"

On the hill above the house, Carver Schramm heard a car and peered through the trees. He couldn't believe it when he saw a car driving up to the very house he had been hiking away from for half an hour or more.

"Oh, man! I've been walking in a circle! I hate these friggin' trees," he growled, then dropped down to stay out of sight of the people in the car.

Seeing four middle-aged women climb out of the sedan, Schramm had an idea. He'd never find his way out of these mountains if he couldn't stay with the road. But if he took that car, he still had a chance to get out of the area without being seen.

He began to creep down through the undergrowth toward Judy's car, as the women approached the house and began to peer into the windows.

When the four went out of sight behind the house, Schramm dashed to the car, where Judy had left the driver's door hanging open.

Carver stifled a laugh when he saw the keys dangling from the ignition. He sprang onto the seat and started the engine, slamming the door shut as he reversed wildly down the driveway and out onto the road.

Alerted by the sound of the engine and the slam of the door, the women came running in time to see Judy's car disappear down the mountain road.

"My car! Someone's taking my car! Ken is going to be so mad."

"Call the police, quickly, maybe they can catch it before it hits the highway," Shirley suggested.

Bunny pulled her phone from her pocket, dialed and asked the emergency operator for the State Troopers.

"Here, Judy. You can describe your car," she said, handing over her phone.

"I left my purse in your car, Judy," Peggy remembered. "Tell them that."

"Never mind your handbag, Peggy. My car's gone."

"But, the question is, who was that and did he have anything to do with Naidenne's disappearance," Shirley said.

"It couldn't have been Naidenne, could it?" Peggy asked.

"Of course not. She would have no reason to steal a car and run away from her friends. Naidenne is either hurt or in trouble, and the person who took Judy's car must be involved. Why else would they be out here all alone at an abandoned house?" Bunny said.

"A trooper is coming to get my statement and take us home. We need to tell him about Naidenne, too. Maybe he can help find her," Judy said.

"Good idea. In the meantime, we can keep looking around. Maybe we'll find something," Bunny suggested.

The women found nothing outside the house except a few beer bottles.

They were hesitant to use their key on the lockbox to open the door and decided to wait and let the trooper go search inside.

After being surprised by the car thief, they weren't completely sure they were alone.

୬

The bump on Naidenne's head made her thinking fuzzy. She kept drifting off to sleep. Each time she awoke she fought against her bonds, trying to get to her feet before being once more overcome by weakness.

Coming around again, she thought she heard voices and a car.

"I must be dreaming," she told herself as she struggled in the dark basement. She soon gave in to exhaustion and slept, once more.

୬

When the trooper arrived, the women told him their story. He relayed the pertinent details to his dispatcher, then agreed to search the house for the women.

Shirley unlocked the front door for the trooper.

"You ladies stay out here," he instructed as he walked inside.

The women could hear him walking around the empty house. He searched quickly upstairs and spent a longer time on the main floor, before they heard him descend the basement stairs.

He soon came out, looking grim.

"What did you find?" Judy asked. "Is there any sign of Naidenne?"

"I didn't find your friend, ma'am. The house is empty."

When Bunny put her hand on the door, preparing to have a look around for herself, the trooper stopped her.

"You don't want to go in there," he cautioned.

"Why not? You said no one's inside."

The officer looked uncomfortable, as though trying to think up a reason without alarming the ladies.

"It may not mean anything, but I saw what might be blood stains in one of the rooms. No one may go in there until the crime scene technicians have a chance to check it out."

"Blood!" Peggy shrieked, while the others went pale.

"It could be from some animal, or a transient may have set up camp in the empty house. You don't what to assume it has anything to do with your missing friend," the trooper said, trying to reassure the women.

Obviously not convinced, the four were becoming more distressed by the second.

"We need to get back to town," Shirley said.

"I'm sorry, but I can't leave until the other officers arrive, ma'am. I'll take you all home, as soon as I'm relieved here."

"Look," Bunny spoke up, "my place is just over the hill. I'll walk home for my car and come and get you. Is that all right, officer?"

"I guess so. I've got all your contact information and statements. None of you went into this house before I arrived, right?"

They all nodded.

"Then, you can go. Someone will probably get in touch, if we need anything more from any of you."

"Would you like me to come with you, Bunny?" Shirley asked.

"No thanks. She travels fastest who travels alone, and all that. I'll be back in a few shakes. Hang in there," Bunny said and walked off across the hill at a brisk clip.

"How are we ever going to tell Scott?" Judy moaned.

"We don't have anything to tell him, yet. No one should say anything about this until the authorities decide exactly what this nice trooper found inside. It may be nothing and speculating will only add to his pain, unnecessarily," Shirley said.

"But this doesn't look good, does it? The person who stole Judy's car was lurking here and now there are pools of blood inside," Peggy said.

Overhearing this remark, the trooper walked over to the cluster of frightened women.

"I never said anything about pools of blood, ladies. There are some stains on the rug that just might be bloodstains. They could just as well be from spilled catsup or something. Please don't go back to town and start a bunch of rumors."

"That's right. 'Least said, soonest mended,' as my grandma used to say," Shirley offered.

The trooper's admonition put an end to the women's speculations. Since there was nothing else on their minds at the moment, they fidgeted silently while waiting for their ride back to town, with the trooper's radio squawking in the background.

The other First Ladies Club search teams had come up empty and were gathered back at Eskaletha's home, waiting for Judy's team to report in, when Bunny dropped them off.

"Will you come in and meet the others?" Shirley asked her.

"I'd like to, but some other time. I want to run by the parsonage and see how Scott's doing. I'm worried about him with Naidenne and Rosamund both missing," Bunny replied before driving off.

Eskaletha greeted them at her door, "You're the last to return. Did you find anything?"

# The First Ladies Club

"My car was stolen!" Judy cried. "And the trooper may have found Naidenne's blood in the last house we looked at."

"Judy! Remember what the officer said," Peggy reminded her.

"What did I hear about Naidenne's blood?" Elizabeth asked, coming up behind Eskaletha.

"Come on in, you guys, and tell everyone what is going on," Eskaletha said, ushering them all in to her stylishly modern living room.

"What's happened?" Olivette asked. "Is Naidenne all right?"

"Did they find her?" Gwennie queried at the same time.

"Let these ladies catch their breath and then they can tell us everything," Eskaletha said.

When everyone was seated, she turned to Judy.

"You said your car was stolen?"

"Yes. It happened at that house the couple from California bought a while back. You know the ones that were practically gutting the place with their remodeling before they ran out of money?"

The others nodded and Judy continued, "It was on our list, so after checking out Bunny's place..."

"Bunny's place?"

"Who's?"

"Bunny Banks, Bunny Elder when she lived in Bannoch, Naidenne's friend from Texas," Shirley began to explain.

"You didn't go clear to Texas?!" Gwennie exclaimed.

"Of course not. She's here. Her vacation home was still on Naidenne's list, because she was managing it for her friend. Anyway, she's here, so when we went to check on the house, we ran into her," Shirley finished.

"As I was saying," Judy interjected. "After Bunny's place we went to the next property on the list, the one I was talking about. I parked in the driveway and we got out to check the house. It is clear out in the country and there's no one ever out there, so naturally I left the keys in the ignition."

Gwennie leaned over and whispered to Elizabeth, "Naturally," with a roll of her eyes.

"We were checking out the windows on the sides and back of the house before going in, like you told us, and we heard the car start up. We got back to the driveway just in time to see my car reverse at high speed out onto the road and disappear."

"My favorite purse is in that car," Peggy added.

"Oh, will you forget about that purse!" Judy snapped. "My car is gone and my husband is going to be furious."

"I think you said something before about blood?" Eskaletha said.

"Listen, the trooper said he wasn't sure it even was blood. But when he went inside he found some suspicious stains in one room, so he sent for the CSI-types to come check it out. He said, very clearly, even if it is blood it could be from an animal or a transient and it might not be blood at all. We should not assume it has anything to do with Naidenne's disappearance," Shirley replied, before Judy or Peggy could say anything.

The women were silent for a moment, each trying to come to terms with this new information.

Elizabeth said, "But what are the odds of a car thief just loitering at that house? It doesn't make sense. Did you get a good look at the thief?"

"I'm afraid not," Judy said. "We couldn't even tell for sure if it was a man or woman."

"I suggested it might have been Naidenne, herself, but the others just scoffed at me," Peggy said. "Women have run away from their husbands before now, you know."

"Not Naidenne," Shirley insisted.

"I agree with Mrs. Griffith," Olivette said. "The Naidenne we all know would never cause her family and friends worry by doing something like that. If she could be home right now, she would be."

"We can't know that for sure, not if she had a nervous breakdown, or something," Peggy insisted.

"I think we had better leave speculation to the proper authorities." Eskaletha spoke in her presidential voice. "We've done all that we can today. Tomorrow we will check those last commercial properties here in town. Let's pray for God's guidance for the searchers, for comfort for Scott and for protection and a safe return for Naidenne."

"And let's pray I get my car back," Judy said.

Seeing Peggy about to speak, she quickly added, "and Peggy's purse, too."

## Chapter Twenty

After dropping the others at Eskaletha's home, Bunny drove the familiar road to the Bannoch Community Fellowship's parsonage, her temporary refuge a few years before when she was the damsel in distress, rather than Naidenne.

Driving up to the house, she experienced a kaleidoscope of feelings and memories. It was here she became friends with Scott and met Rosamund. The adventures begun in Bannoch had led to her marriage to Max.

On this visit she had expected to greet her friends, Scott and Naidenne, in this house and to revel in the happy relationship she had instigated. Now, Rosamund and Naidenne were missing and Max was lost to her forever.

The joyous reunion she'd imagined had become a condolence visit to comfort Scott and commiserate in both their losses.

"Better get out and face it, Bunny old girl. Scott needs all the friends he can get right about now," she encouraged herself before squaring her shoulders and approaching the door.

"Bunny! What a surprise, come in, come in," Rosamund enthused, pulling Bunny inside and embracing her nonplussed guest.

"Rosamund! What are you doing here?"

"I live here, don't you remember?"

"But, they said you were missing..." Bunny protested.

"That was all a misunderstanding. Come on in. There's someone I want you to meet."

"Look who the cat dragged in, Scott!" Rosamund called to her brother, who was in the kitchen pouring yet another cup of coffee.

## The First Ladies Club

Leading Bunny over to Len, she said, "Bunny, I want you to meet Len Spurgeon. Len is our local bank manager and, um, my husband," she concluded with an air of triumph.

"I'm happy to meet you, Len," Bunny shook his hand, and then turned to Rosamund.

"When did this happen? Why didn't you tell me? I would have come to the wedding."

"We, well, we sort of eloped. We only just got back to town and learned of this terrible news about Naidenne."

"Well, congratulations, both of you," Bunny responded.

"Bunny, when did you get to town?" Scott asked from the kitchen doorway.

Bunny was pierced to see how miserable he looked.

"I only arrived today. Come and sit down, Scott, and I'll tell you all about it."

"You mentioned to Rose that you'd heard she was missing, too. That news didn't travel as far as Houston, I hope."

"No, what I thought was a welcome party turned up at our vacation cabin and they told me about Rose and Naidenne. I'm so sorry, Scott. I know you are worried sick. I came over to try to offer moral support."

"A welcome party? Who was it?"

"Shirley Griffith and two ladies from Naidenne's club. They were out searching her empty properties in case she might have been showing a house and had an accident or something. Naidenne keeps an eye on our place when we aren't here, so it was on their list," Bunny explained.

"You know, that's not a bad idea," Scott said. "Did they find anything?"

"Not really," Bunny hedged, not wanting to mention the blood stains.

"What does that mean?" Rosamund asked, sitting on the sofa beside Len and holding his hand tightly.

"Well, when they told me about Deenie, I joined them. When we got to the next empty house and got out of the car to look in the windows, someone stole the car."

"What on Earth?" Scott exclaimed.

"I know, out there in the hills, no one would ever expect it. None of us got a look at the thief. The car was out on the road and gone, almost before we knew what was happening."

"Did you call the Sheriff?"

"We called the State Troopers and an officer came out right away."

"What did he do?" Scott asked.

"We were afraid of more people popping out of the woodwork, so we waited outside for the trooper. Shirley unlocked the door when he arrived and he searched the house by himself."

"And did he find anything inside?" Len asked.

"He found the back door lock was broken, and there were some empty booze bottles and…stains on a rug, that's all. Probably some trespassers had broken in."

"What kind of stains, Bunny," Scott said, holding Bunny's gaze.

"The trooper thought they might be blood stains, but he stressed they could be from anything, and even if it is blood, there's no need to think it was from a human, let alone Naidenne."

Scott sank back in the chair with his eyes closed.

"Were they going to investigate the stains?" Len almost whispered, as Scott got up and left them, climbing the stairs like a very old man.

"Yes, the trooper was going to stay there until the investigative team arrived, to be sure no one went inside. So, I brought the others into town and dropped them off."

"Did he say if he thinks the stolen car is connected to Naidenne?" Rosamund asked.

"He didn't, actually. Just put out a BOLO, I think it's called, then seemed to forget about the car. But one of those women I was with seemed to think it was Naidenne who ran off with the car."

"That's outrageous! Who was she? I'll give her a piece of my mind," Rosamund said.

"I don't remember their names, I'm afraid. It was all so unexpected. But the rest of us told her she was being ridiculous."

"That's good, but it still makes me mad."

## The First Ladies Club

"Look, Rosamund, I'd better go. I came to give Scott moral support when I thought you and Naidenne were both missing, but I'm afraid I just made things worse. He's got you and Len to look after him and I've got a bit more unpacking to do at the cabin, so I think I'll scoot," Bunny said, getting up.

"Oh, wait Bunny. I forgot to ask how Max is. He didn't come with you this time?"

"I don't suppose you had a chance to hear. Max died about six months ago."

"Oh dear, I'm so sorry. I didn't even realize he was ill."

"He wasn't. He was one of the passengers in that plane shot down over Eastern Europe."

"How awful! What will you do now, dear?"

"Oh, I'll be fine. He left me well off, financially. I'm just trying to decide what to do with the rest of my life. That's why I came west as soon as the funeral and other details were wrapped up."

"You should have told us when it happened, Bunny. We would have come to the service."

"It was just a small memorial service for his friends and family in Houston. His body was never recovered, you see."

Bunny hugged Rosamund and nodded to Len and walked to the door.

"It was good to meet you," Len said. "I'm so sorry for your loss."

"Thanks. I'll probably see you again before I leave town. I want to stay until Naidenne turns up. Good-night."

When Scott came back downstairs he was surprised to see Len alone in the living room, watching the news.

"Where did Rose and Bunny go?" Scott asked.

"Rosie's in the kitchen and your friend left a while ago."

"I didn't even tell her how sorry I was to hear about her husband's death," Scott said.

"So you did know about that. Rosie wondered."

"Yes, I only found out after Rose had taken off. His plane crashed. Terrible thing. They hadn't been married very long, just a few years. I am so wrapped up in my own problems; I wasn't much of a friend in time of need."

"I got the idea she came to comfort you, not the other way around," Len commented.

"Yes, Bunny's got a big heart. Did my sister tell you Bunny is the one who got Naidenne and me together?"

"Why, no. Tell me about it," Len urged, glad to see Scott willing to talk about something pleasant.

"I'm afraid I was paying court to Bunny, in my clumsy way, and she only had eyes for Max. But she's too soft-hearted to turn a guy down flat, so she manipulated Deenie and me, in the nicest way, of course, into each other's arms. We owe her a debt we can never repay."

"She seems like a nice woman. Kind of at loose ends, right now, though."

Rosamund came into the room with a plate of warm walnut and apple muffins and a dish of strawberry jam on a tray.

"You know, I can't find a single one of my aprons in the kitchen. I had to wrap a dishtowel around my waist. Here, you two, eat them while they're hot. Lots of good nourishment to get us through the night. I've got some spiced cider simmering to wash them down," so saying, she handed the men napkins and returned to the kitchen for the drinks.

"I'm not very hungry, I'm afraid," Scott said.

"I haven't known my Rosie as long as you, of course, Scott, but I already know her well enough to know she won't let you get away without eating at least two of these delectable goodies," Len said while spooning jam onto half a muffin.

With a rueful smile, Scott nodded in agreement and took a bite out of the nearest muffin. He was hungrier than he'd realized and was putting jam on his second muffin when Rosamund came back with mugs of steaming cider.

"Thanks, Sis. These are good."

"That's why I married her, you know, not just for her pretty face," Len said, giving his bride a squeeze.

Rosamund smiled almost coquettishly, before saying, "Here, drink your cider, but be careful, it's hot."

Watching them together caused an almost physical spasm in Scott's heart from feeling joy for his sister simultaneously with the anguish of Naidenne's continued absence.

Where could she be? And, worse still, what might she be suffering?

"It was good to see Bunny tonight," Rosamund said.

"Yes, I shouldn't have left the room so rudely. Did she say how long she will be in Bannoch?"

"She said she wants to stay until Naidenne is found. This can't be the vacation she was hoping for," Len replied. "She seemed sort of lost."

"Well, she's been widowed twice. What do you suppose Max was doing in Eastern Europe, anyway, Scott? I knew his business took him to Central and South America, sometimes, but I thought he might curtail his travels after he married Bunny," Rosamund said.

"I wonder if Bunny thought that, too. Many marriages run into bumpy roads when expectations don't match the realities," Scott mused.

"Were they having troubles? Is that what Naidenne told you?"

"No, Rose. I was just speaking in generalities. As far as I know, they were a deliriously happy couple."

"Just like us," Len added, with a wink.

Rosamund patted Len's hand and began to clear away the mugs and leftover muffins.

"I'm going to wash up the dishes, and then I think I'll be ready to call it a day."

"Me, too. Traveling always wears me out, even the short flight from Reno, with that long drive from Medford tacked on, has me beat."

"That's right! You two must be dead on your feet. Please, Rose. Leave the dishes. I'll take care of them. You go on up. I don't feel like going to bed, just yet."

"Well, if you're sure. This has been quite a day. Thank you, dear."

Rosamund hugged Scott and patted him tenderly on the cheek before holding her hand out for her husband and leading him up the stairs.

Len called a gruff, "Good-night, take care," to his new brother-in-law as he followed Rosamund.

Scott slowly rose and went into the kitchen. He put suds into the sink and began to wash up. He'd been so happy in this room with Naidenne, whether doing dishes together or sitting across the breakfast table. The room had been filled with sunshine, then, no matter what the time of day or night, as long as he was with his wife.

As his tears dropped into the dishwater, his prayers flew fervently to Heaven, prayers for Naidenne's safety and speedy return.

At that moment, Naidenne's kidnapper was once again thrashing about in the underbrush and briars between the towering pines north of Bannoch.

Cursing to himself as he struggled to keep his bearings and control his frustration, he relived the misadventures of the afternoon which continued to work against him in this ill-fated community.

He'd thought he was home free when those stupid biddies presented the car to him on a silver platter, but he hadn't even made it to the highway when the engine coughed, sputtered and died. He was on a downhill grade and managed to coast to the shoulder beside a shallow ditch.

The fuel gauge indicted the tank was half-full, but the car acted like it was out of gas.

In a rage, he pulled out his knife and slashed the seats before getting out and kicking large dents into the doors.

His tantrum over, he pushed the car into the ditch to try to make it less noticeable, then struck out on foot, once again trying to get far away before the vehicle was discovered.

It was all that tall bitch's fault. It was because she'd tempted him to stay around, instead of sticking with his original plan. He'd be in Canada by now, if it wasn't for her.

Instead, here he was, cold, hungry, on foot again, and for practically nothing.

If he ever ran into her again, or anyone like her, he would kill them quickly. Well, not too quickly, but before they had a chance to get away and spoil things.

Just now, though, he had to find food and a place to shelter for the night.

## Chapter Twenty-one

Following another sleepless night, Scott rolled off the sofa, stretched to get the kinks out of his back and climbed the stairs to shower and change.

Lying awake in the early hours of the morning, he'd decided to go to the Sheriff's Office and get as much information about those bloodstains as they would share with him.

Naidenne had been missing for nearly seventy-two hours, now, so there should be no doubt about officially classifying her as a missing person.

He hoped that detective was over his crazy ideas.

Up to now, the rest of the sheriff's department seemed to think Naidenne had simply run off and would soon turn up in Reno, filing for divorce, or something.

The only one taking his wife's absence seriously was the awful Portland detective who thought Scott was a murderer.

Scott tried to tell himself the blood stains were from a trespasser who'd been camping out in the house. Some squatter probably broke the lock on the door to get in and left the trash and stains. When this guy saw the women and the car with the keys in it, he probably thought lady luck was dropping a gift into his lap.

It all made sense. The blood and the car theft probably had no connection to each other, or to Naidenne.

This line of thought should have been reassuring, but if what happened yesterday was only a random incident, then they were still no closer to finding his wife.

☙

"No, Len, we can't even mention it to my brother while Naidenne is still missing," Rosamund said.

"I suppose you're right, but as soon as all this is over, you are going to have to tell him."

"I pray when that time comes Naidenne will be back, safe and sound. It would be cruel to move out and leave Scott alone, otherwise."

"You are too kind-hearted to be real, sometimes, Rosie. That's why I love you. You've been looking after your little brother all your life and I understand. You've got a husband, now, though…"

"And I should be looking after you, is that what you are saying?"

"Sounds selfish when you say it, but I guess that is what I meant," Len admitted.

"Don't worry, dear. I don't think you're being selfish. A wife's first duty, after God, of course, is to her husband. You may need to remind me of that from time to time, I'm afraid. I'm new at being a wife."

"Don't you worry, we can stay here just as long as Scott needs us, but that doesn't mean we shouldn't start making plans for a home of our own. Will you want to move into my condo, or shall we get a house? I'm willing to do whichever you choose, as long as we're together," Len said.

"I can't think about that just now…although I always used to dream of a cottage of my own with a nice little garden."

"Then you shall have it, my love."

Hearing Scott moving around, they left Rosamund's room and went downstairs to fix breakfast.

Scott was already pouring his coffee when they entered the kitchen.

"Morning, Scott. Did you manage to get any sleep?" Len asked.

"Not much, but I'm okay."

"Here, let me get you some breakfast," Rosamund said, putting away the coffee filters and wiping up spilled coffee grounds.

"Just coffee for me, Sis. I'm going down to the Sheriff's office to see what they discovered at that empty property."

"You really should eat, first. You need to keep up your strength. I'll heat up the leftover muffins and scramble an egg."

"This will do fine," Scott said as he grabbed a cold muffin, quickly downed his coffee and left.

"Oh, dear," Rosamund sighed.

"He'll be okay, Rosie. A nice warm muffin and a scrambled egg sounds good to me, though. After that, I'd better get to the bank and make sure it's still standing," Len said.

In the dreary basement, the early morning light filtering through the dirty windows roused Naidenne to a renewed awareness of the pain in her head and shoulder.

Remembering where she was, the full danger of her situation hit her anew and she moaned.

"I've got to get out of here. I've got to…for Scott and our baby."

Thinking she might die and Scott would never see their child brought tears to her eyes and a sob escaped her lips.

"Get hold of yourself," she admonished. "God is in control, so calm down and think."

So saying, she looked around and noticed a broken wooden stool a few yards away. There were exposed nails sticking out of the seat. These just might cut through her bindings.

With a snort of determination, she rolled onto her stomach and once again began the painful process of inching across the cement.

❦

"Judy couldn't make it this morning, Letha," Elizabeth explained. "She had to go to school with her twins."

"There will be just the two of us, then. Shirley dropped off the keys on her way to work at the arts and crafts shop. I really don't think there's much chance of us finding any trace of Naidenne in these last properties, though. We checked all the most likely places yesterday. Still, I guess we do need to look. Come in and have some coffee before we start out. I confess I'm discouraged, and a little reluctant to cross these last buildings off our list. I just don't know what to do next, if we come up with nothing, again today," Eskaletha admitted.

Elizabeth perched on a stool at the black granite kitchen island while Eskaletha filled their cups and set out a plate of date bars.

"I understand how you feel. I've prayed and pleaded with God like a spoiled child, begging him to show us where she is, then backing off and asking him to show me His will, instead, but I don't feel like I'm getting answers," Elizabeth said, reaching for a cookie.

"It's so frustrating," Eskaletha agreed. "Intellectually, I know this is going to work out for good, somehow, but my heart aches for Naidenne…and for Scott, too, of course."

Joining hands around their cups, the women prayed for their friend's safety and swift return.

With an emphatic, "Amen," they finished their drinks and set out to examine the empty commercial buildings.

Arriving at a disused warehouse a short time later, Eskaletha unlocked the door and the two women entered the dimly lit building.

It was a vast, empty space, at first glance appearing to contain nothing but a scattering of broken pallets on the cracked cement floor. An enclosed office area was just to the side of the entry, its door hanging open.

The women poked around inside, but this space, too, was empty. There wasn't anywhere for someone to be hidden. Reluctant to give up, they paced the full warehouse interior before leaving and locking up.

After wandering through one empty building after another, with no luck, they were getting discouraged.

The last property on the list was an old decommissioned gas station out on the highway a few blocks north of town.

They arrived at this last possibility much sooner than they would have liked and were hesitant to go inside.

Stopping under the awning between the barren pump islands, Eskaletha and Elizabeth sat in the car for many moments without speaking.

"Well, this is it. I guess we can't put it off any longer, Liz," Eskaletha broke the silence and opened her car door.

As they approached the side entry to the service area, Elizabeth paused, clutched her friend's elbow and pointed at a plastic milk crate, surrounded by crushed weeds and scrape marks in the bare dirt, under a half-open window.

"Doesn't that look like someone's been climbing in and out here?" she asked with a mixture of hope and fear in her voice. "Maybe we should call the police."

"Not for litter and some scuff marks, Liz. Come on," Eskaletha encouraged her friend as she unlocked the door.

The interior was shadowy. It was difficult to see in the dim light, but the space seemed to be empty, except for a few display racks leaning against the wall beyond the pit area and grease rack.

Eskaletha led the way carefully through the two bays, staying well clear of the open pit as she approached the door on the far wall.

She hesitated, listening, with her hand on the doorknob.

"I think I heard something," she whispered.

"I did, too," Elizabeth responded.

They stayed very still, alert with a mixture of hope and dread, for the sounds to repeat.

A soft scratching sound and what might have been a whimper came from someplace on the other side.

Opening the door as quietly as possible, the ladies crept into a large room, formerly the gas station's convenience store and cashier's counter.

The large windows had been boarded over, letting in very little light. In the gloom, they could just make out the rows of shelves, the counter area to their right and refrigerator compartments lining the back wall.

Elizabeth peered over the counter and looked at Eskaletha, shaking her head to indicate no one was there.

Eskaletha led the way cautiously down the aisles, both women's nerves on edge, expecting someone to leap out at any moment.

Coming to the last row of shelves, the women found themselves at another door. This one led to the restrooms and storage area.

The muffled sounds seemed louder, as though coming from nearby.

Elizabeth stepped closer to her friend and breathed, "Maybe we should go back."

Eskaletha shook her head and grasped the door handle. She pulled the door open slowly and peered around.

The darkness in the windowless hallway was complete. She was tempted to give in to Elizabeth's suggestion and leave, but thoughts of Naidenne gave her the strength to step through with Elizabeth following.

Before the door closed behind them, shutting off the light from the empty convenience store, they saw three doors opening off the hallway.

Feeling their way, they found the first door and paused again, encouraging one another with a squeeze of their hands.

This door opened into a storeroom. Its lone window, while barred, was not boarded over. The filtered light revealed only bare floor and walls.

The women were relieved, and emboldened to move on to the next door.

Leaving the door open gave them light to see their way more clearly. Another empty storeroom greeted them behind door number two. That left only the unisex restroom ahead on their right.

The sounds were clearer now, definitely whimpers plus rustling and scratching, as from someone struggling while lying on paper.

The women paused to consider what they might find on the other side of the door. If it was their friend, what condition was she in? If not Naidenne, then who was in this abandoned gas station?

A shiver of fear passed over Elizabeth when she thought of all the horrific possibilities and she sent up a prayer before nodding to Eskaletha.

As soon as the door began to open, both women recoiled at the strong, unpleasant odor.

Eskaletha pushed the door wider and a cacophony of sound erupted.

As they emerged into the restroom, squeals and yelps greeted them and they easily identified the source of the smell.

The room was full of puppies!

In a makeshift corral of cardboard boxes, on a carpet of soiled newspapers, were four mongrel puppies, two black, one tan and one white with a black eye like the dog, Zero, in the old "Little Rascals" movies.

An empty dog dish and basin of water, now overturned, sat in one corner of this slapdash kennel.

The dogs leaped over one another in their excitement and eagerness for company.

Eskaletha dropped to her knees beside the row of boxes, reaching in to pet the wriggling pups as they scrambled to try to climb up her arms.

"Whoa, there! I think these guys are hungry!"

"Someone has obviously been taking care of them here, but it looks like they haven't come today," Elizabeth said.

She looked around and noticed a couple of half-full trash bags over in a corner behind the boxes.

The first bag she opened was filled with noisome newspapers and doggy doo. Closing it quickly, she opened the second more carefully and found it full of kibble. She scooped some out into the dish in the puppies' pen and the hungry dogs scampered over.

Discovering rusty water still flowed from the restroom sink's taps, Eskaletha filled the pups' basin.

She put it down inside the enclosure and the tiny movie-star look-alike immediately sat in it, wagging his tail happily and spraying water droplets onto his litter mates.

Elizabeth and Eskaletha laughed, releasing all their pent up tension.

"Well, who do you suppose left these little rascals here?" Elizabeth asked.

"And what are we supposed to do with them, now?" Eskaletha responded.

"We should report them to Animal Control. I'd take the little darlings home with me, but Gil and I really don't have the time for even one puppy…They are cute, though, especially this little beggar," Elizabeth said, scooping up the black runt of the litter, who had already finished eating.

"I'll bet we would have no trouble finding adoptive homes for them, but we don't know who left these guys here. They may already belong to someone," Eskaletha pointed out.

A scrap of damp paper clung to the back paw of the puppy in Elizabeth's arms and she pulled it off. It was lined notebook paper and there was writing on it.

She looked closely and read aloud, "A-S-T-I-L-B-E."

"Oh, no! You don't suppose it was Judy's girls who put the puppies here, do you?" she exclaimed.

"How else would a school paper get here?" Eskaletha said. "If they aren't actually responsible, they must be involved or at least know about these pups. There can't be two girls named 'Astilbe' in Bannoch."

"We have to tell Judy, then, I suppose."

Eskaletha nodded, but the two women continued to crouch beside the puppies, rubbing their little round bellies and scratching their ears.

"I guess we can eliminate this place from our search for Naidenne," Elizabeth said, breaking the spell.

"Yes," replied and Eskaletha stood up. "And now I don't know where else to look."

It dismayed Elizabeth to see her take-charge friend looking so lost and discouraged.

"What do the detectives on TV do when they hit a brick wall?" she asked, with a twinkle in her eye.

Eskaletha thought for a moment before responding with a dry chuckle.

"I guess they go back over everything again to see what they missed."

"Okay, then. We'll go to Judy's to find out what the girls know about these cute little critters, then you can call the Club ladies together and we'll start searching for Naidenne from the beginning."

"What about the puppies?"

"They are fed, watered…quite well watered, in fact…and settling down, now. They should be okay for the rest of the day, while we attend to business," Elizabeth said.

With a definite agenda, they re-filled the dishes, patted the dogs and hurried out, intent on getting things done.

## Chapter Twenty-two

Scott left the Sheriff's substation with precious little additional information.

Preliminary lab tests determined the blood was human, but the sample was so small it would be weeks before the DNA results came in.

Scott told himself the small amount of blood was a good thing, but he was frustrated not to have it ruled out as belonging to his wife.

Scott decided not to wait for the lab results, but to go to the house where the blood was found and see if he could find anything the authorities had missed.

With no proof of a crime, and feeling his men had gotten all the information they could from the house and grounds, the Sheriff had released the scene

Tillamook County wasn't Las Vegas CSI, after all. And local authorities hadn't taken Naidenne's disappearance very seriously in the beginning. They might easily have overlooked something Scott would find meaningful.

He drove back to the parsonage to get a flashlight and the set of lock-box keys his wife kept there.

Naidenne had finally wriggled up against the broken stool, where she was rubbing her sister-in-law's favorite apron against the exposed nails, hoping to shred it apart and free her hands.

"I hope Rosamund forgives me for ruining her apron," she thought.

"Ouch!" she cried out as the nails tore deeply into her skin, causing her to smear fresh blood onto the cloth and giving Naidenne a twinge of regret at this additional damage to the apron.

"Silly, me," she murmured aloud. "I may not get out of this alive and I'm worried about staining Rosamund's apron."

She knew she was in grave peril, but the inconsequential thoughts seemed to take her mind off her fear and discomfort.

Even with her gag removed, her mouth was like cotton and her stomach cramped from hunger. She worried about her unborn child. Was this tiny life hungry too?

※

After spending the morning stumbling through the crowded hallways in the wake of her mortified daughters as they went from class to class, and sitting in the back of each room like a bodyguard, Judy was relieved to be home.

The girls had promised to stay at school for the afternoon, if their mother would go home at lunchtime.

Judy warned them she would be calling the school, periodically, to be sure they were there.

It hurt her heart not to be able to trust them, but she knew Ken would insist on verifying they lived up to their word.

He'd dropped the three of them off that morning and would pick the girls up after school, since Judy no longer had her own transportation.

Thinking about her car, Judy wondered if she should tell the troopers to look out for it in nearby gas stations.

The gas gauge in her car hadn't worked in years. Judy routinely filled the tank once a month, but with all the confusion and upset about Naidenne, she hadn't gotten around to it, lately. It was bound to be getting pretty low.

She fixed herself a vegan macaroni and cheese dish using whole wheat macaroni and a faux cheese substitute comprised mostly of almond paste, with mustard added for color. It was a new recipe she'd found in Vegan Life magazine and she had to admit it didn't taste much like she thought it would.

As she ate, she decided the troopers would have already checked the area gas stations as a matter of course when the car was first stolen, so they wouldn't need any advice from her.

She was cleaning up her dishes, scraping the ersatz mac and cheese off her plate into the compost container, when Eskaletha and Elizabeth arrived and rapped on the window at her back door.

"Hey, you two, what's up?" she greeted them.

"Hi, Judy. We've been checking out the final properties on our list, looking for any sign of Naidenne," Elizabeth told her.

"Well, come on in. Have you eaten lunch? I've got lots of this vegan mac and pseudo cheese…"

"No thanks," Eskaletha replied as she and Elizabeth entered the kitchen.

"At least have a cup of herb tea," Judy insisted.

"Sure, thanks," Elizabeth said.

Turning to switch on her kettle, Judy asked, "So, did you find anything? Even a tiny clue?"

"We did find something, but it wasn't any sign of Naidenne," Eskaletha replied.

"What was it?" Judy set their cups on the table.

Eskaletha tried to stall by taking a sip of her tea and began to choke at the bitter taste.

"Are you okay?" Judy said, while Elizabeth handed over a napkin.

"I'm fine. I guess the tea was still too hot. What kind of herb tea is this?"

"It's my own blend. Isn't it nice? I use some herbs from my garden, of course, but I enhance it with wild herbs I pick in the woods, plus a nice root I found. I think it tastes a lot like sassafras, although that doesn't grow around here. You know root teas are wonderful medicines. They cure tongue sores, bronchitis, peptic ulcers, hiatal hernia, Crohn's, Celiac, irritable bowel syndrome, and even cystitis, kidney, bladder and urinary tract infections. I'm not sure what my tea cures, yet, except I know it is great for constipation."

"How nice," Eskaletha commented, pushing her tea cup away ever so slightly.

"You didn't say what you found," Judy prompted.

"What we found, dear, is a litter of puppies being kenneled in the old gas station," Elizabeth said.

"Puppies? Oh, no! Why would anyone leave little baby doggies in a nasty place like that?"

"They weren't just left there. They were being cared for. They had food and water and a sort of pen. And we think we know who put them there, or at least someone who knows about it," Elizabeth replied.

"Who?"

"We found this in the puppy's pen," Eskaletha handed over the scrap of notebook paper.

"Astilbe? My Astilbe?"

"Is there another?" Eskaletha asked.

"But how did she get a litter of puppies? And why would she keep them in that old station?"

"We were hoping you might ask her. If the puppies don't belong to anyone, we are willing to find them homes. They are darling little things," Elizabeth said.

"You know I don't really believe in keeping our fellow creatures as pets. It's exploitation and dehumanizes them. But I would rather see them cared for in that patronizing way than for them to be abandoned or shut up in a cold empty building. I'll talk to Astilbe when she gets home from school and let you know what I find out."

"Thanks, Judy," Elizabeth said.

"Did you leave the puppies where you found them?"

"Yes, they are safe there, at least for now, but if someone owns them, they had better move them soon. If no one claims these four pups, and we can't find them homes, they will need to go to the animal shelter," Eskaletha said.

"Oh, dear. They kill unwanted animals there, don't they? Well, I'll talk to my daughter today."

Driving away, Eskaletha reminded Elizabeth they were going to renew their search for Naidenne, starting back at square one.

"Sure, but not today, Letha. I'm beat. This whole puppy thing just wore me out, I was up early doing my arthritis exercises and I've got a Bible Study to lead tonight," Elizabeth said."I can't keep up with you younger women like I used to, I'm afraid."

"Okay, I'll try to get everyone together tomorrow. But I hate to think of Naidenne being out there, wherever she is, for another hour, let alone another night."

Scott was backing out of his driveway when Bunny arrived in her rental car. When he saw her, he stopped and stepped out to greet her with a hug.

## The First Ladies Club

"How are you holding up?" Bunny asked with her face mashed against his chest.

"What'd you say?" Scott asked, stepping back.

"I asked how you're doing, but I guess I can tell. I'm so sorry for all you're going through. Has there been any news about Naidenne?"

"Nothing since you and the others found the blood smears. The police lab said there wasn't enough blood for quick tests. Although it is human, we won't know the DNA results for a week or so."

"It was from some trespasser, don't you think? Maybe there were a couple of guys staying there, and maybe they were drinking and got into a fight and the loser...the guy who was bleeding...maybe he ran off and the winner stayed on. Maybe he's the guy who took Judy's car."

"Sure, it was probably something like that...but, Bunny, I had to give them Naidenne's hairbrush for a DNA sample," Scott replied, his voice catching as he spoke.

"Is your sister inside? Maybe we should go in and have a nice visit," she said, trying to distract Scott.

"No, you go in. She'll be happy to see you, but I'm on my way to that house. I have to see for myself if there is anything the police missed."

"Shall I come with you?" Bunny offered.

Scott started to say that wouldn't be necessary, then changed his mind.

"Thanks. I think I could use the company."

"Just let me pop in and let Rosamund know I'll be back to see her when we get done," Bunny said.

She walked up onto the porch and rapped on the door, while Scott waited beside his car.

"Bunny! I'm so glad you came back. Come in, come in," Rosamund greeted her.

"I can't, now. I'm going to keep Scott company while he checks out that house…you know, the one with the blood," she replied, lowering her voice at the last few words. "I'll come back with him afterward, if I may, then we can have a really good visit."

"Of course. Thanks for keeping an eye on him," Rosamund said as she gave Bunny a quick hug.

"See you later!" she called cheerfully to Scott and Bunny as they drove away.

When she turned to go inside her face was downcast. She had little hope the pair of amateur sleuths would find anything useful. With every passing hour Rosamund was becoming more discouraged about Naidenne ever being found.

When Ken returned to the manse with their daughters, Judy was waiting for them.

"Please, all of you come sit down," she said as soon as they came through the door.

"We need to change, Mom," Paisley complained.

"What's this about?" Ken asked.

"Our daughters have something to tell us, Ken. Don't you, girls?"

"What are you talking about?" Paisley asked, wide-eyed.

"We haven't done anything wrong. We stayed in class all afternoon, like you told us to, didn't we, Dad?" Astilbe said, turning to her father for confirmation.

"This isn't about your recent truancy…or maybe it is," Judy said, suddenly putting two and two together.

"I know where you've been going when you've been skipping school," she told the girls.

Hearing this, Ken and the girls sat down, Ken leaning forward, eager to hear, while the girls slumped down onto the sofa, crossing their arms protectively.

"Would you like to explain yourselves, or shall I tell your father what you've been up to?"

Ken turned to look at his daughters, his face like thunder, obviously expecting the worst.

"It's not that bad, Dad. Honest," Paisley protested.

"We didn't know what else to do," Astilbe offered. "We knew you and Mom would never let us have them here."

"Have who here? Are you involved with some bad kids? Drug users? Boys!?" Ken's imagination was running away with him. "Don't tell me you're pregnant!"

"Dad!" the horrified twins cried in unison.

"Now calm down. It's nothing to do with boys; at least I don't think it is. You girls had better start explaining before your father has a stroke. From the beginning, if you please."

The sisters looked at each other, silent messages zipping through the air between them, then, with a nod, Paisley began to speak, "We found the puppies…"

"Puppies?" Ken interrupted.

"We found them on the way to school one morning a couple of months ago," she continued, with a pointed look at her father. "They were really tiny and didn't even have their eyes open."

"Someone had dumped them beside the road in an old cardboard box! We couldn't just leave them there," Astilbe added.

"We knew you wouldn't let us have them here, not with the way Mom feels about keeping God's creatures as pets, and you've told us lots of time, Dad, that animals don't belong in a house. So, we had to figure out what to do with them," Paisley explained.

"We couldn't let the animal control people just kill them. They're innocent babies," Astilbe said.

"When we noticed the open restroom window at that old gas station, we figured we could put them there, just until they were big enough to fend for themselves, you know?"

"So, you have been skipping school to visit and care for these puppies ever since, is that right?" Ken asked.

The girls nodded in unison.

He was so relieved at their relatively innocent offense; it was all he could do to keep from smiling broadly as he spoke.

"Where did you get the supplies; food and water and so on?" he asked.

"We used our lunch money and our allowance," Astilbe replied.

"You lied to your father and me. Even though you were trying to take care of God's helpless creatures, you went about it in the wrong way. We are both very disappointed in you."

"I'm sorry," the girls chorused.

"How did you find out?" Astilbe asked in a small voice.

"That doesn't matter, now. We need to decide what to do about these puppies," Judy said.

"The dogs can go to the pound; that is what it is for. The real question is what to do with these girls," Ken asserted.

"Oh, Daddy, we were only trying to help. And we won't cut school, ever, ever again!" Paisley cried.

"You certainly won't. But there must be consequences for your disobedience and dishonesty. Perhaps having your phones taken away for a month would be appropriate."

"Not our phones," the girls moaned.

"Say, Dad, I know…why not give us community service chores, like they do in the courts?" Paisley suggested.

"That might be a good idea, Ken," Judy said.

"We could polish the pews and throw out the wilted flowers at church!" Astilbe suggested.

"Or help in the nursery," Paisley said.

"No. Let the punishment fit the crime. I think our daughters would benefit from volunteering at the senior care facility. If they are so tender-hearted about dogs, let them learn to have that same concern for the helpless and vulnerable older people in our community. I'm going to call Mrs. Joiner, who works as the activity director there."

His mind made up, he left the room to make the phone call, leaving his stunned wife and daughters gazing after him.

## Chapter Twenty-three

At last! The shredded fabric was finally weak enough for Naidenne to tear her hands free.

She slumped down in exhaustion, holding her chaffed and bloodied wrists tenderly on her lap, lifting a heartfelt thanks to God.

She knew she should hurry to untie her legs, but couldn't quite summon the strength.

After several moments of inertia, Naidenne forced herself to tackle the apron around her knees.

The fabric had become stretched from her various escape attempts, but the knots were still tight and her hands were weak. She was just able to push the cloth down over her calves to her ankles, where it was blocked by the apron-tie hobbles.

These were similarly loosened and she was soon able to push both loops of cloth off over her feet.

For the first few moments, sitting on the hard floor with her legs splayed out in front of her seemed as luxurious as a resort's poolside chaise lounge, as she reveled in her limbs' freedom.

Soon the painful sensation of blood flowing into previously cramped tissues prompted her to try to stand to relax and stretch her knotted muscles.

Her arms were also weak after being tied behind her back for so long. She tried to pull herself up by leaning on a nearby packing box. As soon as she put weight on her right arm, a jolt of pain shot through her shoulder and upper chest.

Her shoulder seemed to have been injured in the fall down the chute.

By keeping her weight on her left hand she was able to get to her knees, balance against the box and get both feet under her, so she could ease to a standing position, wobbling only a little.

This upright perspective gave her a better sense of her surroundings.

She could see there were no exits other than the high, narrow windows and the way she'd dropped in. Even without an injured shoulder, she would never have managed to navigate either option.

Taking a good look, now, at the wall closing off this area from the rest of the basement, she saw there was no insulation or drywall on this side of the framing. She might be able to break through the single layer of sheetrock to the other side.

She was in no condition to attempt it with her bare hands, though. She would need some sort of tool.

She'd seen high-heeled shoes sometimes used as hammers in the movies, but she'd lost her shoes somewhere and they were only soft-soled flats, anyway.

There had to be something buried in the clutter in the cellar which she could use to batter her way out.

Naidenne was very shaky. When she turned from side to side, looking for an implement of some kind, she felt light-headed and had to sit on the packing box until a wave of nausea passed.

She stood again, slowly, and began taking shuffling steps toward the kitchen cabinets, hopeful the careless remodelers left kitchen utensils in the drawers. A cleaver would be ideal, but even a steak knife would be better than nothing.

Moving across the damp, chilly basement was a torturous process, as weak and dizzy as she was, but she finally reached the counter.

While she opened drawers and cabinets, the disused kitchen sink seemed to mock her thirst.

Although the appliances had been removed before the area was walled off, she couldn't resist turning the taps, on the slim chance disconnecting the water from this sink had been overlooked.

Her action was a waste of precious energy, resulting in only silence, instead of the gush of refreshing water she longed for. She would have welcomed even rusty, brackish water to moisten her parched lips and throat. Disappointment almost overwhelmed her.

Swallowing her discouragement, she went back to looking for an implement she could use to attack the wall.

In an upper cabinet, out of sight of anyone shorter than she, Naidenne finally found something. It was an old-fashioned can opener, the kind they used to call a church key when she was a kid. Could it be the key to her freedom that would return her to the church parsonage and Scott?

Grasping for any straw of encouragement, she desperately hoped this was a good omen.

Rolling her eyes at this descent into superstition, she nevertheless felt more assured as she steadily worked her way back to the wall, her leg muscles cramping in protest.

☙

Driving away from the parsonage, Scott turned to Bunny and spoke.

"I should have said this sooner, but I was really sorry to hear about Max. Are you doing okay?"

"Thanks. It was a shock. I was pretty much a zombie, at first. I couldn't quite take it in, you know?"

"Yes. I do know."

"Of course, you do. Losing your first wife and precious daughter, and now Naidenne's disappearance, is so much worse. I'm sorry for being so insensitive."

"No, I'm sorry. I should be trying to comfort you, not whining about my troubles. This business with Naidenne has sort of driven the pastoral care right out of me. I'm afraid I've begun feeling sorry for myself."

"I wish there was something I could do, or say, to make things better. Not knowing what's happened to her has to be driving you nearly insane."

"Nearly? How about completely around the bend? I've had my faith tested in the past, but this…this is just about to break me, Bunny."

"I won't say all the usual platitudes now, Scott, like God only giving us what we can bear, all things working for good and all the rest, you aren't ready to hear those things, even though they are true. But I know you. I know how strong you are, both physically and spiritually. Whatever happens, you will get through this."

"What if we don't ever find her? What if I never even know what happened?"

"I don't believe that is going to happen. Not for one minute. And you shouldn't, either. We are going to find Naidenne, or she's going to come home on her own, somehow, and everyone is going to be just fine."

"Is that what you thought when Max flew off on his last flight?"

"Yes, I did. And because I did, I didn't have to deal with grief and pain one minute before it arrived. Have hope, Scott. We are going to find her. Hang onto that and don't begin to anticipate unhappiness which may never materialize."

Scott drove in silence for a while before responding.

"Did anyone ever tell you that you are a wise woman, Bunny?"

"Don't be silly. Of course, not! Anyway, I only said what you would have said to me, if our situations were reversed."

"Thanks, anyway," Scott said and squeezed her hand, briefly.

"I think this is the turn into the driveway," Bunny said.

Scott parked next to the house and locked the car, slipping the keys into his pocket with a wry smile at Bunny.

"No sense tempting history to repeat itself, I guess," she remarked with a grin.

Sobering up, the two slowly walked around the house, intent on finding any small clue which might have been overlooked.

"What's this?" Bunny asked, picking up a gray button with a scrap of fabric attached. What looked like the top of zipper was still attached to the scrap.

"What did you find?" Scott asked.

"Oh, nothing important, I'm sure. Just a plain gray button."

"Let me see that," Scott took the button. "You're right, there's no way to say where this came from…although Naidenne's favorite slacks are gray. Maybe she was here."

He paused, and then went on, as though to himself, "She always had, I mean, *has* a hard time finding slacks long enough for her legs and said those were just perfect."

Scott stuffed the find into his pocket, refusing to dwell on the obvious conclusion that the button hadn't just fallen off. The fabric attached to it spoke of being removed by force.

The broken back door was boarded up now, so when they completed their amateur version of a grid search on the yard and grounds, they returned to the front door.

Scott opened the lockbox and removed the door key. He paused before inserting it into the lock and turned to Bunny.

"Am I being foolish? How can I expect to find anything, if the professionals couldn't?"

"Those professionals didn't have your motivation, remember. You have every reason to think you might see something of significance to only you and Naidenne. But you won't find it out here on the doorstep. Come on, let's go inside," Bunny urged.

"We made a pretty good detective team a few years ago when we stumbled into that gang of sex traffickers, didn't we? Maybe between the two of us, we'll solve this mystery, too," Scott said, opening the door and letting Bunny enter.

Rather than going straight to what Bunny thought of as the "blood room," Scott wanted them to look at each room as if they had no knowledge of what the others had found, so they began in the empty living room, on hands and knees combing the carpet for any small item which might lead to Naidenne.

"Ouch!"

"What is it, Bunny?"

"I ran my finger into the tack strip on the edge of the carpet, sorry. I didn't mean to scare you…or get your hopes up."

"Looks like we've hit a wall in here, quite literally. Let's check out the dining room," Scott suggested.

They crawled across the dining room floor without finding anything, before moving on to the kitchen, where there were drawers and cabinets to inspect.

Other than a couple of broken pencils, a dead cockroach and uncountable mouse droppings, they came up empty-handed. The utility porch was the same, so they headed upstairs to check the bedrooms and closets.

Scott was purposely avoiding the media room. He wasn't certain he could hold it together while looking at the blood on the floor, knowing it could have come from his wife. However, when their thorough and fruitless search of the upstairs was completed, they couldn't put it off any longer.

Bunny went in first, on tiptoe, as though she thought she might be stepping into pools of blood. Noticing what she was doing, she stopped and looked around, feeling foolish.

She could see where a section of carpet had been cut out by the crime lab people and where a few faint brownish streaks led up to and away from the missing section.

"It looks like someone was dragged across here," Bunny started to say, then seeing the look of dismay on Scott's face, she hurriedly continued, "I mean, like maybe someone cut their knee or leg and scooted across, like they maybe didn't notice it was bleeding, or something," she concluded lamely, looking pained.

"Sure," Scott said, keeping his eyes averted from the stains.

"They lead up to this built-in cabinet," she said, hoping to divert Scott from her previous blunder.

He approached the cabinet and began to examine it.

"That's odd. There are stains on the cabinet under this shelf, but they stop under the lip of the shelf."

"Maybe the shelf was replaced after the stain got there. After all, we don't know this is the same stain as on the carpet, or even if it is blood."

"I suppose you're right, but it looks strange," he said, as he ran his hand up the side of the cabinet under the shelf. When his hand bumped the shelf, the board wobbled.

Scott gave the shelf a tug and it pulled out a bit. He pulled harder and it came away from the cabinet, revealing a square, black hole.

"What's that?" Bunny asked.

Scott stuck his head into the hole and could see a lighter area down at the bottom.

"Looks like an old laundry chute. Come on, I want to check out the basement."

Judy Falls clicked off her phone and placed it carefully on the counter next to a bowl of quinoa she'd been washing.

She stood quietly thinking, a furrow forming between her eyes.

The call was from the State Troopers to let her know her car had been found in a ditch, with flat tires and the interior slashed and ruined. Amazingly, Peggy's precious purse was still on the back seat. Her friend would be pleased about that, but Ken would be furious with her for losing the car, she knew.

He had been holding off judgment about her negligence, hoping the car would be found, none the worse for wear.

Now, she would bear the full weight of his displeasure with her for irresponsibly leaving her keys in the ignition.

Judy had been enjoying their united spirit about the twins' puppy episode; both parents relieved their daughters' truancy sprang from such a simple, childish impulse. And they were in one accord on his choice of discipline, too.

Judy had been feeling like an adult partner for a change, rather than the oldest of Ken's wayward daughters.

If only the car had been recovered in good condition…or it might have been even better if it had never been found, at all. In that case, Ken would have gotten over his annoyance by the time they were resigned to its loss. The insurance would cover the down payment on another car, after all.

To have it found so soon, totally destroyed, meant her carelessness was still fresh in her husband's mind. He would probably feel the need to discipline her, too.

Maybe she should arrange to volunteer at the senior residence now and get it over with.

# Chapter Twenty-four

The knuckles of Naidenne's left hand were scraped and bloody from clawing at the drywall with the can opener. Her arm was weak and her legs were trembling.

She needed to take frequent breaks, leaning against the wall for support. She had managed to scrape away the paper and only about a half inch into the gypsum plaster on a very small section of the wallboard panel.

Assessing her progress with growing dismay, she thought she heard something from the other side of the wall.

Was someone in the house? Had her attacker returned? Or could this be her salvation?

Naidenne stopped scraping and listened intently, straining to hear.

What should she do if someone was really out there? If it was the repellent monster who kidnapped and assaulted her, she had to keep absolutely quiet, but potential rescuers would never know she was behind the wall if she didn't cry out.

She felt ill with indecision, as both fear and hope struggled within her.

Hearing definite footsteps on the stairs, she held her breath, still unable to risk being found by her assailant.

"Don't rush so, Scott. It's dark on these stairs. You don't want to break your neck," Bunny cautioned.

Trotting to the bottom of the stairs, Scott stood shining his flashlight slowly in all directions, clearly disappointed by the mostly empty space.

Without speaking, they did their best to conduct a thorough search in the dark basement, but found nothing except bits of construction trash, spider webs, empty cartons and dirt.

Bunny slapped her hands together, trying to remove the loose grime.

Crouched behind the wall, Naidenne was startled by this sound, lost her balance and pitched forward, landing on her right hand and crying out in pain.

"What was that?" Scott asked. "Did you hear that, Bunny?"

"It sounded like it came from outside, from over there," she pointed to the false wall.

Hearing Bunny's name in the indistinct jumble of words, but not recognizing Scott's voice, muffled as it was by the wall, Naidenne cried out, "Bunny? Bunny! I'm here! Help!"

Her weak voice carried thinly through the plasterboard.

"That's Naidenne!" Scott cried. "But where is she? Naidenne! Where are you?"

"Oh, Scott! I'm here. Behind the wall," she called, scratching on the plaster with her can opener.

Scott put his ear against the wall, trying to locate the source of the sounds.

"Say something, darling. We're going to get you out. I love you!"

"I love you, Scott. I'm here. Oh, thank you, Jesus. I'm here!" she cried.

"Her voice is coming from behind this spot," Bunny said.

"We've got to break through. Naidenne! I'm going to try to kick the wall in. Move back."

"Wait!" she called. "Just a minute…okay. I'm out of the way."

Scott began kicking at the space between the tapes on the wall board. His first kick hit a support and set his foot and leg tingling.

He moved his aim down and kicked a four-inch hole through the lower section of wall, and then he dropped to his knees to peer through.

"Naidenne, are you alright? I don't see you," he cried.

"I'm here, my darling," Naidenne responded, shuffling into view.

"Okay, stay back, I'm going to start kicking again," Scott said with relief and renewed determination.

By kicking and tearing at the drywall with his hands, he soon had a hole large enough to crawl through to the other side.

Scott wriggled through, stood up and took his wife into his shaking arms. He and Naidenne held each other tightly, both of them sobbing.

Bunny peeked through the gap in the wall.

"I called the Sheriff and an ambulance is on the way," she said. "I'm going outside to meet them."

Getting no reply, she grinned and climbed the stairs, leaving the couple to celebrate their reunion in privacy.

ॐ

"But that's amazing. And wonderful. And just the most marvelous, miraculous news!" Rosamund gabbled, hearing Bunny's news.

"You are sure she's really all right?" she asked again.

"She seems to be. I don't know what she's been through," Bunny replied while standing in the driveway awaiting the medics. "She's probably a little the worse for wear, but she was standing and talking. They will check her out at the hospital before she can come home, though. That's standard procedure, at least on the cop shows. The ambulance and all haven't arrived, yet, but I didn't want you to worry a moment longer than necessary."

"Bunny, thank you so much for calling. I'm going to start the prayer chain, right now, to let everyone know we can begin praising God for restoring our sister to us," Rosamund said and hung up.

Before calling the first person on the church phone chain, she called Len.

"Hi Rosie," he responded when his secretary put the call through. "I was just thinking about you. How's my beautiful bride?"

"Naidenne is alive! Scott and Bunny found her. Isn't that wonderful?"

"Where was she? Is she injured? How did they find her? What happened?" he asked without giving Rosamund a chance to reply.

"She was at that house where the Presbyterian pastor's wife had her car stolen. Scott wanted to check out the room with the blood spatters. They found her shut up in the basement. Bunny said she was talking and able to stand, so I'm hoping she's okay. But, she's alive, that is the main thing. All our prayers have been answered."

"Shut up in the basement? How did they find her, then?"

"I'm sure Scott will tell us all about it this evening. I've got to start the prayer chain, and then I'm going to the hospital to meet them when the ambulance brings her in. Bye!"

She called the first number on the list, shared the good news, and then dashed out to await Scott and Naidenne's arrival at the hospital.

❧

"I just got the call on the prayer chain. Yes, it's true. Naidenne has been found," Shirley Griffith said.

Shirley had phoned Eskaletha to let the First Ladies Club know, right after calling her next number on the chain.

Eskaletha let out a whoop of celebration before responding to Shirley.

"Thank you, Jesus! And thank you for calling, Shirley. Do you know where she was found, or any of the details?"

"I'm afraid not. The prayer chain message was just that our prayers for her safe return had been answered. I'm dying to know all about what happened, too, though. I suppose we just have to be patient. The news should spread pretty quickly, if I know our community."

"You're so right. Well, I'd better do my part to spread the good news. Thanks, again, Shirley, for all your help. It's been great getting to know you."

"Thanks. Same here. Bye," Shirley said and rang off.

She called Bunny next.

Since Bunny had married and moved away, she was no longer on the prayer chain list.

"Hello?" Bunny answered after only one ring.

"Hi, it's Shirley. Have you heard the wonderful news?"

"If you mean about Naidenne begin found, safe and relatively sound, I sure have. In fact, I was there when she was found," Bunny said with a satisfied grin which carried plainly through the phone connection.

"Tell me!"

"She was being held in the basement of that house where we found the blood and the car thief scared us."

"Don't tell me she was there when we were? Why didn't she call for help?"

"I don't know any of the details about how she got there or what happened before we found her. The EMT's whisked her away as soon as the ambulance arrived. Scott went with her. I just brought his car to the hospital. I was going inside when you called."

"Well, then, get in there and find out everything. And call me tonight, as soon as you can. I'll wait up."

"Sure thing. You know, I haven't been this happy since before Max died. I just can't stop smiling. Talk to you later. Bye."

༄

In the emergency room, Naidenne was lying on an examination bed with Scott standing at her side. He hadn't let go of her hand for more than a few moments since finding her.

The doctor examined her and diagnosed dehydration, exhaustion, exposure, a broken collarbone, a concussion and a badly bruised shoulder, but nothing she wouldn't recover from, in time.

The cut on her abdomen was shallow, and while showing some signs of infection, had not required stitches.

Naidenne was thrilled and thankful to be safe with Scott at her side, but wasn't completely at peace. The doctor hadn't mentioned how the baby was; not even while checking for evidence of sexual assault, in spite of Naidenne's assurance the man had not been able to actually rape her.

She wanted to ask, but did not want Scott to learn their wonderful news this way…if the baby was still all right. If not, then he didn't need to learn that kind of news under these circumstances, either.

She'd had it all planned how she would tell him over a special dinner on the evening she was abducted. Her attacker had taken that from her, too.

They heard a cough on the other side of the privacy curtain before the Portland detective poked his head in.

"Hello, Mrs. Davidson, I'm Detective Rasmussen. I'd like to ask you a few questions, if you feel up to it."

Naidenne began to agree, when Scott interrupted.

"Do you want to ask her why I kidnapped and brutalized her? Or where she 'ran away' to? Or maybe if I'm a serial killer?"

"Scott, what are you talking about?" Naidenne asked.

"I'm afraid your husband and I got off on the wrong foot at the beginning of my investigation into your disappearance, Mrs. Davidson. Rev. Davidson, I'm sorry if my questions offended you. You must understand we have to look at all the angles in a wife's disappearance."

"You had better not treat my wife the way you did me, not if you want our cooperation."

"Of course. I will be as gentle as possible. Now, Mrs. Davidson, can you tell me in your own words exactly what happened?"

☙

Bunny went into the ER to wait until Scott came out, so she could give him his car keys and find out how in the world Naidenne wound up trapped behind a wall in that cellar.

Rosamund was already in the waiting room, pacing back and forth in front of the doors to the examination rooms.

"Bunny! Hi. I can't get any information out of the nurses, except that Naidenne hasn't been admitted. At least that's a good sign, don't you think?"

"Sure. If she were badly injured, I suppose they would probably want to admit her right away. Why don't we sit over here while we wait for Scott to let us know what's going on? All this excitement is making me thirsty. I'm getting a drink from the vending machine. Can I get you something?"

"No thanks. But, we can sit and you can tell me everything you know. What happened when you got to that house? How did you happen to find her? Was she crying for help?"

Bunny held up one hand to get Rosamund to pause her questioning, and walked over to the machine.

A cup of hot tea-like beverage in her hand, she sat next to Rosamund.

"Okay, shoot. But, one question at a time, please," Bunny said with a smile.

Taking a calming breath, Rosamund started over, "Start at the beginning and tell me everything you know."

"I will, but after that I want to hear all about you and your wedding. Did you and Len actually elope?"

## Chapter Twenty-five

"Thank you, Mrs. Davidson. You've been a big help. In the next couple of days we will want you to come to the station to sign your statement. At that time you can take a look at some mug shots. From your description of the man who abducted you, and from fingerprints on those beer bottles we tested, we may know who it is, but we'd like you to confirm."

"My wife has just been through a terrible ordeal, Rasmussen. She needs to rest and recover, physically and emotionally. I don't want her upset," Scott said.

"No, Scott. It's all right. I won't mind doing as Detective Rasmussen asks. I'm eager to help get that man locked up, before he hurts someone else," Naidenne assured her husband.

"Well, I'll be going now. Thanks again," Rasmussen nodded to Naidenne, and with a glance at Scott, pulled the curtain aside and left.

Naidenne's ER doctor came in before the curtain fell closed again.

"We're finished with your tests and you are all set to go home, Mrs. Davidson."

"Are you sure she doesn't need to be admitted, Doctor?" Scott asked.

"We've rehydrated her and stabilized her fractured clavicle. All she needs now is rest and lots of TLC. I'm sure you can provide her with that better than we can here. I'll just have the nurse remove her IV and you can take your wife home."

"Thank you, Doctor," Naidenne said.

"Yes, thanks for everything!" Scott echoed, squeezing his wife's hand.

Before the nurse came in, Scott leaned down and gently kissed Naidenne.

"I almost can't believe I'm really going home," she whispered.

"Me too. I was afraid I'd never see you again," Scott replied.

Naidenne was pleased to be going home, but before she could tell Scott about the baby, she needed reassurance it had not been harmed during her abduction.

"Dear, why don't you go out and tell Bunny and any others who might be here that I'm being released? Then you can come back and get me after the nurse has unhooked these tubes."

"Sure, if you're certain you will be okay. I'll be right back."

The nurse came into the cubicle a moment after Scott went out.

"Nurse, can you tell me if the doctor mentioned anything about my baby?"

"I'm sorry...your baby?" the nurse responded with a puzzled expression.

"Yes, I'm pregnant. I just found out the day I was, uh, I was taken...No one has said if all this has harmed my baby."

"Oh, I see. I'll check your chart."

"Please don't say anything to my husband. I haven't told him, yet. I don't want him to find out here, not as part of this frightening episode. I want it to be special,"

"Gotcha. I'll be right back," the nurse said with a wink.

Scott came back before the nurse returned.

"Not ready to go, yet?" he asked, looking at the IV still in Naidenne's arm.

"Here's the nurse, now, dear," Naidenne said, looking pleadingly at the nurse.

"We'll have your wife all set to go, right away. If you'll just step out for a moment?"

Scott went through the curtain and as the nurse removed the IV, she leaned down to whisper, "your chart shows you are about sixteen weeks pregnant, with nothing exceptional noted. Looks like the baby is just fine."

Freed from the IV, Naidenne hugged the nurse with her good arm and thanked her.

She slipped out of the hospital gown and the nurse helped her to pull her sweater on, being careful of her injured shoulder and collar bone, then slipped that arm back into a sling.

Naidenne's ruined bra had been discarded.

The small town police hadn't wanted her clothes for evidence, so Naidenne would wear the same filthy garments she arrived in, at least until she got home.

She managed to slide her legs into her slacks one-handed, but had difficulty pulling them all the way up.

"Do you have a safety pin I can use to keep my pants together?" Naidenne asked the nurse, showing her the damage Schramm had done to the zipper.

"I'll get one, honey. Be right back."

Scott saw the nurse's exit as his signal to return to his wife's side. He was dismayed at seeing her in the bloodstained sweater and ruined slacks.

"I should have thought to ask Rose to bring you some clothes. I'm so sorry!"

"My darling, you have nothing to be sorry for. You saved my life this morning, remember?. You are, and will forever be, my hero. Heroes don't need to worry about wardrobe details."

Scott wrapped her gently in his arms, talking care not to jostle her injuries, and kissed her.

"What did I ever do to deserve you?" he asked.

The nurse entered, interrupting the sweet nothings, and handed the safety pin to Naidenne.

"I don't think I can manage. Can you pin my slacks, Scott?"

Blushing, Scott clumsily pinned the waist band together.

"Congratulations, you two!" the nurse said, so charmed by this couple that she forgot her promise to keep Naidenne's secret.

"What for?" Scott asked.

"For being released, of course, silly," Naidenne said quickly.

"Exactly. It's always cause for celebration when a healthy patient leaves us," the nurse adlibbed with a slight grimace of apology to Naidenne.

"Well, thanks for all your help. I guess we'll get out of here and make room for some sick people," Scott said.

Bunny and Rosamund rushed over to the couple as they came out of the examining rooms.

"Oh, Naidenne, I'm so sorry," Rosamund cried. "This is all my fault!"

"What do you mean, Rosie?" Scott asked.

"If I hadn't run off like that, Naidenne wouldn't have been alone and vulnerable."

"Don't be silly, Sis. No one is to blame, except the tool of Satan who kidnapped her," Scott said.

"That's right, Rose. For all we know, if you had been home, he might have taken you, instead, or hurt us both, badly," Naidenne added.

"I know you are dying to get home, Deenie, but as soon as you feel up to it, we want to hear how it all happened," Bunny said.

"Home, first. Story time, later," Scott spoke up. "Naidenne is tired, injured and probably suffering from shock."

"Of course. I don't know what I was thinking. Please forget I said anything," Bunny said.

"That's okay, Bunny. I want to tell you all about it. Just not today. How long are you going to be in Bannoch?" Naidenne said.

"Oh, I'm not on anybody's schedule, except my own, these days. I can stay until I feel like going someplace else."

"That's right! Bunny, I'd forgotten about Max. Can you forgive me?" Naidenne said.

"Let's break up this apology-fest and get you home," Scott said, putting a protective arm around his wife.

"Okay, dear, but can we have Bunny over for dinner tomorrow?"

"Good idea! I'll fix something special. It can be a little celebration, just the five of us," Rosamund offered.

"Five? Oh, yes, I keep forgetting you are married, now," Bunny said. "We've got a lot of things to celebrate."

"Yes, we do," Naidenne added, with a Mona Lisa smile.

"Come on, now. I'll drop you and Rosie home, first, and then take Bunny out to her cabin. Will that be okay?"

"I don't want to take you away from your family, Scott, not today. Tell you what, I promised to call Shirley to let her know how Naidenne is, so I can offer to tell her all about it while she drives me home," Bunny suggested.

"Are you sure?" Scott responded, obviously eager to take her up on the offer.

"Absolutely. I'm looking forward to a nice, peaceful visit with Shirley, after all this excitement. I don't know what it is about you folks, but there is always way too much drama going on in this town," Bunny quipped.

Once Bunny connected with Shirley and arranged to meet her in the hospital parking lot, the others left her.

When the three reached Scott's car, Rosamund exclaimed, "Oh!"

"What's wrong, Rosie?" Scott asked.

"In all this excitement, I forgot. I drove here in my car."

"Bunny!" she called out to her friend who was standing by the ER entrance. "I can drive you home. Silly me. I've got my car right here."

Laughing, Bunny, shouted back across the parking spaces, "You are way too excited to drive, Rosamund. I think I prefer a slightly calmer chauffer. Thanks, anyway."

Noting the time, Rosamund decided to drive by the bank and pick Len up on the way, so Scott and Naidenne rode home in happy solitude.

Several times on the drive Naidenne almost blurted out her news, but stopped, reminding herself she wanted to set the stage, first. Only moments before turning into the driveway, she decided exactly when and how she would tell him.

As they pulled up to the house, Naidenne had a flash of memory from the last time she'd returned home and felt a frisson of fear at the thought of what had awaited her then.

"I guess our Rosie isn't the only over-excited driver today," Scott said. "Bunny left her rental car here. I wonder when she will remember."

"We should call her and let her know," Naidenne said.

"Right…Say now, what's all that?" Scott asked.

"What? Where?" she responded, clearly alarmed.

"It's okay. Nothing to be afraid of, dear. Someone's just left something on our porch. Probably stuff for the next rummage sale," Scott soothed, becoming aware that Naidenne was still deeply affected by what she'd endured, in spite of the brave front she had been putting on.

"You see what it is. I'll wait here," she told him.

When Scott stepped out of the car, Naidenne stopped him, saying, "…no wait! I'll come with you."

When they stepped onto the porch, Scott laughed.

"Looks like we've just had a pounding, my dear."

Naidenne surveyed the boxes and bags filled with groceries and covered dishes which nearly filled their front porch under a hand lettered sign saying, "Welcome Home, Naidenne!"

"Pounding? What do you mean?"

"In the early days of the church, and I'm talking eighteen and nineteen hundreds, not Bible times, it was common for the members of a congregation to get together and give the pastor and his family a 'pounding'. That would be a pound of butter, a pound of flour, a pound of bacon and so on. The old-time preachers were often paid in-kind and these events helped the family in the parsonage survive. After the way some people in this congregation have been behaving, lately, I've got to say I'm surprised…and touched."

Naidenne picked up a small bouquet of fall flowers which had been nestled beside a casserole dish. She tucked it into her sling, smiling.

"What a lovely custom. I'm so grateful for their kindness."

Scott could tell Naidenne's strength was fading as the turbulent emotions from her ordeal caught up with her.

"You go on upstairs and get into bed, now. I'll bring these things in and help Rose put them away when she and Len get home. Scoot," he patted her good shoulder when she hesitated, then she went obediently inside.

Upstairs, Naidenne pulled her nicest trousseau nightgown out of the closet and took it into the bathroom.

She was desperate to scrub every trace of her abductor off her body. She wished she could cleanse her memories as easily.

Washing her hair with the handheld shower attachment and bathing with one hand was exhausting, but she finally felt clean.

By the time Scott came upstairs she was changed and in bed. Her damp ringlets curled around her head as she lay back on the pillows, savoring the softness and comfort. Tears rolled slowly down her cheeks.

"Darling! Are you okay?" Scott asked, rushing to her side.

"I'm absolutely wonderful," Naidenne replied with a smile. "Just a little emotional these days, I guess."

"Who wouldn't be, after what you've been through? But you're home and safe, now, and I won't let anyone hurt you, ever again."

"Silly man. Don't make promises you can't possibly keep. In fact, I know for certain that I will probably suffer more pain in the future, rather than less."

"What do you mean? Is there something the doctor didn't tell me?" Scott looked terrified as he spoke.

"Yes. I'm afraid there is," Naidenne replied, unable to meet Scott's eyes.

"Tell me, please. Whatever it is, we will get through it together."

"That's what I thought, too. I'm so happy you feel the same."

"Of course I do, but what is it? Are the doctors sure? Could it be a mistake? This is just a small town hospital, after all."

"Oh, I've had two opinions. The diagnosis is confirmed and we will simply have to live with it, for the rest of our very long lives, I hope."

When she said this last, Scott was puzzled, and groped for words to ask for clarification.

Feeling sorry for him after all he'd been through, Naidenne stopped teasing him, saying, "In about five months or so, my darling, we are having a baby."

## Chapter Twenty-six

Rosamund and Scott had been fielding visits and phone calls from church and community members all day long. There had even been a call from a reporter from a Portland TV station asking for an interview with Naidenne.

Scott was having a hard time keeping the news about the baby to himself, but they had decided the previous evening to make their announcement at that night's celebration dinner. Still, news of the pregnancy completely overshadowed Naidenne's kidnapping, in both of their minds.

The couple was already looking to the future and putting the unhappy episode behind them. If only everyone would let them.

"I suppose it is a good thing Naidenne decided to wait until tonight to tell us all what happened," Rosamund said after saying a terse, "No comment," into the phone and hanging up.

"Why do you say that?" Len asked her.

"I might be tempted to answer everyone's snoopy questions if I knew the answers, just to get them to quit bothering us."

"Would that be a bad thing? Everyone is simply curious. Most of these folks care about Scott and Naidenne, after all," Len said.

"I'm sure you're right, but this is Naidenne's business. It's up to her to tell us, and everyone else, only what she wants to share. I can imagine there could be some things she would rather keep to herself, under the circumstances."

Scott fairly skipped down the stairs.

"Who was on the phone, this time?" he asked.

"A reporter from the Tillamook newspaper. I told him to talk to the Sheriff."

"I think that's probably best, especially until they catch this guy."

"But will they catch him? He could be long gone, by this time," Len said.

"I talked with Deputy Williams. He said they know who it is. It's that guy who killed a guard and escaped from Pelican Bay a while back. They think he may be the one responsible for the house break-ins along the Coast south of here, also. The Feds who were tracking him said they thought he was making for the Canadian border. They don't know why he stayed around Bannoch, but they found his prints at Maureen's place, too. That's a puzzle, since the autopsy shows she died of a heart attack."

"Will there be a service for Maureen, now the autopsy's over?" Rosamund asked, thinking about the arrangements she would need to make for the funeral meal.

"That will be up to the next of kin, I suppose. I haven't heard anything."

"So, they know who this guy is. But do they know where he is?" Len pressed.

"They know he is the man who stole and wrecked Judy's car, so he was still here a couple of days ago, and probably on foot, since no other vehicles have been reported stolen."

"So that evil being was right there when Bunny and Shirley were at the house looking for Naidenne. How frightful!" Rosamund said.

"Now he's been identified, the FBI is on the scene, not just local cops. He's one of their most wanted criminals, so I expect them to catch him. I feel like tracking him down, myself, but Naidenne made me promise to stay out of it."

"Wise woman. This guy sounds like a majorly bad piece of work," Len said.

"How is Naidenne doing this afternoon, Scott?" Rosamund asked.

"She's sleeping, right now. She said she wanted to be at her best for tonight's party."

"Hardly a party, after all she's been through."

"Well, that's what she said. She's really looking forward to having dinner with friends and family and celebrating our many blessings, large and small," Scott responded to his sister, with a twinkle in his eyes.

"I hope the meal I'm fixing will live up to her expectations. It's just slow cooker pot roast. Maybe I should make something fancier."

"Every dish you cook is fit for the finest banquet, my love," Len said, pulling her hand to his lips for a kiss.

The banker's uncharacteristically romantic gesture reminded Scott of his sister's recent marriage.

Everything that happened while Naidenne was missing had been pushed into the background. Bunny's loss and Rosamund's marriage weren't getting the attention they deserved.

Scott resolved to rectify that, now that his own world was no longer upside down.

"Say, Rosamund. Why don't I bring in something from the Crab Shack, so you don't have to cook tonight? You two are celebrating something pretty stupendous, too, you know," he suggested.

"No, no. I've already got dinner in the crockpot. I don't mind fixing the meal. Naidenne is the star of this little gathering."

"Actually, now that I think of it, everyone here tonight will be an honored guest. Naidenne and I are celebrating her return, of course, but we also have a wedding to celebrate and a recent bereavement to honor. I know! I'm going to get you guys a wedding cake for our dessert. The bakery in the mall should still be open. I'll be right back," Scott said and dashed out.

Rosamund looked after her departing brother, shaking her head, but with a smile on her face.

"That man is so happy to have Naidenne back, he's positively giddy, bless his heart," she said.

Len stood up and put his arms around Rosamund.

"And I am just as giddy with happiness to finally have you for my bride."

ॐ

After a long, restorative nap, Naidenne felt more like herself as she descended the stairs just before dinner.

"Can I help with anything, Rose?" she asked her sister-in-law, as that woman put the finishing touches on the dinner table.

"Nope. You just sit down and relax. Len and Scott have been giving me a hand in the kitchen and everything is all taken care of. We'll eat as soon as Bunny gets here."

As if on cue, Bunny knocked at the door.

Len let her in and she congratulated him, once again, on his marriage.

"Thanks. Let me just tell you again how sorry we are for your loss," Len intoned.

"I appreciate that. Now let's put my bereavement aside and start celebrating," she said before spying Naidenne on the sofa.

"Deenie, I'm glad to see you looking so much better. How are you feeling? Are you sure you're up to this little party?"

"Oh, yes. A celebration is just what I need to put the events of the past few days behind me."

"Dinner is served," Scott pronounced like an old-fashioned English butler.

When the guests were seated around the table, they joined hands while Scott thanked the Lord for their many blessings.

With a unison chorus of "Amen," the group began to pass the food.

By unspoken agreement, the conversation focused on the elopement and Bunny's visits with her sisters. Details of Naidenne's abduction were saved until after dinner.

Scott and Naidenne had discussed how the evening should go and had decided to save their announcement until after she related as much of her unpleasant story as they felt comfortable sharing. Some things were for Scott's ears alone and he had heard every painful detail the day he found her.

But news of the new baby would end the evening on a happy note for everyone.

"When I plunged down that dark chute, I didn't even know what was at the bottom, but I knew what was coming back and figured nothing could be worse."

"Oh, dear! You poor thing," Rosamund moaned.

"You are a brave woman, Naidenne. Not many would have been strong enough to escape under those circumstances," Len said.

"Not brave. Just desperate. And I knew that house, you see. I saw all the renovations and knew about the old boarded-off kitchen. The only risk I was taking, really, was the fall and the chance no one would ever find me."

"Oh, well, then. If that's all," Bunny said with a roll of her eyes.

"But, you did find me, Bunny. You and Scott didn't give up. I can never thank you enough, either of you," Naidenne said with tears in her eyes and a catch in her voice.

"We wouldn't have known to come looking at that house if the Club ladies hadn't sent out search parties, you know. And that nifty blood trail you left us helped a lot," Bunny said.

"Did your attacker stab you? Is that where the blood came from?" Len asked.

"He cut my stomach when he was…playing with me, before he got rid of my car," Naidenne replied. "I knew when he came back he would kill me, though. That's why I had to get out."

"How did you keep your sanity, locked in the dark basement, no water, no food and no way out?" Rosamund asked with her eyes wide.

"I think Story Time's over, ladies and gentleman," Scott said, noticing the effect these memories were having on Naidenne. "I say it's time for our newlyweds to cut the wedding cake. Bunny will you help me bring it in?"

"Sure. Great idea."

Scott carried in a German chocolate cake with "Happy Retirement, Gloria" written in icing on its top.

"It was the last cake in the shop. Sorry about the message," he explained.

"I don't know...seems sort of appropriate. We've both retired from the single life and are looking forward to a Gloria-ous marriage," Len joked, to chuckles and groans all around.

Bunny, who had carried in the plates and forks earlier and returned to the kitchen, came out again with a bottle of sparkling cider in one hand and one of champagne in the other.

"The wine glasses are in the china cabinet in the dining room, Bunny," Scott directed.

When everyone's glass was full, Scott announced it was time for the bride and groom to cut the cake.

Rosamund and Len joined hands on the cake knife and began to cut when Bunny cried, "Wait! Cell phones, everyone. We've got to take pictures."

There was a small scramble as phones were retrieved from pockets and purses, then the newlyweds resumed their pose for the photographers.

The photography session over, Rosamund was dishing up slices of cake when Scott held up his glass.

"Toasts!" he proclaimed, grandly. "First, to the newlyweds. May you have a long and Gloria-ous marriage."

Cries of "Here! Here!" met this toast and everyone clinked glasses and drank the beverage of their choice. Rosamund and Naidenne were the only ones drinking cider.

"To the beautiful bride," Bunny toasted and Naidenne followed up with a toast to the groom.

Rosamund toasted Naidenne's safe return and Len toasted Scott for the great party.

After a slight lull in the general gaiety, Scott looked at Naidenne and she nodded.

"And now a toast to the future aunt and uncle," he proclaimed.

Blank looks and general puzzlement gave way to whoops of joy as one by one the others caught on. Laughter, hugs and congratulations were exchanged.

"How long have you known, Naidenne?" Bunny asked.

"I found out the day I was attacked," she replied.

"Oh, no! That makes everything so much worse, somehow," Bunny said.

"Not really. I'm not sure I would have had the nerve to escape if not for the baby. I couldn't let anything happen to our little girl, no matter what."

"A girl? We're having a girl?" Scott asked, incredulous. "How do you know? Why didn't you tell me?"

"The doctor in Tillamook did an ultrasound and I wanted to save something to surprise you tonight, too."

"I am so happy for you both! This is wonderful," Bunny said.

"A little girl," Rosamund said softly, sadly remembering Scott's first little girl and saying a fervent prayer for God's protection on this new life.

Scott cleared his throat, "As you all know, this isn't my first daughter. When my first wife, Jenny, and little Abigail died, I thought a part of me died forever, too. Finding Naidenne reanimated a piece of my heart. Learning about our daughter tonight has made me a whole man. We can celebrate our joy without being disloyal to the memories of my first family. Please don't ever be afraid to talk about them. I'm convinced they are aware of everything and are sharing in our celebration."

After a moment of silence, while everyone thought about what was said, the general gaiety returned to the group and they began talking about the big changes in each of their lives and their plans for the future.

Eventually, Naidenne's tiredness became obvious and Bunny prepared to leave.

"You are the best friend I've ever had, Bunny. First, you brought Scott and me together and now you've helped save my life. I will never be able to thank you enough," Naidenne said tearfully.

"Well, you've got to promise me just one thing, and we'll be even," Bunny said.

"Anything! What is it?"

"Promise me you won't name that innocent little girl 'Bunny'."

They laughed and Scott piped up, "What about 'Leveline' then?"

"Aargh!" Bunny cried. "Don't even speak aloud my given name in front of the baby. She'll be scarred for life."

There were smiles on every face as the evening ended.

Bunny drove back to her cabin, humming a favorite lullaby to herself.

# Chapter Twenty-seven

Rosamund wasted no time in sharing Naidenne and Scott's great news the next morning. Within a matter of hours the joyous tidings reached all the members of the First Ladies Club.

"This calls for a baby shower. We haven't had one since we formed the club," Judy told Elizabeth, when she phoned to spread the good news.

"I think that is a wonderful idea, and we should invite Naidenne's friends, Shirley and Bunny, too. They are almost honorary members, after all their help."

"Then, we'd better have it soon. Bunny's just here on a visit, isn't she?"

"That's right. I am going to call Eskaletha and get the ball rolling right away. Bye."

Schramm slumped in a dilapidated recliner in the shabby living room of a derelict house tucked among the trees in the hills only ten miles north of Bannoch. He squinted at the snowy screen on the old-fashioned rabbit-eared television, trying to make out the images of the local newscast.

Carver was trying to find out what they were saying about him, but the reception was terrible.

He'd been lucky to stumble onto this place the day before, when he was getting really desperate.

There had been smoke coming from the chimney of the house and from a smoke stack on the barn out back.

Creeping from window to window, he saw there was no one inside, but he heard noises in the barn.

When he got close, the smell of acrid fumes told him right away what was going on.

He grinned as he eased through the door, surprising the scrawny man working inside. At the sight of Schramm's knife he gaped wide in shock, displaying rotten teeth.

Schramm's blade was given full reign, at last, as he vented his frustration on the hapless meth-cooker.

After his fury left him, Carver looked over the make-shift lab for any of the finished product. He scooped up the few crystals he found into a baggie and left the barn to inspect the house.

There were no vehicles in the yard or the barn, leading Schramm to think the dead man had partners who might be out making deliveries of their illegal product.

He decided to take as much food and water as he could carry and get away before the others came back.

While filling a filthy pillowcase with provisions from the kitchen cupboards and refrigerator, he heard a motor approaching.

Dashing to the window, he saw a single man in a rusty, dented pickup truck jolting up the rutted drive.

The driver, a near twin for the ruined specimen in the barn, jumped down from the truck and headed for the house.

Schramm pressed himself against the wall beside the backdoor and waited. When the door opened, he leaped out, slashing and stabbing his startled victim.

Schramm emptied the dead man's pockets of keys and money, then dragged him to the barn and left him beside the corpse of his friend, shutting the door tightly.

He took his time exploring and satisfied himself that the two in the barn were the only ones who had been living in the house, so he no longer needed to rush off.

He'd been hungry and cold since the stolen car ran out of gas.

With the pickup outside, cash in his pockets and plenty of food to see him to the border, Schramm decided to hole up for the rest of the day and get on the road that night.

He'd found a stash of booze in a cupboard and settled in to enjoy a drink or two. The alcohol and the meth combined to make him miss that night's departure date and he'd slept off his hangover late into the morning.

Now, before heading out, he wanted to find out if the locals were still looking for him.

He was trying to make up his mind about whether or not to burn the barn down when he left, making it look like a meth-lab accident.

The flames might bring too much attention before he could make himself scarce, but they might be just the distraction he needed. It was hard to think with his head still pounding.

Rotten reception on the ancient television didn't help. Schramm's anger was mounting by the second as he fiddled with the bent wire coat hanger antenna trying to get a clear picture.

Fed up, he picked up his beer, drank the dregs and flung the empty bottle at the screen, shattering both screen and bottle.

He finished packing up all the useful supplies he could find and took them out to the truck before disappearing into the barn, his mind made up.

He ran out as whiffs of smoke began seeping through cracks in the barn siding.

He was backing the truck out of the yard when a loud boom rang out and flames began to reach out of the hayloft and lick up the front of the barn.

With a satisfied smirk, Carver bounced the pickup over the rutted track and out onto the logging road leading down to the highway.

※

In early afternoon, Bunny and Shirley were in Bunny's rental car on the way to Tillamook.

"I'm so glad she's having a girl," Shirley said.

"Why?"

"It's just so much more fun to shop for girly clothes. We can find some really cute things in Tillamook for the baby shower."

"The shower is just what we need to relax and get back to normal, after all the horror of recent events," Bunny said.

"I wonder if Naidenne can relax, yet," Shirley responded.

"What do you mean?"

"The man who took her, the one who stole Judy's car, he hasn't been caught, has he?"

"Not that I've heard. But, surely he and Judy's car must be long gone, by now."

"Didn't you hear? Judy's car was recovered not far from town. I guess it broke down or something. Anyway, unless he hitched a ride or stole another car, he could still be somewhere nearby."

"What an awful thought!" Bunny exclaimed. "I hope that hasn't occurred to Naidenne."

Bunny's car was catching up to a knot of traffic where the faster cars were attempting to get around a much slower vehicle.

"I know people love their RV's, but I sure hate getting stuck behind one," Shirley observed, looking ahead.

When only one car separated them from the source of the bottleneck, Bunny saw it was not a recreational vehicle, after all.

A beat-up old pickup, its dragging tailpipe shooting sparks, was struggling up the slight incline, its driver hunched over the steering wheel as though urging the truck forward with his own strength.

"I'll be able to pass this guy as soon as the line of oncoming traffic gets by," Bunny said, while being forced to match the truck's speed.

As they passed the pickup, Shirley turned to look inside.

"Did you see all the tattoos on that guy's arms? I'd hate to meet up with him in a dark alley," she shuddered.

"I didn't notice," Bunny commented, concentrating on her passing maneuver.

ૐ

Scott scooted his chair back from the kitchen table and carried his plate to the sink.

"Are you sure you don't want me to stay home this afternoon? I don't have to go back to the office, if you need me."

"I'm fine. Rosamund will be back soon, so I won't be alone. I can't wait to hear what she and Len have decided to do about where they are going to live. If they buy a place, I hope they let me be their realtor," Naidenne said.

"Will you be up to going back to work, so soon, and with the baby coming?"

"Of course, I'm okay to work. Or I will be in a day or two. I can hunt and peck on the keyboard with one hand as long as I need to. Women work right up to their due dates these days, you know."

"But not once the baby's here," Scott stated.

"Babies are expensive, dear. I will stay home with her as long as I can, but that may not be long, at all."

"I didn't want to bring it up, so soon after your terrible ordeal, but, before you were attacked, I had decided to look for another pastorate. The openings I've been reviewing all have starting compensation packages much more generous than I get here."

"But, you love Bannoch Community Fellowship! You wouldn't think of moving just for more money…especially if you made up your mind before you knew about the baby," Naidenne protested.

"You're right. It isn't just the money, but now the financial side weighs more heavily."

"What was it, then? What made you want to leave?"

Scott silently struggled with himself before blurting out, "I got sick of the way I'm being treated!"

Naidenne was stunned.

"What do you mean?" she asked, softly.

"I owe you an apology. I've been keeping some things to myself because I didn't want to upset you."

"Please tell me. We are supposed to bear each other's burdens, you know."

"I know…the trustees have been giving me a hard time ever since our marriage. They think my salary should be reduced because you work and we have more income."

"But, that's ridiculous! What does my working have to do with it?"

"That's what I said. I've been ignoring their gibes and snarky remarks for months, but the leak in the roof gave them a new tack. I know I told you it was just a silly joke, but, at the last board meeting they all voted to reduce my compensation, effective immediately, to pay for a new roof. It was just the last straw."

"Oh, Scott! I'm so sorry you have been dealing with this all alone. I just can't believe the rest of the congregation knows what the board is proposing to do, though. Most of the people love you."

"Maybe so, but most of these good people come to church for comfort, fellowship and to worship God. They don't want to get involved in church politics. That's why so few of them are willing to serve on the boards. It gives people like the Oldhams and our current trustees free rein to do whatever they want."

"I haven't given a thought to poor Maureen. Did the authorities ever say what she died of?" Naidenne asked.

"Heart attack, apparently. No idea how her body came to be wrapped in a carpet in her garage. We know someone broke in. Deputy Williams told me there were signs the trespasser was squatting in the house for a while. Maybe the squatter found her dead of a heart attack and didn't want to stay in a house with a corpse. I don't suppose we'll ever know, but I wouldn't be surprised if all this business wasn't the work of the same man…that escaped convict from California. His fingerprints were found in her house, after all, so he was at least there."

At the mention of her attacker, Naidenne shuddered.

"Did Deputy Williams say whether the man has been captured?" she asked in a small voice.

Scott could imagine what was going through her mind and wanted to reassure her.

"No, but that guy is long gone from here. He probably drove Judy's car clear to Canada before these local yokels even took your disappearance seriously."

"I hope so. I'd like to know when he's caught, though."

"Of course. But, you don't need to worry. He couldn't be stupid enough to come back here again. Although I wouldn't mind getting my hands on him," Scott said, through gritted teeth.

"I can't imagine you ever being violent, Scott, no matter how much you might want to," she said, standing and putting her good arm around his neck.

Scott kissed her deeply, then held her for a long moment.

"You'd better get to your office, dear. Whether you decide to write another sermon or apply for another pulpit is up to you. Whither thou goest, I will go…or stay, with you," Naidenne said.

Rosamund came in the back door, eager to share her future decisions with her family.

"I've had a good look around Len's condo and we've discussed everything, including finances and retirement and we've decided to buy a house," she announced as she entered the kitchen.

"Oh, Rose, that's wonderful! Will you let me help you find your dream home?" Naidenne asked.

"Of course," Rosamund replied.

"Congratulations, Sis. See you girls later," Scott said and went out the back door on his way to church to try to decide his own future.

# Chapter Twenty-eight

Gwennie Barthlette, Peggy Burt and Judy Falls were sitting at Judy's kitchen table, surrounded by scissors, glue guns and snips of pink-colored construction paper. They were crafting nut cups in the form of tiny diapers for the next day's baby shower.

"Who is in charge of the games?" Gwennie asked. "I know some really clever ones, if anyone needs suggestions. There's this one where you smear peanut butter or creamed peas in preemie diapers and…"

"I'm sure Eskaletha has all that under control," Peggy interrupted.

"I think she's planning a more, um, sedate party, in consideration of all Naidenne's been through, lately," Judy added.

"This whole town has been through a lot. First, that rash of break-ins, then Mrs. Oldham's funny death…I don't mean 'funny ha-ha', just funny-odd, and then Naidenne getting snatched by that escaped convict," Gwennie said. "Has anybody heard just what all he did to her while he had her in his clutches?"

"I don't think we need to even think about that," Peggy replied. "I wish we would hear the police have captured him and thrown him back into Pelican Bay, though."

"They couldn't keep him there, before," Gwennie said.

"I just want to know he won't ever come back here," Judy commented.

☙

Scott was in his study at the church, staring in consternation at his old-fashioned computer monitor, trying to compose a cover letter to send with his pastor's profile to the pulpit committees on his list.

He had a hard time selling himself as the best man for the job, while feeling his failure here in Bannoch so bitterly. He was convinced, if only he had been able to reach these people, they never would have considered treating their pastor with such disdain.

Someone rapped on the office door and he quickly minimized the computer display.

"Come in," he called.

Orville Locke entered the study, head down and with his grimy baseball cap in his hands.

"Hiya, Pastor. I was in the neighborhood and thought I'd stop by and see how your missus is doing."

"My wife is as well as can be expected, Locke," Scott responded, without getting up.

"That's good to hear. You mind if I set down?"

Scott nodded toward the chair, without smiling.

Locke cleared his throat and fidgeted with his hat, but didn't speak.

"What can I do for you, Locke? Is something on your mind?"

"Yeah, sort of, I guess," he replied. "Uh, well, there is something…I just wanted to make sure you weren't still miffed about our little joke at the last board meeting."

Orville spoke quickly, without making eye contact.

"Joke! What joke?" Scott almost shouted, making Orville cringe.

"Why, that silly business about the roof, of course," he blustered. "You never thought we were serious, did you?"

"Mr. Locke, I have no doubt you were all very serious. You were united in your determination to take the cost of a new roof for the church out of my compensation, and I am serious, now, too. I'm so serious that I am considering turning in my resignation."

"Now, Pastor, I know you've been under a lot of stress with what happened to your wife and all, but, Scott, how can you think we'd do something like that after all these good years together? We're your family, after all."

Scott was dumbfounded.

After taking in what his trustee was saying, he stood and came around his desk to stand beside Orville's chair.

"Is this the official position of the entire board, or are you speaking only for yourself?"

"Well, some on the board maybe got the impression you might not have appreciated our little joke and asked me to come clear the air a bit. We all talked it over, and, yeah, it's unanimous. We're real sorry if you took our bit of fun the wrong way."

Scott looked steadily at Orville until the man met his gaze before speaking.

"If you are representing the board, here, then I accept your apology. It took some courage to come to me and admit your misdeed..."

"I didn't say..." Orville interrupted.

"And, since we are in agreement that you all behaved abominably toward your pastor, can I assume there will be no repeated threats to cut my salary in the future?" Scott continued without pausing.

Orville squirmed, looking everywhere but at his pastor, then shrugged and nodded.

"Thank you, Orville. I appreciate you coming here today. I confess I wasn't looking forward to leaving Bannoch. This town and this church are home, and most of the people here are, as you say, family."

Scott held out his hand and Locke, recognizing he was being dismissed, rose and shook it limply, before going out.

Scott walked back around his desk where he settled down with a deep sigh of relief.

He sensed he'd just witnessed a shift in the dynamics of the congregation.

He was filled with hope as he lifted up a prayer of thanks before picking up the phone to relay his good news to Naidenne.

❧

Driving back to town after a hugely successful shopping trip, Bunny passed a pickup truck parked on the shoulder of the northbound side of the highway.

"Isn't that the same pickup that was slowing everyone down earlier today?" Shirley asked.

"Sure looks like it. I don't see anyone in it, though."

"Well, if that driver is trying to hitchhike, promise me you won't pick him up."

❧

Carver Schramm was on foot, once again. The stolen truck had broken down shortly after the ladies passed it earlier in the day.

He'd tried to figure out what was wrong and fix it, but Schramm's tool of choice had always been a knife. He was completely out of his element under the hood of a truck.

Eventually giving up on the pickup as a lost cause, he was forced to retreat once more to the shelter of the woods bordering the highway, this time carrying two heavy bags of provisions.

"Why the Hell can't I get away from this place? It's like I've got a curse on me," he fumed as he trudged along, stopping frequently to rest his arms and shoulders.

He was still many miles south of Tillamook, where he hoped to find another car to steal, so he could finally leave Oregon and all his bad luck behind him.

☙

Dinner at the Davidson's that night was festive.

Len and Rosamund were excited about buying a new home and Naidenne was enjoying the opportunity to give them some pointers.

Scott felt a weight had been lifted from his shoulders.

The prospect of leaving Bannoch had been casting a gloom over him which wasn't completely lifted by Naidenne's rescue. He'd felt guilty about not sharing his troubles with her, too.

She was right that he'd been wrong to try to shield her.

"So, you have a big party tomorrow, eh?" he asked during a lull in the conversation.

"That's right. The Club ladies are throwing a baby shower for me, isn't that sweet?"

"Are you going, too, Rosie?"

"No, I wasn't invited, but I am sure the church will want to have one, too. So, I'll get my chance to welcome this precious new baby."

"You should come, Rose. The ladies would be happy to have you," Naidenne said.

"No, thanks. I've already got plenty to do tomorrow."

"That's right. I've lined up a couple of places for us to look at tomorrow afternoon," Len said.

"Hey, I thought I was your realtor," Naidenne protested.

"Oh, you'll be the realtor of record, don't you worry. I lined these up before we knew you'd feel like taking us on. If we decide to make an offer on either of 'em, you'll get to handle the deal."

"Where are these places?" Scott asked.

"One is not far from here; right on the edge of town, but the other is about half-way to Tillamook. I'm not sure Len will want such a long commute. It will have to be pretty special to get us to move so far out," Rosamund replied.

"I've got a big day tomorrow, and I'm pretty tired. I hope you will excuse me if I go up to bed, now. I'm not sure if my lack of energy is because of all the, you know, or from the pregnancy, but I will be so happy when I get my strength back," Naidenne said as she reached to carry her dishes into the kitchen.

"Leave those, Deenie," Scott said. "I'll take care of the clean-up, tonight."

"You heard the man, Rosie. Let's you and me take a little moonlight stroll before heading up to bed," Len suggested, standing and holding out his hand to his bride.

"If Scott doesn't mind…there are a lot of dishes and I'm afraid I left the kitchen in a mess."

"You honeymooners just go, Sis. I think I can handle everything on my own. I'm a big boy," Scott said with a smile and turned to kiss his wife on the cheek.

As Naidenne turned away, he patted her bottom, gently, saying, "You go on up, dear. I'll be along shortly."

༄

## The First Ladies Club

Walking hand in hand, Rosamund and Len strolled along the lanes near the parsonage as a fat, yellow late September moon hung in the plush night sky.

Stopping at the intersection with a road leading down to the main highway, the couple admired the view of the twinkling lights of the town below them and the dark ocean beyond.

"We have so much to be thankful for, Len."

"That we do, my love. That we do.

At the main Sheriff's Office in Tillamook, Detective Rasmussen was talking to the sergeant on duty.

"We've had a report of a man matching our guy being seen working on a disabled truck on the highway between here and Bannoch this afternoon. When it was checked out, the troopers found a pickup registered to one of those meth cookers we found in the burned out barn, earlier today. Looks like our perp may have had a hand in that, too. At the very least, he stole their truck."

"Do you think he's still in the area, then?" the sergeant asked.

"If the witness was correct, he was seen this afternoon and, now, he could be on foot. I want as many deputies as you can spare to begin a house to house search, right away. I've notified the FBI of the sighting, so their men will be out there looking, too. Don't get in each other's way. We've got to get this guy before he does any more damage."

## Chapter Twenty-nine

Carver Schramm was fed up, frightened, and dangerous. After a night huddled against the damp, rough bark of a pitch-dripping pine tree, feeling bugs crawling up his pants legs and jumping at each and every menacingly indecipherable noise in the darkness, he was exhausted, his temper on a hair trigger.

"I just hope I run into somebody today," he growled. "Any yokel crossing my path dies."

Trying to keep out of sight while staying as close to the highway as possible, so as not to get lost, was forcing him to slog through underbrush and rough terrain.

The tattoos on his arms were crosshatched with scratches and smeared with trickles of blood. Irritating insect bites on his back and neck added to his foul mood.

He had eaten the major portion of the food in the sacks and jettisoned the rest as not worth carrying.

A heavy marine layer obscured the sun and dripped damply from the trees as he passed under them.

The gray-misted day was a perfect backdrop for Schramm's black thoughts.

A large collie broke from the trees above the deer track Carver was following.

Catching the fugitive's scent, the dog barked and began to trot nearer.

Schramm gripped his knife, tightly, while waiting for the animal to reach him where he crouched in a brushy hiding place.

# The First Ladies Club

Before the dog was within range, it stopped with ears perked and a whistle pierced the quiet. The obedient canine bounded away.

Schramm held his breath in anticipation of the appearance of the dog's owner. After a few moments when he neither saw nor heard anything, he relaxed and walked on, adjusting his route further down the hill.

This brought him to a bluff behind a rather remotely situated house at the end of a winding private drive.

It was close to midday and Carver was hungry. He decided to check out the house for something to eat, before moving on.

&

"Come on, Rosie. I want to see this place and get back to work in time for my staff meeting this afternoon," Len urged his wife.

"I'm almost ready. I had to find my camera. I want to take pictures, so we can look at them, later, when trying to decide where to buy."

"Doesn't your cell phone take photos?" Len asked.

"I think so. I'm afraid I haven't quite figured out how to send them to my computer, so I can look at them. The phone's screen is so tiny, it hurts my eyes," Rosamund replied.

"I don't have time right now, but this evening, if you remind me, I'll show you how to take advantage of all your phone's features. No point in paying good money for all the bells and whistles, if you aren't going to use them."

"Thanks, dear. I'm ready. We're leaving now, Naidenne," she called up the stairs.

Naidenne came out onto the landing.

"Have a nice drive, you two. I wish I could go with you," Naidenne said.

"Well, you have fun at your baby shower. We'll tell you all about the house this evening. We'd better leave, now, Rose," Len said and held the door open for her.

"Bye!" Naidenne called before returning to her room to finish changing clothes for the party. It was getting hard to find outfits to fit her now rapidly changing shape.

Discarding a pair of slacks she couldn't zip up one-handed, she shrugged and reached for a loose beige knit shift hanging in the back of her closet.

"I guess it is lucky I never sent this dowdy thing to Goodwill, after all," she said with a smile. "This weekend I'm going to ask Scott to take me to the mall in Tillamook to shop for maternity clothes, sling or no sling."

Awkwardly tying a royal blue patterned scarf around her neck in a loose knot, she decided the shift didn't look half bad, after all.

She rearranged her curls, swiped a smear of gloss on her lips and skipped down the stairs just as Scott came in to take her to the baby shower.

"You must be more careful on the stairs, Deenie, and hold onto the bannister. You're walking for two now, remember," Scott grinned.

"Yes, dear," Naidenne replied, in mock obedience, before smiling up for a kiss.

"I'm sorry you need to play taxi today. I know you were busy at church," she said.

"Not a problem. I'm happy to break away for a quick smooch with my wife, anytime."

"Do we have to wait until my car is found before we can file an insurance claim and replace it? What if…that man…drove it off a cliff or into the sea, or something?"

"I'm waiting for a call from our insurance agent about that. When he gets back to me, I'll let you know what he says. I wish we could afford to just replace the car, but, well, you know how it is. Staying here in Bannoch is emotionally and spiritually satisfying, but not such a boon to the budget, I'm afraid."

"We managed before and we'll manage, now. God always gives us what we need," Naidenne said.

"Thanks for the sermonette," Scott responded. "Let's get you to that shower. Not a good idea for the guests of honor to be late."

"Guests? Are you staying, too?"

"Heaven forbid! No, I meant you and our daughter. You'll never catch me at a baby shower. I'm allergic to giggly gossip and girly games," he teased.

Bunny Banks wrestled a large package out of the trunk of her car and lugged it to Eskaletha's front door, along with a bag of smaller gifts slung over her shoulder.

Unable to reach the shoulder-high doorbell with her hands so burdened, she tried depressing the button with her shoulder. When that didn't work, rather than setting down her packages, she slipped off one of her flats, backed up a few paces and rang the bell with her toes, nearly losing her balance, just as Olivette walked up behind her and put a steadying hand on her shoulder.

"Now this is the first time I have ever seen anyone do that," Olivette said.

"Oh, I didn't see anyone coming," Bunny responded. "Sorry about that. Guess I should have waited. Patience has never been my highest virtue, I'm afraid."

The two were laughing when Eskaletha opened the door.

"What's so funny?" she asked.

"Oh, Olivette just caught me in a 'Bunny moment', I'm afraid."

"Eskaletha, you won't believe what this woman can do. How do you stay so loose, Bunny?" Olivette asked.

"I started doing yoga a few years ago. But I'm a little embarrassed you saw me taking advantage of my limber legs," Bunny said.

"Now, I'm really curious. Come on in, you two, and you can explain to everyone at once," Eskaletha teased.

"What's in your big gift box, Bunny?" Judy asked when Bunny dropped her small presents on the display table and set the large box on the floor beside it.

"Naidenne isn't here, yet, is she? I don't want to spoil her surprise. I got her a diaper disposal system. Isn't that an amazing invention? I never had kids, but when I saw this thing, I just knew it had to be the perfect gift."

The women chatted happily and greeted each later arrival, until finally it was the guest of honor, herself.

"Naidenne! You look radiant! Come sit by me!" a mix of voices called out when she entered the room.

"The decorations look so elegant, Eskaletha. Thank you all so much for doing this for me," Naidenne said before sitting down.

"I think everyone's here, now, so we can begin," Eskaletha pronounced. "Olivette, will you read the minutes of the last First Ladies Club baby shower?"

Olivette, flustered for a moment, caught the twinkle in Eskaletha's eye and admitted, "There are no minutes, Madam President. This is our first ever club shower."

"Exactly, so, in lieu of the minutes, I will make a speech," she replied to a chorus of good-natured groans and protests.

"When we established this club, we all knew how isolating life can be for a pastor's wife, especially in a small town like ours. But I had no idea just how much I needed the companionship and support of other women who share the same blessings and trials I do. This past week, when Deenie went missing, it brought home to me exactly what this group has come to mean in my life. I think we all share that feeling. We are more than the sum of our members, but each one of us is so necessary to all of us. I'm afraid I'm not saying this as well as I would like to…This baby shower is also a 'thank you' celebration for Naidenne."

Turning to Naidenne she went on, "It was your idea to start the First Ladies Club and it was you who showed us how much we have come to depend on each other. You, Naidenne Davidson, make a difference to me and to all of us. We are so glad you are here."

Smiling through the tears rolling down her cheeks, Naidenne got up and hugged Eskaletha.

"Thank you, thank you all. You mean the world to me, too," she said and sat back down.

"And now, the presents!" Judy exclaimed. "I'll help you unwrap."

Carver Schramm was peering through the windows of the house he had spied from the hill above. He was disgusted to find the place empty. No furniture, so no food.

Turning away to climb back up to the trail, he heard the sound of an approaching car.

It was coming quickly up the drive and there was no way he could cross the open field between the house and the trees before it was in view. There were no outbuildings to hide in and, possibly thanks to the owner's fire safety tactics, there weren't even any concealing shrubs near to the house.

Frantic to get out of sight, he kicked in the back door, ran through the house and hunkered down beneath the front windows, hoping the people in the car were simply lost and would leave once they realized the place was empty.

"Well, here it is. What do you think, so far?" Len asked Rosamund.

"It took an awfully long time to get here, don't you think? I'm not sure I even want to look inside," she replied.

"What do you mean? Why not?"

"If it is really wonderful inside, I will be torn between having a lovely house with a long commute and being close to Bannoch in a house which might not be as nice. I hate hard choices, like that."

"You are a silly goose, sometimes, but I love you. Do you want to get out and look around, or wait for the real estate lady?"

"I think I'd like to get out and stretch my legs and get an idea of what the grounds are like."

"As you wish, my lady," Len replied, coming around the car and opening Rosamund's door.

"Thanks, Agent Phelps. I'll radio my men in the area to rendezvous with you," Detective Rasmussen put down the phone and turned to his sergeant.

"A hunter in the woods up above the old Williamson's place on East Beaver Creek Road said his dog almost flushed a fellow who looked like our suspect. When he caught a glimpse of the guy, he called his dog off and hightailed it. Smart man."

"Is the FBI team going there to check it out?"

"Yes, call our nearest search team to head over there to give them back up."

≈

Schramm saw a pair of rich-looking wrinklies pull up in a silver Cadillac sedan. They just sat there for a few moments, giving him hope they were checking directions on a map, or something, and would soon leave.

When they got out of their car, he slunk back down and tried frantically to work out a plan.

This could be the break he'd been hoping for. With a car like that, he would be long gone before this privileged old party was ever missed. Killing people like them would be just that extra bit of recreation he'd been looking for.

Carver stood beside the window, hidden by the drapes, and watched as Rosamund and Len wandered around the front yard. When they began walking toward the back, he hurried into the kitchen.

When they opened the back door, he and his faithful blade would be happy to give them a special welcome.

## Chapter Thirty

Rosamund loved the views from the front and side of the house she and Len were viewing. She tried to picture the two of them living here surrounded by the woods and mountains.

It was very quiet and so peaceful.

When their stroll around the grounds reached the backyard, she was pleased to find a lovely sunny patch which would be perfect for her vegetable and herb gardens.

This house was becoming a real possibility, in spite of its remoteness.

"Hey, someone's been vandalizing the place, even way out here. I guess there's nowhere safe from miscreants and vagabonds, these days," Len said when he noticed the broken lock on the back door.

He began to walk over to the door to check the extent of the damage.

"I suppose not," Rosamund replied. "It's hard to imagine anyone wanting to do evil deeds in this peaceful valley, though, isn't it? Look at these woods. How much of the hillside comes with the house, do you know?"

Len changed course to join his wife at the rear of the property, where he put an arm around her waist and pulled her close.

"You always see the beauty in things, Rosie. That is one of the reasons I love you."

The couple stood together listening to the wind in the trees and just soaking up the serene atmosphere, until they heard another car approaching.

"That must be the realtor. Guess we'd better get out front and greet her," Len said.

A large black SUV pulled up behind Len's car and two men in FBI jackets stepped out.

As Len and Rosamund rounded the front of the house, the driver call out to them.

"Special Agent Phelps. You people live here?" he said, flashing his identification.

"Why, no. We are here to view the property for potential purchase," Len replied, walking up to the men, as Rosamund stepped up onto the front porch.

"Have you seen anyone hanging around here?" the agent asked.

"No. But I noticed the lock on the back door is broken. I was about to check it out when we heard your car."

"You didn't go inside, then?"

"No. What's this all about?" Len asked.

"We're looking for an escaped prisoner. He was reportedly seen in this vicinity recently."

"Is this the same man who kidnapped the pastor's wife in Bannoch?"

"That hasn't been established. You folks should head on home, now, and see this house some other time. If our guy's here, you don't want to have anything to do with him."

Schramm had heard the car, too, and crept back to the front window.

When he saw the FBI men, he was frantic.

As Rosamund stepped nearer to the entrance door, he knew what he had to do. He jerked the door open and pulled her inside, holding his knife to her throat.

Rosamund screamed, Schramm hit her with the hilt of his knife and she fell to the floor inside the house as he slammed the door.

The FBI agents jumped into action at the sound of her scream.

Len started toward the house, but Agent Phelps stopped him and ordered him to get into the SUV and stay there.

The other agent got on the radio to call for backup and a hostage negotiations team, while Phelps crept up on the house to try to see inside.

Len sat in the agents' vehicle, shaking and gray-faced, praying for his wife's safety.

He was stunned by the sudden transition from peace to horror.

"How could this happen? I never should have brought Rose out here," he mumbled to himself between prayerful pleas for her protection and safe return to his side.

Two sheriff's units pulled into the driveway behind the agents' car and, within what seemed either hours or minutes, a helicopter swooped overhead.

Finally remembering his cell phone, Len called Scott. He needed his pastor and Rosamund needed all the prayers she could get.

&

"That party was such fun, Bunny! Thanks for bringing me home. I told Scott I'd call him for a ride when it was over, but I'm happy not to need to bother him," Naidenne said as she and Bunny hauled another load of baby shower loot into the parsonage.

"I think that's got it all," Bunny replied, putting down an armload of packages. "You were given so many nice things. Your little girl is going to be all set."

"Everyone was so generous. And I love that diaper gadget you gave us. It's not only practical, but I adore the pistachio color. All the other gifs were pink. I've just decided the nursery will be pistachio green set off with touches of pink."

"I'm so happy you like it. Anything else I can help you with before I go?"

"Don't go, yet. Let's sit and have a really good talk. We haven't often been alone since you got here, and there's so much to catch up on."

"I'd love to, but that sounds like Scott's car, if I'm not mistaken. I guess our tete-a-tete will have to wait," Bunny said.

Scott entered, greeted the two women and kissed his wife.

"Wow, you made quite a haul! Does one little baby really need all that?" he asked, only half in jest. "What an embarrassment of riches."

"That reminds me, Scott. I've been wanting to tell you something," Bunny said.

Scott sat on the sofa next to Naidenne.

"Shoot!"

"Well, you are aware that Max was fairly well-to-do, financially, right?"

Scott and Naidenne nodded and Bunny continued.

"After he died, I discovered he was heavily invested in lots of commercial properties in Houston, as well as other investments. Then, there's the life insurance and all and, well, it really is sort of embarrassing to say it out loud, but I am what is known as a woman of some means. Heck! I'm filthy rich, is what I am."

Scott and Naidenne simply stared, looking dumbfounded.

"Well, say something!" Bunny cried.

"Is this a joke?" Scott asked.

"I'm afraid not. If I never even lift a finger, I can live on the interest payments, and live very well, indeed, for the rest of my life…even if I live to be one hundred or more."

"But that's wonderful, Bunny!" Naidenne said. "We're so happy for you."

"I think you can be happy for yourselves, too, just a little."

"What do you mean?" Scott asked.

"Shirley and I were chatting at the shower and she told me about the church needing a new roof," Bunny said, reaching for her handbag on the floor at her feet and pulling out a slip of paper.

"Here," she handed the paper to Scott. "That should cover a new roof on a building of the church's size, according to what my business manager told me when I called him. If you need more, just let me know."

"But, you can't do this. It's too much," Scott protested.

"Sure, I can. You can't stop me. If God wants me to have this kind of money, there has to be a reason. So, I'm going to spend it for His glory, every chance I get."

"This is so generous. How can we thank you?" Naidenne said.

"Don't thank me, thank God. I didn't do a thing to earn this money, the best I can do is spend it wisely. Oh, and I'm switching my tithe to the Bannoch Community Fellowship, until I can decide where I'm going to settle. You can count on a check every month, from now on. Oh, and a one-time 'catch-up' check, too. I hadn't begun to tithe from the inheritance to the local Houston church we attended, yet, so you'll get that, too."

"Bunny, I'm overwhelmed," Scott said.

"I expect the Board will want to negotiate a new compensation package for you, now. At least, I will include a little suggestion to that effect along with the 'catch-up check'. I don't usually approve of folks tacking strings on gifts, especially to the church, but I'm going to make an exception, just this once."

Naidenne gave Bunny a one-armed hug, laughing.

"This is even better than the diaper disposal," she chuckled.

"I'm so happy to be able to do this for two people I really care about. Now, I'm afraid I've grown weary in my good works and need to get home and rest on my laurels…to mix metaphors and sins," Bunny quipped and left her friends still shaking their heads in amazement at the gift she had just given them and their church.

Naidenne was humming to herself and starting to sort her gifts when the phone rang.

Scott answered, listened for a moment and cried, "What? Rosie? Oh, no!"

૭

Scott knocked on the passenger window of the FBI SUV to get his brother-in-law's attention.

Len sat without responding, but Scott's continuous rapping finally got through to him and he turned toward the sound as if in a trance.

"Hey, Len. Let me in," Scott said.

Len slowly unlocked the door and Scott slipped onto the seat.

"How are you holding up?" he asked.

"It's all my fault. I finally had her, and now I've lost her, just because I always need to have my own way," Len said.

"You haven't lost her. I spoke to one of the deputies when they stopped me down at the road. This guy needs Rose as a hostage. He's not going to hurt her."

"She screamed and he hit her. I saw it. He hit her so hard. What can I do, Scott? I can't lose her!"

"Try to calm down. You can't help her if you fall apart. I want to pray with you, then I'm going to see if one of the FBI people will tell me what's happening and how they are planning to get Rosamund back to us, safe and sound."

When Scott approached Agent Phelps, the agent was speaking on the phone. He finished the call and turned to Scott.

"What are you doing here? This is no place for civilians," he said.

"I'm the brother of that woman in there, but I'm also the chaplain for the local Sheriff's department. I know enough to stay out of the way. I just wanted to know if you can give me any information I can share with my brother-in-law. He's in a pretty bad way, worrying about his wife."

"I'll tell you this. Our hostage negotiator is here, now. He's going to try to get a conversation going with the suspect. We are going to do our best to end this without anyone, especially your sister, getting hurt. Now get back there and stay in the car, or I'll have to force you to leave."

"Got it," Scott said and returned to the SUV.

With no telephone in the house, the negotiator was forced to use a bullhorn as he tried to get a response from Schramm.

"Attention, you in the house. We know who you are. You cannot get away, so let the woman go, unharmed, and come out with your hands up. Any resistance will only make it worse, Carver Schramm."

Inside the house, Carver was jolted to hear his name. Maybe there was no way out, but he was not going back to prison, not without a fight.

Rosamund moaned and Schramm jerked her to her feet. Holding her as a shield, with his knife to her throat, he stepped up to the window and began to shout.

"Let me out of here or the woman dies. Give me safe passage to Canada…and a million dollars, or she dies. Do it in one hour, or she dies."

He pulled her away from the window, but continued to hold her tightly as they stood out of sight waiting for the response.

Len heard the demands. Turning to Scott he declared, "Let him take my car! He can give me my Rose and drive the car away to Canada."

"The authorities aren't going to let him leave here, Len. And he would never let her go before getting to Canada, if they did. She's his insurance. We have to let these guys take care of it. They know what they are doing."

Len put his head in his hands, rocking back and forth, while Scott patted his back.

"We've talked it over, Schramm. You let the woman come out and we'll try to work out a deal for you."

Schramm screamed out, "No way, Fed. I want a car and a million bucks or the old bitch dies!"

# Chapter Thirty-one

Naidenne called the prayer chain as soon as Scott left the parsonage. Next, she called her best friends, Shirley, Bunny and the First Ladies Club.

These women surrounded her, now, offering prayer, comfort and distraction from the worry about her sister-in-law.

Judy brought in cups and a teapot from the kitchen.

"I didn't see anything herbal, but I found some Constant Comment teabags, I hope that's all right," she said to Naidenne.

"That's Rosamund's favorite, so I suppose it is the most appropriate drink we could have," Naidenne replied.

"Are you doing okay, Deenie? Not feeling too tired or in pain? The baby doing okay?" Peggy Burk asked, hovering over Naidenne's chair.

"Do sit down, Peggy," Elizabeth said.

The phone rang and all the women jerked.

"Hello?" Naidenne answered. "Oh, Scott, what's happening?"

She listened then nodded.

"Okay. Thanks for calling. Please tell Len the ladies are here praying…I love you, too."

She hung up the phone and took a breath before speaking.

"There's no change. Rosamund is still being held hostage by the same man who took me. They identified him from the description I gave them of his tattoos. Now he's threatening to kill her, if they don't give him safe passage to Canada and a million dollars."

"I can give him the money, if he'll let her go," Bunny offered. "Call Scott and tell him to let the police know. I can give him two million, if that's what it will take."

The other women looked at Bunny in amazement, before beginning to talk all at once.

"Where'd you get that kind of money?" Shirley asked.

"They won't pay any ransom!" Gwennie insisted.

"Wouldn't Canada just send him back?" Olivette offered.

"Ladies! Please," Eskaletha stood up and brought the group to order, as if they were having a regular meeting.

The women responded instinctively by obediently coming to attention.

"This is in God's hands. We've prayed and we're going to stay and give Naidenne moral support, but other than that, we have nothing to offer. That was a kind gesture, Bunny, but I think Gwennie is probably right. The authorities won't give this man what he wants."

"We've got to be able to do something!" Judy cried.

"We can help Naidenne put away all these gifts. She can't do it with her bad arm. Deenie, you tell us where these things go and we will put them away for you," Elizabeth suggested.

"Have you decided which room will be the nursery, yet?" Bunny asked, catching on and joining in Elizabeth's attempt to take Naidenne's mind of Rosamund.

"We thought the small bedroom next to ours," Naidenne replied.

"Oh, perfect!" Shirley bubbled, joining in the effort.

Each woman picked up a gift and stood in line awaiting Naidenne's instructions, chatting happily about nursery decorating and the coming baby, effectively diverting her from her memories and fears.

Rosamund's legs were quivering, forcing her to lean into Schramm for support. It repulsed her to be in physical contact with this man who had kidnapped and abused her sister-in-law.

Schramm felt her tottering against him and pushed her to the floor.

"Don't move, or I'll slit your scrawny throat," he growled.

Looking at his face for the first time, Rosamund felt a jolt of recognition. He looked like that man on the dark highway the night she ran away.

If she had given him a ride, he would probably have killed her...but then Naidenne would never have been attacked.

"Carver Schramm!" the bullhorn blared.

He jerked Rose back to her feet and pushed her toward the window.

"Have you got my money? And I want a helicopter and pilot, too!" Schramm yelled.

"You can't change your terms, now, Schramm. We're getting your money together and arranging a car. Why not just let the woman go?"

"No way. I let her go and you'll kill me. Forget that!"

Rosamund's legs began to tremble, again, as she was arched back against Schramm, with his knife on her neck. She could feel the sting and a trickle of blood where the sharp blade pierced her skin.

Through the window, she could see the rows of police and FBI around the front of the house and three men with rifles on the rise across the driveway.

If she could see those sharp-shooters, they could see her. If she moved out of the line of fire, they would be able to see Schramm clearly, too.

Rosamund exaggerated the quivering of her legs, leaning back heavily into Carver's chest. As before, he roughly thrust her away.

She dropped to the floor and shots rang out. Schramm collapsed beside Rosamund, trapping her legs with his weight.

Pulling herself free, she crawled away from the body and was getting shakily to her feet when the door crashed open and FBI agents burst in.

One man rushed to the fallen convict and the other approached Rosamund.

"Are you alright, ma'am?"

"Yes, I think so. Thank you, so much," Rosamund replied, with tears coursing down her face.

"There's blood on you. Are you hurt?" the agent asked.

Reaching up to her throat, Rosamund felt the wetness on her fingers. When he pushed her away, Schramm's knife must have sliced her neck more deeply. The cut was bleeding freely.

"I think maybe I am," she said, staring at her fingers.

The agent called for a medical team who soon trotted into the house with a stretcher and emergency gear.

"This guy's in no rush. Take care of the lady," the agent said as he looked down on the fugitive's body.

There was a small bullet hole in the side of his forehead and a gaping wound in his neck. Lying there awkwardly, eyes glazed and blood oozing, Carver Schramm was obviously dead.

When the medics rolled their stretcher out of the house with its black shrouded burden, Len let out a deep moan.

"Rosie! They killed my Rosie!" he cried as he stumbled from the car toward the gurney.

"No, Len, that's not Rose. Look," Scott called, pointing toward the house.

The EMT was helping Rose walk to the waiting ambulance. Her neck was bandaged and she was weak from shock, but she appeared to be fine, otherwise.

"Rosie!" Len cried again, only this time in relief, as he rushed to her side and wrapped her in his arms.

"Oh, Len," she gasped and clung to him, beginning to sob.

※

Naidenne answered Scott's call with some trepidation. As she listened, her expression became radiant.

"Thank the Lord!" she exclaimed.

After ending the call, her friends gathered around, eager to hear her good news.

"Rosamund is safe! She has bumps and bruises and a cut on her neck, but she's okay…and that man, that evil man, is dead."

"God is good," Olivette said, while the others expressed their relief and praised God in their own way.

"Do you need a ride to the hospital, Deenie?" Bunny asked.

"No. Thanks, anyway. Scott wants me to wait here. He said they are just going to check her out and see if she needs stitches in the gash on her neck then they will be right home."

Naidenne suddenly felt her legs go week and needed to sit down. The horror was past, at last.

"Are you okay?" Shirley asked when she saw how pale Naidenne was as she sagged into a chair.

"Oh, yes. For a moment I was overcome, absolutely overcome…"

## The First Ladies Club

"With relief, of course." Shirley said when Naidenne failed to finish her thought.

"No, not just relief. I was overcome with joy. Now, we can really get on with our lives."

"I suppose the rest of us should be getting on with our lives, too," Gwennie suggested.

"Good idea, Gwennie. Naidenne has had enough excitement to last for quite a while. We should let her have some peace and quiet." Eskaletha said.

"Thank you all, so much, for being here. Without your support, prayers and friendship, I just don't know…"

"That's what the First Ladies Club is all about," Elizabeth replied.

The women took turns hugging Naidenne and departed, leaving Shirley and Bunny the last ones to go.

"Would you like me to stay, Naidenne?" Shirley asked.

"No, Jack's waiting for you at home, Shirley. I'll stay until Scott brings Rosamund home," Bunny insisted.

"Thanks, Shirley. For everything. I'll call you tomorrow and let you know how Rosamund is," Naidenne assured her.

Shirley gave each of her friends a hug.

"I guess you're right. My dear husband will be on pins and needles wondering what's happening. I'd better go share the good news and put him out of his misery. Bye!"

"You have some wonderful friends in this town, Deenie. I'd forgotten just how much I loved my time living in Bannoch. It's all coming back to me, now," Bunny said as she settled back on the sofa.

Naidenne began to clear away the cups and saucers and Bunny jumped back up.

"Oh, for Heaven's sake! What am I thinking? Let me do that. You sit down and rest. I'll clear this mess, then go up and turn down Rosamund's bed for her. She's going to need some coddling, too, after her experience. I just may have to stick around to take care of you guys, indefinitely."

Naidenne chuckled to herself as Bunny bustled around. She was so right about all her good friends. In spite of the recent unpleasantness, Naidenne felt extraordinarily blessed.

Bunny trotted down the stairs with an armload of sheets.

"I heard a car in the drive, just now. I think they're here. I'll just pop these into the washer and get out of the way. Rose's bed is all fresh and ready," she said as she scurried out to the utility porch.

Naidenne went to open the door for her returning family. They were still clustered in the doorway when Bunny came back from starting the washer. She gave Rosamund a quick hug then made her escape, leaving the family to recover and rejoice in private.

"Sit down, Rosie," Len said while he eased her into a chair. "What can I get you, my dear?"

"You're spoiling me. All I really want is to go to bed, but I'm too tired to climb those stairs, just now."

"You haven't had anything to eat since lunch, have you?" Naidenne asked.

Rosamund shook her head, and realizing that was true, she began to feel a little hungry.

"Once you have something to eat you will feel more up to getting ready for bed. What would you like?"

"A cup of tea and a slice of toast sounds heavenly," Rosamund replied.

"I'll get it," Scott said. "No need for you to try to do it one-handed, Naidenne. Both of you sit here and just take it easy. Len and I will fix the food."

When they were alone, Rosamund took Naidenne's hand.

"I owe you another apology."

"Whatever for, now?" Naidenne asked.

"I saw that man on the highway the night I ran off like a schoolgirl. He wanted a ride. If I'd let him get in he would have driven right past Bannoch and never attacked you, like he did."

"Why, if you had picked him up, he might have killed you!"

"Maybe that is what was meant to happen…"

"Never. Don't even think like that. Everything has worked out for the best and it is behind us, now. You know, Bunny told me once that she believes everything which God allows to happen in a believer's life holds both a blessing and a lesson for the believer, but we have to look for them. I think I've found the blessings in this for me. It's the wonderful love of friends and family and a greater trust in His mercy."

"If that's true, I know what the lesson is for me, too," Rosamund said. "Never, ever try to buy a house out in the country."

# Epilogue

On a rare windless day in June, Naidenne Davidson knelt on a beach blanket, happily changing her daughter's diaper. Hearing her name called, she turned and waved to her approaching friend who was slogging towards them through the dry sand.

"Hi! Scott said I'd find you here," Bunny Banks said as she crouched on the blanket and tickled the baby's feet.

"When I saw the glorious sunshine this morning, I had to bring Talitha to the beach to enjoy it. She loves it. See what she can do?"

The fresh diaper now secured, Naidenne took her daughter's hand and pulled her into a sitting position. Talitha wobbled a bit, but stayed up for a moment before reaching for a flower in the blanket's pattern and falling over.

Bunny clapped, "What a big girl you are, Talitha Joy! We are all so proud of you."

As the baby groped happily at the blanket, the two friends sat back to admire her.

"I'm glad you came, Bunny. I have been meaning to apologize."

"Whatever for?" Bunny asked.

"When you came to visit last fall, we were all distracted by, well, first, the…troubles, then this little dumpling and Rosamund's marriage and then you went back to Houston to take care of things there, so we never did get a chance to really catch up with all the things in your life; Max's death and all. Since you've been back, I've been so absorbed in Talitha, I'm afraid I've dominated every conversation."

"We've got all the time in the world, now that I'm living here permanently. Don't worry about it. And I love to hear about the baby. You know that."

"Well, you've seen her trick for today, and there's nothing here to distract us, so let's talk, now."

"What do you want to know? Max died over a year ago. It was a shock at the time, but I'm pretty well accustomed to widowhood, now."

"But, what was he doing in Eastern Europe? How did you find out about the crash? You never had a chance to share about any of it."

"At the time, I didn't really want to talk about it. I was too confused. I hadn't known Max was in Eastern Europe. I thought he was on another trip to Brazil."

"Really? Why didn't he tell you where he was going?"

"That was what I wanted to know. I'm afraid I was suspicious he was seeing another woman."

"Oh, dear! Why would you think that?" Naidenne asked.

"Past history, I'm afraid. But, now, I don't think that was it, at all."

"Why not?"

"Max never wanted to talk about his life in the years before we got back together. I thought it was because of all his other women, but he didn't talk much about his business, either. He said he didn't want to bore me. When I got back to Houston after coming here last fall, I found our condo had been broken into."

"Oh, no!"

"Yes, all our computers and other electronics were taken and Max's study was trashed. I just thought random robbers had taken advantage of my absence, but now I'm not so sure."

"Why is that?"

"I got some strange phone calls, after that. They didn't make sense, really, but added to all the other odd things, it's made me suspicious. I think Max was involved in something 'covert', something he didn't want me to know about. I think that's why he was in Eastern Europe and it might even be the reason he died."

"Don't you think you are letting your writer's imagination run away with you? What sort of covert business could Max have?"

"Oh, you're probably right. There are just so many things which don't quite add up, that's all," Bunny said.

"Sudden death is like that, isn't it? We always want to make sense of it, somehow. It's too hard to accept the randomness."

"I guess. Speaking of my writing, I've started work on a new book," Bunny remarked.

"Did you finish the pirate story?"

"Nah. I gave up on it. I couldn't quite reconcile a romantic pirate adventure with my real life pirate experience. This is a straight romance, but not one of those salacious bodice rippers. It will probably never sell, but it will keep me occupied on the odd lonely afternoon."

"Are you lonely since returning to Bannoch?" Naidenne asked.

"Oh, not usually. Singing in the choir and serving as treasurer on the church board keep me fairly busy, now."

"It was such a shock when Orville Locke's wife ran off with Bill Odem. I suppose no one was quite as shocked as Orville, though," Naidenne said.

"I heard he'd had a stroke. Was that what brought it on?"

"That, and a really toxic life-style, I suppose. If you believe my friend, Judy, it was the white flour that did him in."

"I've been doing my best to straighten out the financial records. Orville's wife left things in a bit of a mess."

"It was a tragic episode for the church, but I can't help thinking things are running much more smoothly under our current board."

"It was quite a coincidence when Josiah Watkins left the Trustee board at the same time as Bill's and Orville's positions came open. It's not often a church finds itself replacing all the trustees at once," Bunny said.

"It couldn't be helped, though. When Josiah tripped over that rake and broke his hip, he couldn't live alone, anymore. Fortunately, his son in Eugene was able to take him in."

Just then a big brown dog bounded onto the blanket, knocked Bunny backwards and straddled her, licking her face.

"Oof! Get him off!" she cried.

It's such a nice day, we decided to join you. Hope you don't mind.

"Texaco! Down. Sit!" Scott commanded his wayward pet, and the dog obeyed instantly, tail wagging and tongue lolling happily.

"I've never asked you before, but why Texaco? Why'd you name him that?" Bunny asked Scott as he strode up and clasped the leash to the dog's collar.

"That's right; you left for Houston before we adopted him. He was part of the litter Eskaletha and Elizabeth discovered in the old abandoned gas station north of town. As far as the vet can tell, he's a high octane blend of Rottweiler, Lab and Boxer. Today the Lab seems to be dominant. Sorry for the rude greeting, but he obviously likes you," Scott said, grinning.

"What happened to the rest of the litter?" Bunny asked, looking over her shoulder, as though expecting them to descend upon her at any moment.

"Elizabeth and her husband adopted the little black runt of the litter and named him Rascal. Eskaletha has one of the pups and Judy lets the white bull terrier stay with the Falls family," Naidenne said.

"Lets him stay? What's that mean?" Bunny asked.

"Judy doesn't believe in keeping pets, but her girls begged for the pup, so Judy said he could stay as a guest. They named him Mr. Jones and they treat that dog like an equal, even ask his opinion on everything. Fortunately, Ken treats him like a dog and took him to obedience school. Judy has the poor thing on vegan rations, so Ken slips him some meat, now and then."

"I've met him out walking Mr. Jones, and I think Ken is really quite fond of the dog, in spite of himself," Scott added.

The fog began to roll in, so the little group gathered their things and walked up to the parking lot.

"Rosamund called before I left the house, Naidenne. She's got a basket of ripe tomatoes for us, if you can use them," Scott said.

"That sister of yours has a green thumb, Scott. She gave me a big bunch of spinach and some of her green beans just yesterday. I love taking her garden's abundance off her hands," Bunny commented.

"Len's been lending a hand with the hoe, too, since he retired from the bank. Turns out he's a regular Mr. Green Jeans," Scott quipped.

"I'll walk down the road to their place and get the tomatoes after I put Talitha down for her nap. Would you like to stay for dinner, Bunny?"

"Thanks, but I can't tonight. I've got a book club meeting in Tillamook. It's just a bunch of wannabe writers who get together and read and critique each other's work, but I wouldn't miss it."

As Bunny waved and drove off, the Davidson family turned and, with Naidenne pushing the stroller and Scott leading their boisterous dog, the happy family strolled toward home.

Other books available in print and for Kindle
by J.B. Hawker include
The Bunny Elder Adventure Series:

Hollow
Vain Pursuits
Seadrift
…and Something Blue

☙

Dear Reader:

If you enjoyed The First Ladies Club, please tell your friends and post a review on Amazon.com.

To learn more about J.B. Hawker, see her author page on the Amazon website.

For updates on future books in The First Ladies Club Series and other writing you may *friend* her on Facebook or follow her author blog, **The Works of JB Hawker**, jbhawker.wordpress.com

To be added to the mailing list to receive notices of new releases and special promotions
Email: j.b.hawker2012@gmail.com

Cover design for **The First Ladies Club** by Candida Martinelli, candida.martinelli@italophiles.com

Acknowledgements

Special thanks to my excellent proof-readers and editors, pastors' wives Donna Reed and Joyce Goldthwaite, for sharing their editing skills and a firsthand perspective on life in the "stained glass fishbowl" of a small town parsonage.

•

Turn the page to read a sample of the second book in the First Ladies Club series, *The Body in the Belfry*.

## Prologue

The woman peered through the wooden slats at the rugged coastline below her as her companion knelt and picked up a rusty counterweight from a pile nearby, turned and brought it up swiftly against the side of the woman's head.

She emitted a surprised grunt and crumpled to the dusty floor. Her assailant stared at the weight for a moment, as though surprised at what it had done, and then cast it away into the shadows.

It had been a sudden, irresistible impulse which left the woman's body on the floor with blood oozing from her temple.

Looking about and spying a coil of rope, the attacker threw one end toward a ceiling beam, but missed. After two more unsuccessful attempts, the rope finally soared over the beam and was immediately pulled down and slip knotted tightly around the unconscious woman's neck.

Several pulls on the free end of the rope finally had the body swaying freely, it's toes a foot from the floor.

A wooden crate was pulled away from the wall and tipped onto its side under the twitching body, as though it had been kicked over by the woman as a final, desperate act.

Leaving the words, "FORGIVE ME," scrawled in the dust, the killer disappeared down the stairs into the darkness.

# Chapter One

"I can't breathe," Indigo Merrillanne Bishop gasped and flung off the blankets smothering her.

Stumbling up from the mattress, she shuffled around the chaos of her bedroom and down the narrow hall into the narrow bathroom, where she began pawing through packing boxes in search of over-the-counter decongestants.

This was the pits. She'd arrived in Bannoch, Oregon, only the day before, driving a rental moving truck containing all her goods and chattels from California's Bay Area.

Her brothers, Wolf and Sage, had driven down from Seattle and Springfield, respectively, to meet her here and help unload the truck at her new home. When the last box and piece of furniture were safely off the truck, and the beds and appliances were setup, they needed to leave to get back to their work. Wolf ran the finance desk at a Seattle newspaper and Sage was a contractor in the middle of a big job.

Just as she was waving good-bye, Merrill had felt an ominous tickle in the back of her throat and emitted a not very lady-like sniff. She'd tried to tell herself she was just being sentimental about her brothers leaving, but when the chills and fever set in later that night, she knew she was the victim of a full-blown head cold or, if she were really unlucky, the flu.

In spite of congestion, aches and pains, Merrill was determined to carry on. She had unpacking to do and only one week to get settled before she assumed her duties as the new pastor of the Bannoch First Baptist Church.

Fortunately for Merrill, she had been raised by a pragmatic, no-nonsense mother who never coddled her children just because they might be ill. If two aspirins, plenty of weak tea and a coating of petroleum jelly didn't bring about a swift recovery, she might resort to the only two OTC medicines Merrill could remember from her childhood: the delicious cherry-flavored cough syrup, absolutely loaded with codeine, was a sure cure for a cough, guaranteed to provide an afternoon of blissful sleep, as well; and for occasional tummy troubles, there was a banana-flavored, off-white liquid with extract of opium as a main ingredient. That last nostrum stopped diarrhea in its tracks with a single dose.

Looking back now, Merrill supposed she and her brothers were lucky to have survived such medicines. Today's children were fortunate government regulations and warning labels protected them from the danger of Reyes Syndrome, associated with aspirin, or a potential life of drug abuse from non-prescription dosing with opium byproducts.

Her parents hadn't been too worried about the drugs in those medicines. They had survived a youthful flirtation with the hippy culture early in their marriage, hence Merrill's and her brothers' unusual names, and had lived to become confirmed members of the establishment who considered themselves none the worse for their previous dabbling in an alternative life style.

A glance into the spotty mirror on the medicine cabinet inspired Merrill to wonder if she had escaped unscathed, after all. A middle-aged face, flushed and splotchy with fever and framed by tangled and faded shoulder-length blond hair certainly didn't reflect blooming health. Still, she and her brothers had survived their unusual upbringing to become strong characters who faced each new challenge with courage and faith.

Victoriously clutching a bottle of FDA approved non-drowsy cold and flu medication, Merrill tottered down the steep stairs to the kitchen of her new home, the parsonage apartment built onto the back of her new church.

A window above the kitchen sink looked out toward the ocean and Merrill admired the view of sky and sea as she washed down a dose of medication with her brother's discarded Starbuck's coffee cup filled with water. She groaned when she spied her scrawled "fragile-glassware" on the sagging carton containing her everyday drinking glasses, now peeking out from the bottom of a stack of heavy boxes labeled "cookbooks" and "pots and pans." She could only hope at least a few of her dishes remained intact.

With a rueful glance at the disorder in her kitchen, she headed back up the stairs, intent on pulling herself together and tackling the unpacking.

After a steaming shower gave the cold medicine a boost, she was partially restored; at least enough to dress in jeans and an old shirt of her late husband's and return to the kitchen, where she hoped to find enough of her utensils to be able to fix a light breakfast before digging in.

Knee-deep in old newspapers, with newsprint smudges on her red stuffy nose, Merrill was putting the last of the spices away in the tiny pantry, when she was interrupted by a knock on the door.

"Who can that be? The congregation knows I don't officially start my pastorate here until Sunday," she muttered as she walked across the kitchen to open the door, wiping her hands on the seat of her jeans.

"Yes?" she asked the two women standing on the step, thinking, "These better not be door-to-door proselytizers from some cult or other."

Although taken aback by Merrill's abrupt manner and her disheveled appearance, Elizabeth Gilbert and her friend, Judy Falls, managed to smile.

"We've come to welcome you to the community," Elizabeth said.

"Have we caught you at a bad time?" Judy asked. "Moving is such a pain. Do you need any help?"

Relieved and a little embarrassed by her own unfriendly greeting, Merrill stepped back, gesturing for the women to come inside.

"It's a bit of a mess, I'm afraid. As you see, I'm still unpacking. Would you like something to drink? I think there's still coffee in the pot."

"No, don't bother. We won't stay. We just wanted to welcome you to the community and invite you to join our group," Elizabeth said, moving an empty carton from a kitchen chair and sitting down. "Shall I flatten this for you?"

"Thanks! I'm just about up to my ears in empty boxes and there's not much storage here. What group do you represent?" Merrill asked.

"We call ourselves the First Ladies Club," Judy explained. "We are both a community service organization and a support group for pastors' wives."

"There hasn't been a pastor here at First Baptist for quite a while, so when we heard your husband had been called, we were all excited to have you join us," Elizabeth added.

"Oh, but I'm not the wife of the new pastor," Merrill began.

"What! Oh, dear, I guess we'd better be going, then," Judy interrupted. "We are a diverse and eclectic group with a wide range of theological interpretations and traditions, but I don't think any of the ladies would be willing to add a pastor's, uh, well, uh, 'domestic partner'," she finally completed.

Merrill laughed when she realized Judy thought she was 'living in sin' with the new pastor.

Baptists come in all shapes and sizes and range from conservative fundamentalists to liberal progressives, but there were none she was aware of who accepted a pastor with a live-in girlfriend.

"No, you misunderstood me," she finally managed. "I'm not the pastor's wife, you see, I'm the pastor."

"*You* are the Rev. Dr. I. Merrill Bishop, like it says on the welcome sign on the message board in front of the church?" Judy asked.

"That's me," Merrill nodded.

"Hallelujah!" Elizabeth shouted, startling the others.

"Dr. Bishop, until you arrived, I've been the only female pastor in this community. My husband and I co-pastor the Methodist Church downtown. You will be joining the Ministerial Association, I hope?"

"Of course, but please call me Merrill. Why do you ask?"

"When Gil and I came to Bannoch, many years ago, I accompanied him to the Ministerial meetings. Of course, I was treated very politely; exactly as any pastor's wife would have been, and then completely ignored, unless they needed some sort of hostess duties. I couldn't fight it, so I stopped going. Those men couldn't see me as an equal. I was Gil's wife and nothing more. With you here, another ordained female, I'm ready to take another stab at breaking through the wall of preconceptions."

"I understand," Merrill replied. "My late husband was a minister. When I felt called to seminary, I encountered the attitude you described."

"Well, then, since you were once a pastor's wife, couldn't you represent your church in our group?" Judy said, and then quickly added, "You don't have a pastor's husband, now, do you?"

"No," Merrill said with a grin. "Would that be so bad?"

"I guess not, but I'm not sure how a pastor's male spouse would fit into the First Ladies Club," Judy explained.

"Would you consider joining us, Merrill? You are going to need a support group outside your congregation and we would love to have you."

"I don't know if my schedule will let me attend on a regular basis, but I would love to come whenever I can. Thank you."

"Good. That's settled. We'll let you know when and where the next meeting will be. Now, what can we do to help you get unpacked?" Elizabeth asked.

Merrill was about to decline this generous offer when she was overcome by a coughing spasm. When she was able to catch her breath, she gave her new friends directions for unpacking the books in the living room and excused herself to take another shot of cold medicine.

Several hours later the three tired women were sitting around an open pizza box nibbling on a few leftover crusts.

"I cannot thank you enough for everything," Merrill avowed. "I could never have finished this today by myself."

"Certainly not, when you aren't feeling well," Judy said. "Besides, this has been fun. I always love looking at other people's stuff."

"Even 'stuff' as boring as mine?" Merrill grinned.

"Oh, it isn't boring. Every item has a past, and a use. And when its useful life is over, it can get a future by being re-purposed. For instance, that ratty bathrobe hanging behind the bedroom door will make a throw pillow or even a stuffed animal when you get rid of it."

"Ratty bathrobe, eh?" Merrill asked, raising one eyebrow.

"Omigosh! Did I say that?" Judy cried.

"Yes, dear, you certainly did. Merrill, you will have to forgive Judy. There doesn't seem to be any filter between what she thinks and what she says, but her heart's in the right place," Elizabeth teased.

"It's alright," Merrill said. "I know that robe is ratty. It's just that it is really comfy. It was a gift from my late husband. I wore it all through seminary, during those late night study sessions and while writing and researching my doctoral thesis. It's sort of a good luck charm."

"Was it really hard getting your doctorate? I'd love to go back to school and finish my BA degree, but I don't seem to be able to concentrate very well since the twins were born."

The three new friends chatted about their families for another half-hour before Elizabeth glanced at her watch and got slowly to her feet.

"Come on, Judy. We've got to let Merrill get to bed."

"Gosh, yes!" Judy responded. "You look awful, Merrill. Do you need help getting up the stairs and into bed?"

"No, thanks," Merrill chuckled. "I apparently don't feel quite as bad as I look. I can make it. Just the thought of a nice soak in that old claw foot tub will carry me up those stairs. Thanks, again."

After her bath, and a very brief devotional, Merrill lay in her freshly made bed waiting for the night time version of her cold medicine to kick in, and looking back over the day.

Only in her new home one full day and she already had two new friends.

She lifted up a prayer of thanks and drifted off to sleep.

## Chapter Two

A low rumble of sound penetrated Merrill's illness-and-medication-befogged dreams and pulled her from the arms of Lethe. She groggily recalled where she was and was amazed that the bedroom walls of her new home seemed to be vibrating with the deep tones of a fog-horn. When these were followed by high pitched whines and moans, she became fully awake and sat up, throwing off the covers.

Trying to locate the source of the sounds, now melding into a sort of muffled harmony, Merrill walked into the hallway, holding her hands over her ears. As she moved further from her bedroom the noise grew less painful.

In the bathroom with the door shut she was finally able to discern the notes of a pipe organ and realized they were coming from the sanctuary on the other side of the shared wall.

She showered and dressed as quickly as possible, feeling all the time as if she were in the bowels of a monstrous calliope.

Making her way to the downstairs sitting room, she unlatched and opened the private connecting door to the church proper. This door opened into to a hallway separating the sanctuary from the choir room, janitor's closet and at the far end, near the front of the church, the Pastor's Study. A door on her left opened into the sanctuary near the pipe organ.

She stepped through and found a thin, blond-haired young man engrossed in playing a complicated classical sacred organ composition. With eyes closed and head swaying, his fingers flew over the keyboards and his feet danced on the pedals.

In the sanctuary the sound was no longer overwhelming to Merrill's ears, but the beauty of the performance overpowered her in a very different way. The young man's talent and passion were exceptional.

Merrill quietly took a seat on the front pew and settled in to enjoy the music. During a quiet passage, she suddenly erupted in a violent sneeze and the music instantly ceased.

"Who are you?" the musician challenged. "You can't be in here, you know. This isn't a shelter."

Hastily blowing her nose on a crumpled tissue from her pocket, Merrill smiled crookedly; dressed as she was in sweatpants and over-sized t-shirt, the man's misapprehension was understandable.

"I'm sorry. I didn't mean to startle you. I'm just getting over a cold," she explained.

"Well, that's too bad, but you can't stay here. If you are ill, you should go to the clinic."

"I came in because I heard you playing. You have a beautiful gift."

"Thank you, but how did you get in here, anyway? I know I locked that front door."

"I came in through the private door. I think we should introduce ourselves," Merrill said, standing up and reaching out her hand. "I'm Doctor Merrill Bishop, the new pastor of this church. And you are?"

"Oh, my goodness!" He jumped down from the organ and began to shake Merrill's hand, with great enthusiasm.

"I'm Peregrine Bostwick, the church organist. Forgive me for being so rude. Welcome, Dr. Bishop. Welcome."

"The church is blessed to have you as the organist, Peregrine."

"Oh, well, not so much these days, I'm afraid. I only get to play an electronic keyboard during our worship services, these days."

"Why is that?" Merrill asked.

"With the congregation so small since the last split, folks felt lost in this big old sanctuary. It's too expensive to heat, too, so the Deacons decided we would meet in the Social Hall. We can't move the pipe organ, of course, and our baby grand is too big to fit over there," he said, gesturing across the stage at a large shape covered by a canvas tarp.

"What a shame for these lovely instruments to be idle," Merrill said.

"It breaks my heart to see these grand old ladies neglected. I come over and play them whenever I can, just to keep them tuned and in good shape."

"About that. Do you suppose you could play them later in the day? The pipes are right against my bedroom and the sound is quite overwhelming as it comes through the wall."

"Oh, gosh! It's been so long since we had a pastor in the parsonage apartment, I didn't think. I'm so sorry, Dr. Bishop" Peregrine said, coming to sit beside her in the pew.

"Call me Pastor Merrill, Peregrine, please."

"And you can call me Peri."

"Thank you, Peri. I understood it was only six months since your last pastor left."

"That's right. He wasn't living in the apartment, though. He had a place in Tillamook and just drove over on Sundays and Wednesday evenings," Peri explained.

"Oh?" Merrill said. This was news the pulpit committee had not shared with her.

"Yeah, he was a substitute teacher in the school district there."

Merrill was intrigued to learn what other church history might have been withheld by the search committee in their interviews.

"Say, Peri. I haven't had breakfast, yet; would you like to join me? I'm afraid my apartment isn't fit for guests, yet, but there must be a good coffee shop in town where we can eat and get better acquainted."

"Sure. We can go to the Boatworks. I've had breakfast, but I can always eat one of their homemade muffins and their coffee is first rate. Shall we go in my car, it's just outside?"

"Sounds great. Let me dash in and get cleaned up. I'll meet you out front."

Peri closed up the organ while Merrill retreated into the apartment.

When they met in the parking lot she was dressed in neat black slacks and a plaid blazer, looking a great deal less like a homeless person.

"Is this your car?" Merrill blurted, seeing Peri standing beside a shiny red vintage Jaguar like the one Inspector Morse drove in the BBC television series.

"You like it? I inherited it from my grandfather. It's a dream to drive. Want to try it?"

"Oh, I wouldn't dare! Just riding in it will be a treat," Merrill said as she slid onto the creamy leather passenger seat.

As Peri drove, Merrill imagined herself cruising the streets of Oxford with the great Inspector and chuckled to herself.

"What's so funny?" Peri asked.

"Oh, I was just indulging in flights of fancy, I'm afraid; trying to imagine myself on the roads of rural England in this beauty."

"I do that all the time! Did you ever watch that British TV show, Inspector Morse? He had a car just like this one."

Merrill admitted this was the source of her fantasy, as well, immediately endearing herself to at least one member of her new congregation.

The Boatworks coffee shop was situated in the town's seaside shopping mall, a converted fish processing plant. Merrill found the seafaring décor charming and was impressed with the menu.

After ordering a spinach omelet, she shook a packet of sweetener into her coffee and looked around. It was still early and the café was busy with breakfast orders. It was easy to tell which of the customers were finishing up before going off to work and who were the retirees just settling in for their morning social hour.

Merrill wondered if any of these people were current or former members of First Baptist. She'd been given enough church history to be aware that almost all the other Baptist churches in town, plus the non-denominational Bannoch Community Fellowship, were founded on splits from the First Baptist Church.

These were not what are usually referred to as church plants.

It is a good sign when a congregation grows to the point where it is able to plant new young churches in a new mission field. However, when new churches pop up in the same town, as the result of disagreements within the church family, it harms the membership of both the original and new churches, as well as the community at large. It did not reflect well on the denominations involved, either.

Merrill knew this divisive history was the reason her new congregation was so small. It was also the only reason they were desperate enough to call a female as their new pastor. It was a challenge and she hoped she was equal to it.

After years on the staff of a large Bay Area church, Merrill was eager to have a pulpit of her own. When the call came from Bannoch First Baptist, she had prayed long and hard before accepting. She thought she knew what she was taking on and felt this was God's will. It would help her to find out as much about her new flock as possible.

"So, Peri, how long have you been a member of First Baptist?" she asked, taking a sip of her coffee.

"I grew up in this church. My grandparents grew up in it, too. They raised me after my mother left me on their doorstep," he replied cheerfully, popping another bit of muffin into his mouth.

"What do you mean? She just left you? Not literally on the doorstep, surely."

"I guess that was a bit of hyperbole. I tend to add color to my humdrum existence from time to time. But my mother actually did abandon me. One day she came for a visit, left me with the grands to go buy cigarettes and never came back. I was nine months old."

"Did your grandparents try to find her?" Merrill was aghast. Her own children, two daughters, were grown with families of their own. She couldn't imagine one of them leaving a baby like that.

"They looked. Even hired a private detective when the police couldn't find her. She just faded away without a trace…like a wisp of smoke on the evening breeze," Peri added, with a dramatically poetic expression and a wistful sigh. He was obviously enjoying telling his story to a new audience.

"I'm sorry to hear that. And she's never tried to contact you or her parents in all these years?"

"Oh, the grands weren't her parents. My father, their son, died before I was born. Gran and Gramps tried to help my mother, so they could be close to me, you see, but she was a wild creature, according to all accounts. Something of a gypsy, I imagine."

"You said you inherited your Jag from your grandfather. Is your grandmother still living?"

"I'll say! You'll meet her at church on Sunday. Gran's a real corker. I love her to death. She's such a darling, I'm sure you'll adore her, too."

When she'd finished her breakfast, Merrill felt she'd played hooky long enough and asked Peregrine to take her back to the church, so she could finish unpacking and get her study set up.

Once that was done it would be time to begin work on her all-important first sermon for Sunday.

"This has been delightful, Peri," she said, as she got out of the car in front of the church.

"Fun for me, too, Pastor Merrill. I'm looking forward to telling Gran all about our little visit. Ta! See you Sunday!"

Merrill watched him drive away, thinking this theatrical and very gifted young man was going to make her life in Bannoch very interesting.

Made in the USA
Monee, IL
02 May 2025